THE SECOND GRAVE

Also by Jeffrey B. Burton

The Cory and Crystal Pratt K-9 thrillers

THE DEAD YEARS *

The Mace Reid K-9 mysteries

THE FINDERS
THE KEEPERS
THE LOST

The Drew Cady series

THE CHESSMAN
THE LYNCHPIN
THE EULOGIST

* available from Severn House

THE SECOND GRAVE

Jeffrey B. Burton

SEVERN
HOUSE

First world edition published in Great Britain and the USA in 2025
by Severn House, an imprint of Canongate Books Ltd,
14 High Street, Edinburgh EH1 1TE.

severnhouse.com

Copyright © Jeffrey B. Burton, 2025

Cover and jacket design by Nick May at bluegecko22.com

All rights reserved including the right of reproduction in whole or in part in any form. The right of Jeffrey B. Burton to be identified as the author of this work has been asserted in accordance with the Copyright, Designs & Patents Act 1988.

British Library Cataloguing-in-Publication Data
A CIP catalogue record for this title is available from the British Library.

ISBN-13: 978-1-4483-1243-6 (cased)
ISBN-13: 978-1-4483-1242-9 (e-book)

This is a work of fiction. Names, characters, places and incidents are either the product of the author's imagination or are used fictitiously. Except where actual historical events and characters are being described for the storyline of this novel, all situations in this publication are fictitious and any resemblance to actual persons, living or dead, business establishments, events or locales is purely coincidental.

All Severn House titles are printed on acid-free paper.

Typeset by Palimpsest Book Production Ltd., Falkirk,
Stirlingshire, Scotland.
Printed and bound in Great Britain by TJ Books,
Padstow, Cornwall.

Praise for Jeffrey B. Burton

"A mighty impressive thriller"
Booklist on *The Dead Years*

"The twists and turns will keep you reading"
Kings River Life Magazine on *The Dead Years*

"So inventive, it's so creative . . . A lot of fun to read"
NPR's Radio Pet Lady (Tracie Hotchner) on *The Dead Years*

"Another solid dog thriller from Burton, that makes good use of the dogs, the lead characters pasts, and twists you don't see coming. Fans of his previous books will enjoy this one"
Red Carpet Crash on *The Dead Years*

"Will keep readers turning the pages. Dog lovers are in for a treat"
Publishers Weekly on *The Lost*

"For fans of Paula Munier's or Susan Furlong's books featuring dogs"
Library Journal Starred Review of *The Keepers*

"A wonder of a thriller"
Booklist Starred Review of *The Finders*

"Will entice fans of Margaret Mizushima and Paula Munier's K-9 mysteries"
Library Journal Starred Review of *The Finders*

About the author

Novels in **Jeffrey B. Burton**'s critically-acclaimed Mace Reid K-9 mystery series include *The Finders*, *The Keepers*, and *The Lost*. His Agent Drew Cady thrillers include *The Chessman*, *The Lynchpin*, and *The Eulogist*. *The Second Grave* is the second instalment in his new Chicago K-9 thriller series preceded by *The Dead Years*. Jeff lives in St. Paul, Minnesota, with his wife, Cindy, an irate Pomeranian named Lucy, and a happy galoot of a Beagle named Milo.

www.jeffreybburton.com

For my mother, Virginia E. Burton –
Sorry about all the naughty words

Acknowledgements

I can't thank the editing team at Severn House – from Tina Pietron to Rachel Slatter to Eleanor Smith – nearly enough for all of their meticulous work. Plus, a special shout-out to designer Nick May for the stunning cover art. Finally, hugs and kisses to my wife, Cindy, who moonlights as my biggest fan, beta reader, photographer, and bodyguard in case any library chats or book clubs turn rowdy. If I could clone the lot of you, we could take over the world.

Let sleeping dogs lie.
– Sir Robert Walpole

PROLOGUE

'I gotta take a leak.'

'Lyle – help your grandfather to the restroom, will you?'

'Oh for crying out loud, Diane, I can get there myself. The Cornhole tournament's about to start and Lyle's taking it home this year.'

'You took your pills with the food, right, Dad?'

'Of course,' he said. Of course, he hadn't, not today and, quite frankly, not since he'd finally acquiesced to attending the family reunion earlier in the week.

Jim Severson pushed himself up from the picnic table and slid out from the bench. He nearly forgot his cane but reached for it as an afterthought. Even though he'd not taken his meds, today had been a good day.

A good day, indeed, he thought.

A perfect day.

The Seversons had held their family reunions at Kankakee River State Park – four thousand acres splashed across both Kankakee and Will counties in northeastern Illinois – for fifty-eight years, counting today's get-together. He knew that for a fact because he and Ann, his beautiful bride of sixty-two years, had begun the tradition those many, many moons ago. It had been Ann's idea, of course. The reunions were held over Memorial Day weekend – often on Sunday, like today – as it allowed time for travel and was an excellent way to kick off the summer.

Jim glanced across the campsite, from the picnic tables to the canopy tents to the still-smoldering barbecue grills to the playground, where two of his grandkids watched over six of his great-grandchildren, to where Jerod and Lyle and Steve and Rudy and Don and Walt and the rest of the clan were setting up the Cornhole boards.

The men in the Severson family took their annual Cornhole tournament seriously. Bets were made, money would exchange hands, and the winner would have an entire year of bragging rights.

Jim watched as his progeny placed what little food remained in the various containers of potato salad, coleslaw, and Jell-O back into the picnic coolers. Diane, the worker bee of the tribe, tossed paper plates, spent cans of soda, plastic utensils, nibbled cobs of corn, and empty bags of potato chips into an oversized garbage bag. If there were so much as one napkin floating about the campsite, Diane would be all over it in an instant. Obsessive-compulsive or not, Jim loved his daughter deeply. She shot a glance his way and the two shared a smile.

Jim worked his way across the grass and on to the sidewalk leading to the campsite's restroom. When he reached the facility he turned and leaned his back against the coolness of the brick exterior, once again taking in the scene. Ann – God bless her – would be so proud of what the two of them had set in motion so long ago. Family meant everything to Jim and his wife, and the sight of a flock of Severson offspring and in-laws eating and playing together, backslapping and laughing, visiting and catching up on the past year's gossip as though there was hardly a care in the world warmed his heart.

This is what we begot, Ann, he thought to himself, *this is what we begot.*

Jim hoped that after today – God willing – the tradition he and Ann had initiated at Kankakee River State Park would last another fifty-eight years.

Ann was the glue that held the whole shooting match together, that is, until the leukemia took it all away nearly three years ago, leaving Jim alone with the hearing loss and hypertension, the osteoarthritis and osteoporosis, Type 2 diabetes and arrhythmia, and the half-dozen other ailments the various doctors chided him over as though he held any sway in the matter.

Truth be told, his medicine cabinet would make a drug lord proud.

Yes, Jim missed his wife, more than he ever thought possible. He spoke to her all the time – not giving a hoot in hell what any casual observer might make of the crazed old geezer walking around muttering to himself – updating Ann on events of the day, both large and small.

He'd even told Ann about his *plan*.

And it wasn't too shabby a plan for a man in his mid-eighties.

Jim continued watching the Severson family reunion unfold before him. His gaze finally settled on Diane again, his firstborn child. He remembered as though it were yesterday, holding Diane in his hands on the day she was born, and looking from her to Ann as Ann stared back from the hospital bed with a smile that lit up the room.

After the past few years he knew Diane would understand; he prayed she would forgive him.

Jim slipped around the campsite's restroom and headed into the forest.

PART ONE

The Nephew

The dog is a gentleman; I hope to go to his heaven not man's.
— Mark Twain

ONE

I spotted Stretch standing over the body as his German shepherds circled nearby.

Kankakee River State Park is one of my favorite spots, not only because I can get the dogs here in under ninety minutes for human remains detection training, but because it has a little of something for everyone – from picnicking to camping to communing with nature to fishing and hunting to canoeing or biking or hiking. Kankakee's got nature trails and pathways that unfold for miles along both sides of the river. That said, today felt as though my dogs – Alice, my bloodhound, and Rex, my springer spaniel – and I had meandered endless miles through copses of pine trees and maples, white and red oak, hickory and American beech with nothing to show for it but thirst and exhaustion. The ground we traipsed upon a floor mat of wilted leaves and dirt, peppered with scrubs and undergrowth, branches downed by storms and high winds, shrubs and wildflowers and a wide array of other brush I could neither remember nor pronounce. I'd never ventured this deep into Kankakee before – was getting that *Hansel and Gretel* vibe – and I glanced at my watch for the fiftieth time in the past hour.

I figured if we kept hiking in this direction, we'd eventually trip over an ocean.

My name is Cory Pratt, and I am bone weary. Weary not only from trudging about Kankakee River State Park all the livelong day, but as a result of the crappy-choppy sleep I'd gotten last night. Said crappy-choppy sleep was the direct result of my detective sister venturing downstairs into my quarters of the household – my fortress of solitude – and waking me up at one in the freaking morning to *inform* me that my attendance would be required at Kankakee State Park, at the first crack of dawn, in order to help the Bourbonnais Police Department and investigators from the Illinois State Police in their continued search for some elderly gent who'd wandered off from some kind of family gathering. I mumbled my acceptance to keep my sibling from further shaking at my shoulder, praying she'd exit stage left, but my sister paused a long moment before stating, 'You know I'll be back in a few hours to make sure you're up and at 'em.'

I knew she would . . . and, of course, she didn't disappoint.

My sister-tormentor, Detective Crystal Pratt, is an investigator in the Violent Crimes Section inside the Area 3 Detective Division in the Chicago Police Department. And though I'm the CEO and president, treasurer and secretary, sole proprietor and all-around gopher at the COR Canine Training Academy, I'm also a fulltime student at Harper Community College, having recently wrapped up a spring semester of computer science courses and currently entering the second week of Harper's summer session. As a result, my instructor-led dog obedience sessions have been cut in half, and Alice and Rex and I only help out on the cadaver dog front, on rare occasions, when some poor soul goes missing and is presumed dead.

Today being one of those rare occasions.

And what better way to spend Memorial Day than slogging about Kankakee River State Park.

When Bourbonnais PD set up the grids in which the human remains detection dogs would search, they informed us the missing person was an elderly gentleman who suffered from an extensive list of medical conditions. I checked my watch again and figured the entire day was shot, a complete bust . . . kaput. There's no way some old-timer could have made it this far into the forest. His family had panicked – I couldn't blame them one bit – and turned the campsite upside down and inside out looking for their absent patriarch before contacting the local authorities. The Bourbonnais Police then searched the surrounding woodlands and nearby trails well into the evening before putting out the call for a few dozen other search-and-rescue and HRD dogs, such as Alice and Rex, as well as their handlers to arrive at Kankakee at first light to assist in the hunt.

As we continued our march deeper into the forest, I fixated on how when I got back home, I'd slip under the covers and snooze like Rip Van Winkle. Then my thoughts returned to my working hypothesis on how the old coot had actually OD'd on family merriment and good cheer, trekked back to the park's main entrance, and phoned a cab or, if he was a particularly contemporaneous octogenarian, an Uber or Lyft to come and whisk him the hell away from his kinfolk. In fact, I was genuinely confident as to the legitimacy of my theory when Alice and Rex latched on to the scent. A couple of snouts rose in the air for the briefest of seconds, then the two pitched forward, narrowing the space between them, coming together as one and breaking into a full-out sprint, springing forward like an arrow from a bow, now racing side by side . . . beelining toward the scent's origin.

I jogged after Alice and Rex, scratching past tree branches, leaping thick undergrowth, not an all-out sprint as I didn't want to roll an ankle on the uneven terrain, but keeping the dynamic duo in my line of vision. The crowns of the trees, the branches and leaves – the forest canopy – robbed us of considerable daylight, leaving us veiled in murk and shadows, a perpetual twilight. My heart pounded as I passed an abandoned windbreaker and then, sixty yards further on, I spotted a cane. I cut right around a pine tree and that's when I caught sight of Stretch and his German shepherds.

And the missing patriarch from the family picnic.

He sat in a patch of weeds, his head slouched forward, his back against a maple tree.

Motionless.

Deceased.

Stretch nodded as I slowed to a walk. Though I'd known my dog handler colleague for several years, I've only known him as *Stretch*. Never knew his first name and couldn't come up with a surname if you held a gun to my head. Just Stretch. It didn't help that he rarely, if ever, uttered a word, much less a complete sentence.

'Hey, Stretch,' I said, nodding back and letting one of his German shepherds sniff at my fingertips. My colleague tilted his smartphone my way and shrugged. I read his mind. At his height, you'd think Stretch would never have issues with phone reception. The guy's nearly seven feet tall, hence his moniker. He's also lanky and sports a tumbleweed of blond hair. Stretch pointed from where I'd just arrived and headed off in that direction in search of an elusive cell phone bar, his dogs following in his wake.

I once had Stretch fill in for me when I was out sick and couldn't teach one of my obedience classes. Boy did I get feedback when the next class rolled around. One canine owner informed me Stretch may have mumbled all of eight words throughout the entirety of the two-hour session, mostly a whispered *yes* here or a hushed *no* over there. Another dog owner asked if the man was mute.

Needless to say I've not had Stretch fill in for me ever since.

And I can only imagine how lively his chat with Bourbonnais PD was going to be.

One of the benefits of handling cadaver dogs is I get to recede into the background as soon as a discovery is made and let the authorities and medical examiners take control of the scene. In fact, I get to take a powder not terribly long after a body is discovered. It's not that I don't have a strong stomach for this kind of stuff, but, well – certain things cannot be unseen.

The old man hadn't been dead long. He'd been missing less than twenty-four hours and I figured he'd passed away sometime during the night from either exhaustion or exertion or fright in conjunction with his advanced age and varied illnesses. I began walking away, checking my cell phone to see if my reception was any better than Stretch's – it wasn't – but I'd spotted something in the old man's hands, and I turned back to verify.

Sure enough, the old gent gripped a small piece of paper, a message of some kind, in a rigor-mortised right hand.

I tried to shake the notion from my head, but curiosity – cat killer that it is – got the better of me and I stepped behind the maple tree, leaned forward, and peered over the old man's shoulder as though I were inspecting his schoolwork. The light wasn't great, so I tapped the flashlight app on my iPhone, shined it down on the poor guy's note, and read.

> *Life's a trap of ER visits, doctor appointments, medications and side effects. Nothing works and I have no desire to cope with everyday actions.*
> *I want to be with Ann.*
> *I've prayed hard for release.*
> *Please forgive me.*

I stood up and again headed away from the maple tree. Suddenly, I wanted to be anywhere but here. I checked my phone again to see if any bars had stealthily crept back into the picture. None had and I hoped Stretch had reached a location where he could call the number Bourbonnais PD had provided us.

Now I understood why the old man had made it this deep into the woodland, the miles he had hiked before sitting down a final time. He must have been beyond spent, completely drained. From the looks of him I imagined he'd staggered on through a heart attack or two . . . and I realized the old man was doing one last thing for his family.

He was making damn sure they weren't the ones that found him.

Alice barked, drawing me back to the here and now. My head snapped up. I had to squint as she was sitting maybe seventy yards away, staring back in my direction, and patting at the ground with a right paw. Rex circled nearby, sniffing at the soil.

'You've got to be kidding,' I said aloud, and began heading in their direction.

Tests indicate a cadaver dog's nose can alert to the scent of human remains as deep as forty feet underground, with ten to fifteen feet being child's play. Yup – it's freaking supernatural. And I've trained Alice and Rex to detect the scent not only in bodies but in blood, in teeth, in hair . . . and in bone.

'Good girl,' I said and patted Alice's head and handed her a treat. 'You, too, Rex.' I tossed him a doggie snack.

Whatever Alice alerted to was anything but fresh. No soil had been overturned, no uneven smears of dirt, no disturbance in the matting of leaves – the ground my bloodhound patted looked exactly like the rest of the forest floor. The nearest tree was thirty feet away, far enough where one wouldn't spend hours chopping away at thick roots.

Alice and Rex orbited away from me, both sniffing the ground as though they were still on the clock. They were likely inhaling remnants of their discovery, but I tossed a hand in the air and issued the command, 'Find.'

I could whistle them back if they strayed too far off the beaten path, but I was more interested in marking the spot they'd just uncovered. I needed a branch, preferably something with a little strength and less like kindling. It took thirty seconds to find the perfect stick, about two feet in length. Then I kicked at the topsoil with the heel of my hiking boot. After loosening the dirt,

I corkscrewed the branch into the ground until it was standing upright of its own accord. Then I dragged my heel in an oval around the perimeter of Alice's find. There was now no way their discovery could be lost in the shade and gloom of the forest canopy. Even if I got twisted around as the police and medical personnel arrived, I could tell exactly where I'd have to drag the lead officer to and inform him or her they'd best call in shovels or some kind of ground-penetrating radar.

I was returning to the maple tree where the old man sat alone with his note, hoping Stretch would return soon with reinforcements, when I heard Alice bark again. I squinted harder this time as the pups now seemed a football field away, two dark shapes off in the distance. Alice sat pawing at a new spot on the forest dirt as Rex stood close by and sniffed at the ground.

'What?' I said. If my jaw dropped any further, it'd bounce off the woodland floor. I scratched at my cheek. 'Now you're just showing off.'

I began heading toward my dogs, glancing about for another branch I could use to mark their second discovery.

Stretch and his HRD dogs found the old man.

But Alice and Rex found the graveyard.

TWO

'Are you making bacon, lettuce, and tomato?' Crystal asked. She'd just arrived home.

'No.'

'Scrambled eggs and toast?'

'No,' I repeated.

'Just a package of bacon for dinner?'

'You say that like it's a bad thing.'

'Not the most nutritious of meals.'

'I'm in my twenties,' I said. 'I'll worry about that when I'm fifty.'

'Save a few slices for my BLT, would you?' Crystal looked at Alice and Rex, sitting at the border of where the kitchen connects to the living room, smelling bacon smells, thinking bacon thoughts, and surveilling my efforts with ever-hopeful eyes. Then Crys spotted my near-empty can of Rolling Rock on the countertop as well as a completely empty one sitting in the sink. 'That kind of day, huh?'

I nodded.

I'd been at Kankakee River State Park until two in the morning, got home around half past three. Then I couldn't sleep. I tossed and turned, eventually began to fret about school until I rolled out of bed at six and paged through my data structures and UNIX assignments. It wasn't keeping up with homework that had me tossing and turning all night, rather certain visions – of anything but sugar-plums – that danced in my head. Visions of what the Bourbonnais PD had uncovered last night after a couple of their beefier cops dug deep enough into one of the spots where Alice and Rex had alerted me regarding human remains.

What the diggers uncovered looked like something out of *Tales from the Crypt*.

Like me, the dogs were exhausted, and when Rex gets pooped, he tends to snore like a whale clearing its blowhole. I'm surprised neighbors from two suburbs over didn't call the cops. I'm toying with getting the goofball a sleep apnea machine for Christmas.

Fortunately, Harper Community College is in Palatine, just a hop, skip, and jump from Casa-de-Pratt in Buffalo Grove. I can even sneak home for a sandwich at lunch, like I did today. I let the dogs out and then sacked out on the couch and rested my eyes a half-hour before zipping back for my afternoon course.

My father had been a veterinarian, the proud owner of Pratt Pet Clinic. Dad sucked me into training dogs at age ten. I loved it and he began offering the occasional obedience class, which took place after hours in the clinic's parking lot. Dad initially performed the bulk of the song and dance – introductions to the differing exercises – while I roamed about the lot offering up tips and tricks, and awarding treats to eager puppies whenever a task was successfully performed. After a few years of this, Dad settled into the backseat and let me lead the circus.

My mother was a certified public accountant. Along with her expanding list of clients, she worked as the clinic's bookkeeper in addition to preparing its quarterly taxes. I figure what's driving me to take up a career in computer programming is the math-numbers half of me that stems from Mom.

My parents died in a car accident when I was a junior in high school. The two were out on a date night – a movie and dinner – when a winter storm swept off Lake Michigan and covered the entire city in ice. Dad was pronounced dead at the scene, Mom died in the ambulance on the way to the hospital.

I've never recovered from their deaths.

And I doubt I ever will.

Life insurance and the sale of Dad's veterinary clinic allowed us to pay off the two-story my sister and I had grown up in. Crystal moved back home so I could graduate high school in Buffalo Grove as opposed to being shipped off to Minneapolis, where my mother's parents lived, or Sioux Falls, South Dakota, where my father's parents resided.

My sister took ownership of the second floor, which was fine by me as I'd previously migrated to the basement – my man cave. Crystal and I get along so well as a result of respecting each other's privacy. I rarely go upstairs and only on Crystal's say-so when she needs me to drag furniture and mattresses about in her never-ending quest to remodel her childhood bedroom.

Although, on this last go-round, we finally carted all of her stuff into the master bedroom – into Mom and Dad's old room. Not that my sister needed it, but she asked for my permission. It had been seven years – our parents would have been OK with the move – and I had no issues, well, except for the hernia I darned near got lugging her stuff down the hallway.

Crystal's always been the go-getter of the family, an A-student whose report cards my parents could juxtapose against my B-minus grade point average. After my parents' death, my mostly Bs GPA sank as though it were the Titanic. The last year and a half of high school – train wreck that it was – found me graduating more on sympathy and pity and Crystal meeting with most of my teachers and, in some instances, nearly plucking her sidearm from her holster in order to make sure my homework got handed in.

My sister is not quite five-eleven to my not quite six feet in height. She's got an athlete's build, whereas I tend to maintain a wiry physique. We both share the same dark brown hair; Crystal's is shoulder-length, while mine is close-cropped.

A few years back Crystal nudged me into expanding my canine repertoire by working with search-and-rescue dogs. More specifically, I work with human remains detection dogs, or, as they are more commonly known, cadaver dogs. Yup – I teach my hounds to hunt for the dead. My pack and I help law enforcement – CPD, other local PDs, various sheriff departments, even the FBI on rare occasions – when some poor devil's gone missing.

Alice, my seven-year-old bloodhound, is black and tan, eighty pounds, and full of equal parts affection and protectiveness. She's named after my mother's middle name, one of Mom's great-aunts I've never met. Rex is my five-year-old springer spaniel. He's named after my father's middle name, which I don't believe was based on anyone in the family tree.

I've never met a better sniffer dog than Alice. Certain canine breeds have three hundred million scent receptors in their nasal cavity, whereas we mere mortals bop about town with only five million. This absurd amount of scent receptors allows them to decipher thousands of different smells, thus sniffer dogs are able to find illegal drugs, locate explosive materials or IEDs – Improvised Explosive Devices – discover survivors after some kind of natural disaster . . . or lead a dog handler such as myself to human remains.

Rex is a good boy, too, but he morphs into T-Rex whenever his knotted sock comes into play. Take it from him at your own peril. Rex is chocolate with white, has floppy ears, goes without saying, and a moderately long coat. He's no slacker, either – forty-five pounds of continual motion. And though Rex is not at Alice's level in the human remains detection department, he has his moments of inspiration, and the three of us can cover a chunk of ground in no time flat.

Yes, Alice may be my A-student, but whatever Rex lacks in gray matter, he triples in enthusiasm.

Speaking of A-students, it pains me to report I am not among them at Harper Community College. When all was said and done with spring semester – my first semester at Harper – I wound up with an equal mixture of Bs and Cs. Crystal was surprised, yet pleased, when I informed her I would be attending school this summer. My reasoning, which I didn't see the necessity to inform my sister, was that I wanted to see if I hated taking programming courses any less in summer than I had in winter and spring.

I'd gotten burnt out on the endless busywork involved in running a canine training academy – booking facilities, hauling gear all over tarnation in Dad's decades-old Chevy Silverado, the taxes and paperwork, working the phone lines, dealing with the occasional deadbeat who refused to pay up no matter how many notices I sent out, staying atop the bureaucracy . . . rinse and repeat. However, halfway through spring semester at Harper, I began to question myself. What the hell am I doing in computer science? Do I want to design and test software? Am I really *passionate* about writing code for mobile apps? Plus, won't AI eventually smother any career in the industry?

Perhaps running a canine obedience school isn't the only vocation that's a pain in the rump?

I didn't bring up any misgivings or second guessing with Crystal out of fear that, unlike with my high school assignments, her Glock 22 would truly work its way out of her shoulder holster.

'These are actually pretty good.' I had relented and let Crystal slice up tomatoes and lettuce as well as toast some pumpernickel for a couple of BLTs instead of just mainlining bacon. We sat at the kitchen table, eating dinner and chatting.

'So you and Stretch kept walking the dogs in case there were even more dead bodies?'

'Yeah, the cops thought I was full of crap until they dug up the one closer to the trail and hit paydirt.' The first spot the police excavated was actually the second grave Alice and Rex had discovered as it was forty yards or so nearer the trail, thus quicker to get shovels and supplies to in the late-evening light. 'After that they got on the horn to bring back the medical examiner who'd been working on the old man as well as some other investigators out of Bourbonnais. A sergeant on the scene got the bright idea that as long as the dogs were handy, they should see what else they could find, if anything.'

The sun had gone down by that point, but law enforcement officers had already lugged in shovels and spades, tarps, bottles of water, and energy bars on the back of a couple all-terrain vehicles. The cops used the ATV headlights to illuminate their dig at the gravesite. Then Stretch and I were each paired with an officer carrying one of those Stinger flashlights that put to shame any illumination kicked off by the light on my phone app.

We paraded our dogs further and further away from where the old man had been found, from where Alice and Rex had made their two discoveries. We hiked what seemed a few hundred laps – back and forth and up and down – to the outer reach of the park in case the pups sniffed out more gravesites.

It was my idea of purgatory . . . and I've got the shin splints to prove it.

After an eternity, Stretch pulled the plug, had us all return to the basecamp that had been set up around the excavated grave, and informed the police sergeant we were both done for the evening. If not for Stretch, I'd probably still be out there. Quite frankly, I don't think I'd ever heard Stretch talk so much in my life, must have been two entire sentences in a row, a personal best – Stretch's equivalent of Hamlet's soliloquy. I'd never been more proud of him.

Crystal said, 'So they left the other grave for the morning?'

'It was late and dark, and Bourbonnais had their hands full with the bones from the first dig.' I shrugged and continued, 'I bet those two graves have been out there since before you and I were born. Whoever's in that other hole isn't going anywhere.'

'Then you haven't heard?'

'No,' I said. 'I'm the dog guy. No one tells me anything.' I set the remainder of my BLT down on my plate and stared back at my sister. 'What did you hear?'

'They did find something in the other hole.'

'Yup,' I said and nodded. 'Another body.'

'No, Cory,' Crystal said. 'Three more bodies – it was a mass grave.'

THREE

Four Bodies Unearthed in Kankakee River State Park

Chicago Tribune

Cadaver dogs discovered two separate gravesites containing the remains of four bodies in a desolate northwest corner of Kankakee River State Park late Memorial Day afternoon.

The dogs were originally brought in to aid the Bourbonnais Police Department and the Illinois State Police in their search for a missing octogenarian, Jim Severson, who had wandered off from a family reunion on Sunday afternoon. After locating the deceased Severson in this section of the state park, the dogs then alerted their handler to the location of two nearby graves. Bourbonnais PD found the remains of a single body in the grave excavated Memorial Day evening, and three additional bodies in the grave excavated Tuesday morning.

A preliminary examination by the forensic anthropologist/bone detective assisting the Kankakee County Coroner's Office is that all four bodies uncovered were adult males due to extended bone lengths as well as the sexually dimorphic features of skeletal size and shape. Time of death has not been established as after soft tissues have decomposed, skeletal remains do not break down in a predictable manner. The decomposition process for bones, referred to as diagenesis, can take years or several decades. If the bones are not dug up, moved, or destroyed by animals, a skeleton can take twenty years to dissolve in fertile soil or hundreds of years in neutral soil or sand.

Bourbonnais Police Chief Mike Thorsen said his department is currently combing through missing person case files going back fifty years, not only from Kankakee County but Cook County as well as the five collar counties bordering Cook. 'If we can connect four missing males,' Chief Thorsen said, 'we can then check dental records or perform DNA analysis in order to see if the missing males match these victims.' Thorsen went on to say how mitochondrial DNA in bones and/or teeth can be used to confirm the relationship of skeletal remains with living or deceased descendants.

Goddammit! The figure in the office chair dropped the *Chicago Tribune* on to the desk. *How on earth did the old man venture that deep into the woods only to sit down and die? The guy had to have trudged a few dozen times the distance it would have taken him to locate a trail and hike back to the park's entrance. And the old man led the damned dogs right to the burial spots.* The figure wanted to pound on the top of the desk. *About those dogs – how in hell did they sniff out those graves because*, the figure in the chair knew for a fact, *they were anything but shallow.*

FOUR

'Can you show me on the map where it took place?' the retired parole officer asked me.

Several days passed before a forensic dentist working for Bourbonnais PD ID'd one of the four dead men, more specifically one of the three cadavers in the mass grave my dogs had uncovered. The body's oral characteristics matched the dental records of a young man by the name of Kenneth 'Kenny' Tharp, who had been twenty-one at the time of his disappearance in August of 1994. Tharp had served a two-year stint at the Stateville Correctional Center in Crest Hill – from where they'd received Tharp's dental records – for aggravated robbery prior to being released on probation and supervised by Chuck Sims, the retiree currently showing me a diagram he'd printed of Kankakee River State Park.

'Right here,' I said, pointing at the northwest corner of the park where the two graves had been discovered.

'Well,' Sims looked up from the map, 'if you don't want bodies popping up anytime soon, you could do worse than planting them out in the boondocks.'

I'd received a text message from Crystal while I was in class informing me she was on her way to pick me up from school and escort me to a retired probation officer's home in Evanston, a suburb along the north shore of Lake Michigan, who had requested to meet with me. *WTF?* I immediately texted back. *We'll chat in the car*, she shot back and, sure enough, there was my sister, behind the wheel of her Honda HR-V, waiting for me in Harper's parking lot after my UNIX course came to an end.

The dead guy, Kenny Tharp, she informed me, had been a Chicago native. He grew up in a single-mother household – no father of record – in Douglas, on the South Side, but spent a chunk of his youth at a juvenile detention center in Warrenville prior to turning eighteen. With Tharp identified, Chicago PD was now officially involved in the Kankakee case much to the delight of Bourbonnais Police Chief Thorsen. Crystal dove in and contacted Chuck Sims, apprised him of the *Kenny Tharp* situation – Sims recalled *the mouse-faced little shit* – and even told Sims about how my pups had discovered the two graves. Sims coughed up his address in Evanston and requested my presence as he had several questions to ask me.

'What the heck does he want me for?' I said. 'I'm not a parolee and he's retired.'

Crystal shrugged. 'I think he's got some ideas about the case.'

I seized my opportunity. 'Sounds like Taco Bell is on you tonight?'

She shot me a stern look but nodded.

Sims was big, a full head taller than me, with muscles atop muscles in his red Bulls jersey. African American, he sported a shaved head with a graying beard and mustache. Even with the gray, Sims looked more fifties than seventies. If he were my probation officer, I'd move heaven and earth to remain on the man's good side. Sims had spent the entirety of his law enforcement career in Chicago, wanted more than anything to migrate south – to Arizona – but an aging mother in an assisted care facility said otherwise.

'Arizona's a pipe dream,' Sims informed us as we exchanged pleasantries and took seats on the front porch of his two-story. 'Mom will outlive everyone on planet earth.'

Sims then started quizzing me about HRD dogs, revealing a more than working knowledge of what I did for a living. He then moved on to our search for Jim Severson at Kankakee River State Park before digging out his map for more specificity. Sims finished by asking if I knew how deep the grave they opened that night had been.

'Deep enough that nothing got at the remains for thirty years.'

'Tell me about the old timer – this Jim Severson fellow.' Sims switched to a new line of questioning. 'He'd have been fifty-something back when those bodies were dumped there. Any way Severson ties in to Kenny Tharp and the other bones?'

I figured nothing got past Sims back in his parole officer days but slowly shook my head.

'Severson had been a welder in Matteson, where he'd lived with his wife until she passed away a few years ago,' Crystal said. 'He was a deacon in their church.' My sister also shook her head. 'I've found no connection between Severson and Tharp; believe me, I've looked. I doubt their paths ever crossed.'

'Yet Severson winds up in that secluded section of Kankakee,' Sims said and looked my way, 'leading you to the two graves.'

'Out of respect for his family they didn't mention it in the news coverage,' I said, 'but the old man had a goodbye note in his hand.'

'Severson didn't wander off and die from a heart attack or exposure – the guy committed suicide?'

'Well, he didn't want to live anymore. Severson had some serious health issues, and he missed his wife. I suspect he pushed himself onward, way beyond overexertion, and then sat down under a tree and let nature take its course, which, hopefully, didn't take too long.' I thought for a second and then said, 'Severson wound up in that remote spot not only because he hiked his butt off, but so no one in his family, no one from the reunion, would find his body. I'm sure he wanted to let the police or park rangers or a dog handler like me deal with that.'

Crystal added, 'It's unlikely, Chuck, that Jim Severson had any type of link to the four bodies in the two graves.'

'Damn,' Sims replied. 'It was a shot in the dark, but I thought maybe the old guy was in on it.'

'What do you mean?' Crystal asked. 'In on what?'

'July 26, 1994,' Sims said, glancing from me to Crystal. 'The Crown National bank robbery.'

FIVE

'It was a five-man job with four inside the bank,' Sims said as though presenting an academic dissertation. 'The men wore suits and those cheap ski masks you can pick up at any sporting goods store. Two of them worked crowd control. Their main focus was getting the guards on the floor with their hands zip-tied behind their backs. The other two worked the bank manager and tellers. The crew had to have known about the armored trucks and the bags of cash and the delivery schedules, and how much was stashed in the vault at that particular time. They were out in under five minutes. The robbers knew exactly what they were doing.' Sims added, 'It almost went like clockwork.'

Crystal said, 'Wasn't a bank guard shot?'

'Not only shot. He was killed.' Sims pointed at the papers littering his desk. 'And the bank guard's name was Andy Benson. He had a wife, two daughters, and three grandchildren at the time of his *execution*. The poor guy was a year away from retirement,' he said. 'One of the scumbags shot Benson in the face on the way out. It was unprovoked, in cold blood – evidently, just for shits and giggles.'

We'd migrated inside, from Sims's front porch to the retired parole officer's home office, where he had what he called 'some fun stuff' for us to see. On the trek to his desk we passed a wall of photographs. The first portrait in the series was of a younger Chuck Sims. He still had hair up top, two small children, and what I took to be his spouse as they both sported wedding rings and smiled for the camera. As I passed later pictures, the children grew taller, appeared victorious in sporting events, eventually graduated high school and college, and began having families of their own. Somewhere along this hodgepodge of imagery, Sims ceased wearing a ring and the spouse had vanished from the portraits.

I didn't ask.

Sims ran a tidy office – not so much as a single candy wrapper, empty can of pop or beer, or errant dust bunny on the hardwood floor, all books positioned neatly on shelves – until you approached his desk. At that point I couldn't tell if the tabletop was solid wood or laminate over particle board on account of it being covered with ancient newspaper clippings, an open notebook with two pages in what I assumed was Sims's penmanship, two photographs of Kenny Tharp – blond hair, a peach fuzz mustache, intense eyes – as well as photocopies of other Tharp-related documents I imagined worked their way into Sims's car on his final shift as a parole officer.

Sims continued filling us in, 'A white Econoline van was waiting for them as soon as they hit the curb. One of the perps aimed his assault rifle at the traffic behind them as they jumped into the back of the van, into its cargo area, with the duffel bags.

He did this to deter any do-gooders from nursing gallant notions of pursuit,' Sims said. 'The first robber out the door jumped behind the wheel, while the original driver slid into the passenger seat. Counting the driver, it was a five-man crew.'

Crystal had been scribbling in her pocket notebook – which she never left home without – but, once at Sims's desk, she jammed the notebook into a breast pocket and switched to snapping pictures of articles and other documents with the camera app on her iPhone. Crystal paused in her flurry of activity, looked up at Sims, and said, 'The four men in the two graves.'

'Yup,' Sims said. 'The Crown National bank heist was huge, not only due to the murder of the bank guard but because of the D.B. Cooper nature of their getaway. The crew made off with nearly four million dollars that day; they got away scot-free.' Sims lowered his voice. 'It's considered one of the great crimes of the twentieth century.'

I'd been scanning one of Sims's clipped articles, a five-year retrospective on the unsolved robbery that had been published in the *Chicago Sun-Times*. The article contained nothing beyond what Sims had summarized; instead, it spent column space detailing dead ends CPD and the FBI pursued. I said, 'The thieves got the money, they got away with murder, and then they fell off the face of the earth.'

'The investigators at the time had to be thinking it was an inside job,' Crystal said.

'Yes, the FBI even polygraphed bank employees, but nothing came of it,' Sims said. 'So either an inside job or loose lips or the perps cased the bank and/or the armored vehicles. Reward money was offered – a hundred thousand – for any tip that led to an arrest. They got a shitload of tips, but no one ever collected the reward. No arrests were ever made, no one ratted anyone out . . . and that was that,' Sims concluded his dissertation.

'When did you suspect Tharp was part of the robbery?'

'He didn't check in with me – failed to report – that first week in August. I let a day slide by, but the little shit remained AWOL. I reported him to the court, which would tack on more time to parole or even trigger a return to prison.' Sims shuffled through some of the desktop documents with his fingertips. 'It was impossible not to hear the news about the bank robbery and a day or two later, while watching the coverage on TV – poof – a lightbulb goes on over my head. The timing of Tharp's disappearance got me thinking. Crown National happens and then Tharp doesn't show up for his next check-in. And what's Tharp's MO?' Sims said, and then answered his own question. 'He was in Stateville for aggravated robbery, but also did time in a juvenile detention center for armed robbery.'

'You raised your concerns, right?'

'Of course,' Sims said. 'One of CPD's investigators went along for the ride when we checked the dump Tharp lived in, but nothing there pointed to Crown National.' He shrugged. 'Not much in the apartment to begin with unless you counted the stack of *Penthouses* by the floor mattress Tharp used as a bed. More bare hangers than clothes in the closet and he didn't own a car, so I figured the little shit packed what he needed and jumped town.'

'Nothing linked him to the robbery?'

'There was no evidence, just a gut feeling.' Sims shrugged again. 'An FBI agent called me six months later to see if Tharp had shown up. He hadn't, and I told the agent, but nothing came of that, either. I'm sure CPD and the FBI were double-checking every tip that came in, turning over every rock.'

'If Tharp was in on it, could he have been the one to kill the guard?'

Sims frowned. 'I don't know, but I know he had it in him. If I'd been in the bank that day and the little shit spotted me, I'd be dead. Of course Tharp and I didn't have the greatest of relationships. We were the opposite of friends.'

I pointed at all the papers on Sims's desk. 'Thirty years later and you've hung on to all these files.'

Sims looked at Crystal. 'After you called, I dug these folders out of my cabinet.' Then he turned to me. 'The other cases in my career had closure, all wrapped neatly together with a bow on top . . . except for this motherfucker. Parolees I supervised either turned things around, went back to prison, died or, in more than a few cases, took their own lives,' he said. 'It's embarrassing for me to admit a little shit like Kenny Tharp has been my white whale all these years. Call me crazy for thinking he was involved in one of the greatest crimes of the twentieth century, but, well – there you have it.'

'You don't make it sound like the guy was bright enough to plan the heist.'

'Nope.' Sims chuckled. 'Tharp robbed a liquor store of three hundred dollars, and then he goes to a bar a few blocks over, gets shitfaced, buys shots for some of the barflies, and then brags about the robbery. That's what got him sent to Stateville. The little shit was a dunderhead,' Sims said. 'Don't get me wrong, Tharp had the stones to march into a store, threaten violence, and demand cash. Not many people can do that, but Tharp could. And not only could he threaten violence, but he'd follow through. In the armed robbery that got him parked in a juvie center at sixteen, the cashier, evidently, wasn't moving fast enough for him, so Tharp came around the counter and kicked the poor woman in the baby-maker.' Sims shook his head. 'Not a good guy.' He took a breath and continued, 'I've spent decades assuming he'd met someone like George Clooney in *Ocean's Eleven* who planned the bank heist and then got everyone the hell out of Dodge. I figured Tharp was lying on a beach in Cancun or Belize or someplace far away, spending the bank's money, but it turns out the little shit never made it more than an hour south of Chicago.'

'Instead of George Clooney,' I said, 'Tharp gets *Evil Danny Ocean*. And Evil Danny Ocean didn't like loose ends, especially after a member of his crew kills a bank guard.'

Sims nodded my way and then turned back toward Crystal. 'What's the thing with the two graves? Seems like a lot of added work. What the hell is that about?'

My sister set her iPhone down on the desk. 'Two of the three males in the first grave the dogs found were shot in the face. Point blank at a downward trajectory. I'm told executioner style; the two died instantly. But the third male sharing the grave got shot in the back, in his upper right shoulder. I'm thinking he made a run for it while the other two were killed, but didn't make it far, and then he got the coup de grâce in his left eye,' Crystal said. 'The man in the second grave – the single-occupancy grave – was shot once in the chest at point-blank range.'

'The mass grave must have come first, right?' Sims said. 'It doesn't make sense for four or more guys to shoot a member of the crew, dig a grave, bury him, and, after all that excitement, mosey on deeper into the forest only to have another shootout.'

'Yeah,' Crystal said. 'They'd be so paranoid; they'd have their guns drawn. But what if Evil Danny Ocean had a right-hand man? I forget who Brad Pitt played in the movie, but what if Evil Danny Ocean and Evil Brad Pitt lured Tharp and the other three into the woods and ambushed them. Now they get much bigger shares of the Crown National Bank funds and don't have to worry about Tharp or the others getting caught and making plea deals. But even a bigger split wasn't good enough for Evil Danny, so he kills Evil Brad on the way back to the trail and keeps all the money for himself.'

'And it's a clean getaway,' Sims said, 'because dead men tell no tales.'

'Do you remember those West Garfield Park drug dealers charged with homicide last year?' Crystal asked. 'They forced heroin addicts into robbing banks, knowing bank tellers are trained to comply in order to avoid violence. You know – give them the cash, don't mess around, don't die over a few thousand dollars.'

Sims and I both nodded.

Ironically, I'd read somewhere, it turns out the best places to sell drugs are on the streets outside treatment centers. And homicide rates in West Garfield Park have been astronomical due to turf wars over selling powder or crack cocaine to snort or smoke, heroin to snort, smoke, inject, or, as I'd also read in a news article, introduce into the bloodstream via the rectum – wow, the guy doing that must be the life of the party. Anyway, whenever an open-air drug market gets shut down due to a police sting, another one inevitably opens up elsewhere in the neighborhood. It's like *Whac-A-Mole*. I've even heard the Eisenhower Parkway has been nicknamed the Heroin Highway due to users coming in from the suburbs to score drugs.

Into this mix, a handful of drug traffickers got the bright idea to induce heroin addicts into robbing tellers for them in exchange for drugs. Knowing junkies are unreliable, and would dime them out in an instant, there's suddenly a spike of addicts OD'ing – and, sure enough, the dealers were making certain the addicts involved in the bank robberies were getting a fix all right, the final fix of their troubled lives. Word of this spread like wildfire in the druggie subculture and, ultimately, came to the attention of CPD.

In short order, the drug dealers were arrested.

'So what if Evil Danny Ocean did the same thing to his crew these drug dealers did to theirs? He eliminated them.' Crystal added, 'You're making me a believer, Chuck.'

Sims shrugged. 'Now if we only had the receipts. You know, that evidence thingy – pesky little stuff like proof.'

SIX

My sister came straggling home a little after ten at night. Even at that hour she got the rock star treatment from the pups-slash-groupies. Crystal gets greeted by Alice and Rex as though she were the Beatles arriving in America whereas I receive the dive bar wedding singer treatment. I suspect this is because, unlike me, Crystal shells out snacks without first requiring tasks be completed.

'I spent all night cooking a Big Mac and French fries for you,' I said. 'They're in the fridge.'

Crystal opened the refrigerator, grabbed the McDonald's bag, glanced about the shelves, and said, 'Where's my Coke?'

'Yeah, um, that survived until about eight o'clock, and then I figured you wouldn't want the caffeine keeping you up all night.'

'You drank mine?' she said. 'You drank two Cokes?'

'They only serve medium drinks with the meals, not those supersized ones. And the guy filled the cups with more ice than pop.' I added, 'You'd have been pissed off.'

'Gee, thanks for thinking of me, I guess.' Crystal sat at the kitchen table and began tearing open ketchup packets. My sister didn't mind cold burgers or fries. 'We ID'd a second guy today.'

'You did?' I settled into the chair opposite her. It had been two days since our conversation with the retired parole officer and not much had moved the case forward.

'We cross-checked those who served time in Stateville when Kenny Tharp was there – other convicts Tharp may have known.'

'Other cons that went missing?'

Crystal shook her head. 'We hit a dead end on additional Stateville alumni reported missing around the same time of

Tharp's disappearance but found a guy who was there for armed robbery and overlapped six months with Tharp. Then I spent all afternoon down a rabbit hole, trying to find out whatever happened to him only to discover that he did in fact go missing in the summer of 1994 . . . only no one gave enough of a shit to report his disappearance.'

Alice and Rex and I watched as Crystal chewed on a bite of her burger. When she grabbed for a French fry, I said, 'Don't leave us hanging.'

'The ex-con was named Ronald Lamprecht. He did eight years for armed robbery and served his full sentence. He got out over a year before Tharp and, by the time of his disappearance, had finished what time remained on his probation – so there was no Chuck Sims to jump up and down over any failure to check in – and then, like Tharp, the guy vanished into thin air.' Crystal got up, grabbed a glass from the cupboard, filled it with ice water, and returned to her chair. 'Lamprecht was thirty-one at the time of his disappearance and had been estranged from his family since he dropped out of high school and left home. Both Lamprecht's parents have since died, but I contacted an aunt who basically said, "Good riddance." She told me she'd always assumed her nephew was serving time in prison in some other part of the country.'

'If Lamprecht wasn't reported as a missing person, how do you know he disappeared in ninety-four?'

'Because I am a genius,' Crystal said. 'I tripped over an ancient credit report that nuked Lamprecht for skipping out on an apartment lease he had in a suburb of Milwaukee – Metcalfe Park, not the nicest of neighborhoods. The report would have screwed him the next time he tried renting an apartment and they ran a background check. A red flag would have gone up, but, of course, that never occurred on account of Lamprecht's new lease being a hole in the ground at Kankakee State Park.' Crys snarfed a few more fries and then flicked a couple at Alice and Rex. None were flicked in my direction, likely as a result of the whole ugly Coke incident. 'I got nowhere with the property management company that currently runs the apartment complex,' Crystal continued, 'as ownership has turned over several times since Lamprecht bailed on his lease. They couldn't find any records the building manager or onsite landlord kept from back then. But in the credit report, Lamprecht was listed in October of 1994 as having been in arrears on a lease that ran through April of 1995. If a tenant ditches out on a lease, it gets flagged on their credit rating, and, evidently, it took them a couple months to sort out Lamprecht's absenteeism, hence the October 1994 date.'

'So the landlord assumes Lamprecht's walked out on the lease – I'm sure they get a few of those every year – but the guy's dead and buried,' I said, thinking aloud. 'Wouldn't Lamprecht leave an apartment full of furniture and clothes and pots and pans?'

'The woman I spoke to at the current management company mentioned they'd have likely stored Lamprecht's belongings for a few months in case he returned. They've got a basement storage area near the laundry machines, and, if Lamprecht didn't show up to claim his property, it'd go to Goodwill or some other charity or, more likely, into the parking lot dumpster.' Crystal took a long sip of ice water. 'Like Tharp, I'm thinking Lamprecht only had some basic stuff – just a trip or two to the dumpster.'

'And like Tharp, you matched the body with Lamprecht's dental records from Stateville?'

Crystal nodded.

'You *are* a genius,' I conceded. 'Which grave was Lamprecht in?'

'The one with three bodies; he was in with Tharp.'

'OK, so you've got two ex-cons – connected per similar MOs, overlapping time in Stateville penitentiary, and disappearance dates – who shared that mass grave,' I said. 'You're on a roll, Crys. Have you got dental records to compare with the two remaining bodies?'

Crystal shook her head. 'Four of us were working Stateville and we got lucky with Lamprecht.' She crumpled up her burger wrapper and tossed it into the fast-food bag. 'I need to step back and look at the overall picture.'

'What do you mean?'

'Sims's theory makes perfect sense. It does. But then again, two ex-cons that knew each other from a Dallas prison could have been murdered right after JFK's assassination, but that doesn't mean they were part of it.'

'No,' I said, 'but what if they were expert marksmen and buried in a spot where nobody would ever expect them to turn up?'

My sister shrugged.

'What happens now?'

'Keep trying to track down known associates, but – well – it's been over thirty years,' Crystal said. 'We're going to flood the news media – both here and in Milwaukee – with photos of Tharp and Lamprecht, and hope like hell that'll shake something out of the tree.'

SEVEN

'I'm FBI Special Agent Zackary Mueller,' the fixer said, holding up a badge in his right hand. 'Please call me Zack.'

The woman behind the screen door – Catherine Dando – was somewhere in her seventies, thin, with gray hair and black glasses. She stared at Mueller's badge a long moment and said, 'Does this have to do with the bodies they found at Kankakee?'

The fixer nodded. 'Would it be OK if I came inside and asked you a few questions?'

She opened the screen door and said, 'Was one of the bodies my son?'

The fixer glanced sideways as he slipped his badge back into the inside breast pocket of his suit jacket, checking to see if any of her Logan Square neighbors were out and about. 'No, we've not identified Thomas,' he said, following her into the house. 'I apologize for showing up out of the blue and startling you. Identifying remains – comparing them against individuals reported missing during that timeframe – is a time-consuming process.' He added, 'And it wouldn't be an FBI agent stopping by if there was a positive ID. More likely it would be Chicago PD along with someone from social services.'

'I kept Tom's room as it was for the first decade or so after he went missing . . . as though it were frozen in amber,' Ms Dando said in a low voice after letting the FBI agent in. 'Later, I got rid of Tom's bed and, though I never sew anymore, I turned it into a sewing room.'

The fixer glanced around the room – from the pictures peppered about the walls, to the trophies and knickknacks displayed on shelves, to a couple of military medals in a gold frame, to old yearbooks sitting atop a bookshelf – and said, 'Your son had quite the list of accomplishments.'

'Yes, he did,' she said, and looked about the space. 'I guess the room's more for memories than sewing. I put all of Tom's pictures in here, in order to keep them in one place.' She turned toward her visitor. 'Tom was my only child.'

The fixer walked over and studied a photograph near the displayed medals. 'Tom cuts a dashing figure in his dress blues.'

'Four years active, a couple in the ready reserve before he . . . well, you know . . . disappeared,' she said. 'My son was in the first Gulf War. He saw combat. It was bad, and he came home changed. Still a good kid . . . but changed.'

'Post-traumatic stress disorder?'

She nodded. 'Irritable. Night terrors. Depression.'

'I'm sorry to hear that.'

'He began drinking too much.'

The fixer said nothing.

'I kept at him to get treatment,' she said. 'I think it's what drove him away, why he left here for Milwaukee.'

'You were his mother; you were trying to do good by him.'

She blinked away wet eyes and said, 'Why exactly are you here?'

'The bodies at Kankakee River State Park have us combing through a list of those who went missing in the mid-nineties, such as your son,' he said. 'I'd liken why I'm here to working a cold case. Perhaps having a fresh set of eyes, an agent like me looking through some of Tom's belongings in case anything jumps out or bites me on the nose.'

'Everything I have of my son's is in this room.' She swallowed hard. 'His Marine uniforms are in the closet as well as his old sports gear, and some games he liked to play.'

'Do you mind if I look around?'

'Help yourself,' she said. 'Would you like a cup of tea? I was going to make some for myself.'

'I'd love some tea.'

As soon as Ms Dando left the bedroom, the fixer began examining the photographs hung about the four walls. Thomas Dando was a handsome young man – tall, a look of confidence in his eyes, must have been a chick magnet as they say – clearly popular amongst his high school classmates, apparently hung with the jocks. The fixer respected Ms Dando. He felt sorry for her, living alone in a house full of reminiscences and other such ghosts. His hope was to spend ten minutes in Ms Dando's chamber of memories – her ode to the son she'd lost – and find nothing. He'd then be able to report as much back to his client, that the coast was clear, that there was no need for worry.

His client had been *adamant* about Ms Dando – about what *needed* to be done – but he'd had adamant clients before that he'd reasoned with, occasions where calmer heads prevailed. Often, an objective take is all that's called for. Several clients even expressed their appreciation after the fact, providing him an additional bonus for talking them out of their haste . . . and those *matters* hadn't involved occurrences from three decades in the past.

Time heals all wounds, they say, but the fixer knew time also clouded memories.

If there was nothing here . . . he'd reason with his client.

Unfortunately, a picture on the third wall put an end to that notion. There stood Thomas Dando, good-looking black-haired man that he was, surrounded by what had to be a group of his closest friends. They grinned ear to ear at whoever was taking the photo, arms splashed across each other's shoulders – probably closing in on high school graduation.

The world was their oyster.

But next to young master Dando was the fixer's client. Though three and a half decades had passed, his client was still recognizable. Plus, the fixer stared at the floor and shook his head, the woman in the kitchen making tea would be able to confirm their friendship and point out who his client had become . . . and reveal how the two had never *truly* drifted apart after high school.

And then some of the smarter folks at CPD or the Bureau might start making connections, they might then put his client under the microscope.

Damn, now he'd have to go through every scrap of paper in Thomas Dando's childhood room, but first he had a cup of tea to drink.

* * *

The fixer sat at the kitchen table. 'Those pictures in the room,' he said. 'Do you know all the people your son was posing with?'

'Of course – they were his best friends,' she replied. 'I'm still in touch with a couple of them today.'

The fixer nodded slowly. 'You know I was never a big tea drinker until I was stationed in England many years ago and got introduced to dumping a shot of milk into the cup,' he told Ms Dando. 'Now I can't touch the stuff without it.'

She began to rise. 'I've got some two percent in the fridge.'

'Absolutely not,' he said, and motioned her back into her chair. 'Let me get it. I've been a big enough burden for you today.'

She smiled and said, 'Did anything of Tom's jump out and bite you on the nose?'

'Not really.' The fixer opened the fridge, grabbed the jug of milk, but set it near the sink instead of bringing it to the table. He slipped on a pair of powder-free surgical gloves – a best practice – and stared at the elderly woman from behind. 'I owe you an apology, Ms Dando,' he said. 'I am forever sorry about this.'

'What?' She began turning in her chair.

But by then his fingers were around her throat, squeezing inward, cutting off oxygen, strangling her. The fixer could have used his belt or a dishtowel or even yanked the cord off the toaster, but this way felt *more personal*.

He owed her that much.

For Ms Dando, he wanted to make it more personal.

EIGHT

The woman in black entered the Chicago Police Department Headquarters off South Michigan Avenue, used the handrail as she took the stairs up to the lobby, and stepped toward the front desk as though she were leading a funeral procession. She dropped the top half of the *Chicago Tribune* – the columns above the fold – before one of two sergeants manning the desk and tapped a forefinger on the article containing pictures of Kenneth Tharp and Ronald Lamprecht.

'I need to speak to someone about my son,' the woman in black told the desk sergeant and blinked back moist eyes. 'God help me – I think he's part of this.'

Crystal's conference room chair was rolled back from the table, hugging a side wall. She scribbled notes as she listened. The woman in the black dress was Viviana Walsh, though she requested that Detectives Horton and Andreen, who sat across from her at the conference table, call her 'Viv.' Walsh was in her early seventies as her gray hair and lined face would attest. The woman was bone thin. Crystal would be surprised if Walsh weighed more than a hundred pounds soaking wet.

Several decades of grief could do that to a person.

'Connor was heading into his senior year at Marquette University, pursuing a degree in architectural design.' Viviana Walsh dabbed the corner of an eye with a crumpled Kleenex. 'He was following in his father's footsteps. His grades were top of the class. We'd never been more proud of him.' Her voice trembled. 'Never.'

Detective Horton checked his notes. He was running lead on the interview. 'I see you still live in Winnetka.'

'Yes, even after my husband's death – in the same house where Connor grew up.' She added, 'Aiden died of a heart attack at his office five years after our son went missing. I'm told he was dead before the paramedics arrived.' Mrs Walsh twisted her wedding ring with a thumb and forefinger. 'I'm of the opinion your heart can destroy you in more than one way. Our son's disappearance killed Aiden.'

The room sat in silence for several seconds before Horton said, 'I am truly sorry to hear that, Viv.'

She dabbed at her eyes again. 'Connor planned on working at his father's firm once he graduated Marquette.'

Detective Horton, a stone's throw from retirement, had thin, white hair. Crystal had nothing but respect for the man, knew him to be meticulous, thorough. She'd once heard he'd counted the peanuts in a canister of mixed nuts as their label claimed they used less than fifty percent peanuts by weight. Detective Horton's count determined otherwise. Legend has it he notified the manufacturer and had been given a modest stipend to keep his mouth zipped shut while they remedied the situation. Crystal wasn't sure whether the story was true. But then again, she wasn't sure it wasn't.

Detective Andreen, a crimson-faced man with a beard, nudged the box of Kleenex an inch closer toward Mrs Walsh. Crystal didn't know Horton's partner as well as she knew Horton, but when it came to dispensing tissue, the man held his own.

Crystal had worked the Kenny Tharp angle, had relayed retired probation officer Chuck Sims's theory to Horton and Andreen, and assumed – beyond helping to identify Ronald Lamprecht – that would be the extent of her involvement in the case. That is until the photographs in the newspaper indeed shook something out of the tree; until Viviana Walsh marched into CPD headquarters with a strong suspicion that her only child might be one of the two yet-to-be-identified victims in the Kankakee State Park graves.

Crystal glanced at the conference room speakerphone sitting on the table between the detectives on one side and Mrs Walsh on the other. She knew Horton and Andreen's counterparts were physically located in Milwaukee and Bourbonnais; nevertheless, they were glued to the conference room phone.

Detective Horton continued, 'The last time you and your husband saw your son was in mid-July of 1994?'

'Yes. Connor came home for the weekend to work on his Ford Mustang, his pride and joy. Something to do with brake pads and shoes,' Mrs Walsh said. 'Like I told you,' she tapped the picture of Ronald Lamprecht in the *Chicago Tribune* that lay on the table, 'he brought this creep along with him.'

'To help with the car repairs?'

'Yes.'

'And you're still able to recognize Lamprecht after meeting him only once over thirty years ago?' Horton asked gingerly.

Walsh didn't bat an eye. 'I remember every single thing about the last time I saw my son.'

Horton nodded. 'And your son told you Lamprecht was a fellow student at Marquette?'

'Yes. He looked a decade older than Connor – like he does in that photograph – but my son made it sound like he was one of those students that return to college in their late twenties.'

'Did Connor introduce him as Ron or Ronald Lamprecht?'

'No, he introduced him under a different name.' Mrs Walsh

thought for a moment. 'John something or other. I gave the name when we reported Connor missing. It should be in your cold case file. Either way, they weren't able to track down anyone with that name, not at Marquette.' She added, 'Aiden and I got bad vibes off Lamprecht, right away. We brought the two of them cheeseburgers for lunch, out in the garage, and Lamprecht was wearing a sleeveless T-shirt – I believe they're called wife-beaters – and he had tattoos that looked anything but artistic.'

Detective Andreen asked his first question, 'Like prison tattoos?'

'I don't know anything about prison tattoos, but more markings than images,' she replied. 'Lamprecht's behavior, though – the hair went up on the back of my neck. Disturbing. No eye contact, incomplete answers about where he was from or what his parents did.'

'Viv,' a voice spoke through the conference phone, a Milwaukee detective chiming in, 'we've opened Connor's record in NCIC, that is, the National Crime Information Center database. He'd told you Lamprecht's name was *John Brand*. And you're correct – no student by the name of John Brand or Ronald Lamprecht began class at Marquette University either that year or in the fall of 1993.'

After Horton and Andreen had ascertained the woman who showed up unexpectedly at CPD's headquarters was not a flake, that Viviana and Aiden Walsh's son, Connor Walsh, had in fact been reported missing to Milwaukee PD in the early days of September 1994, Crystal figured she'd been summoned to this ad hoc meeting for one of two reasons. First, her knowledge of all things Kenneth Tharp in case his involvement became linked to Connor Walsh. Secondly, in case Mrs Walsh broke down and they thought it wise to have a female presence in the room.

Crystal hoped it was reason number one. Reason number two, though, appeared a moot point as, outside of dabbing away the occasional tear, Viv Walsh was no shrinking violet.

'Connor was a good kid; he was an A-student.' Walsh tapped again at Lamprecht's photograph with a forefinger. 'This piece of garbage is responsible for my son's death . . . this piece of garbage got him killed.'

'Let's not get ahead of ourselves, Viv,' Horton said gently. 'No positive ID has yet been made.'

'Lamprecht disappeared at the same time Connor did, and he

now turns up in a *mass grave*,' she said and dabbed again at her eyes. 'Now I'm no detective, but . . .'

Viviana Walsh did not complete the thought – she didn't have to – everyone in the room and on the conference phone heard her loud and clear.

Horton then said, 'You mentioned Lamprecht stayed with Connor at your house that night?'

'Yes, and when the two headed back to Milwaukee Sunday afternoon, Aiden and I went downstairs, where they'd camped out and watched movies all night. It smelled like marijuana.' Walsh looked at Horton. 'I'm not deluded, Detective. My husband and I assumed Connor imbibed now and again, mostly alcohol, maybe some recreational drugs – he was in college for Christ's sake – but we knew it was Lamprecht that pushed smoking weed in our basement.'

'Where do you think your son met Lamprecht?'

Walsh shrugged. 'Connor was a night owl; he had been since high school. And by night owl I mean Connor would be up until three or four in the morning. He'd lived in Milwaukee for three years by then and knew all sorts of night spots. I imagine he bumped into Lamprecht at some such spot.' Walsh dropped the tissue in the bin next to the table. 'I wish Connor had never met the man. It was obvious Lamprecht was nothing but trouble. I doubt my husband slept a wink that night. I know I didn't. I almost called my brother to come over,' she said, then shrugged again, 'but, well, it's best not to wake him up.'

Horton nodded and checked his notes again. 'Why did you wait until September to report your son was missing?'

'Connor told us he was taking a road trip before school kicked in, camping at Mount Rushmore or Devils Tower. We lived in Chicago and Connor was in Milwaukee, and this was before everyone had a cell phone attached to their palm. But when August passed and we hadn't heard from him, we drove to his apartment. No one answered the door, but we had an extra key. Connor's mail had piled up, food had gone bad in the fridge, his answering machine was filled with messages, and his Mustang was gathering dust in the parking lot. Aiden and I got frightened at that point – seriously frightened,' she said and tilted her head toward the speakerphone, 'and that's when we went to the police.'

Crystal sat still as the conversation turned toward checking the two sets of unidentified remains against Connor's dental records or performing a DNA analysis. Something gnawed in the back of her mind. She glanced through her notes and, at a pause in the interview, Crystal said, 'Earlier, you mentioned another friend of Connor's stopped by to check the work on the car. Can you tell us anything about him?'

'Well, he wasn't this man,' Walsh said, her finger now tapping Kenny Tharp's picture in the *Tribune*. 'He stopped by after we'd eaten dinner, got under the Mustang for half an hour, and then took it out for a spin,' she said. 'When he left, he took the Chilton manual with him, so I think he was the real brains behind the car repairs.'

'Did you get his name?'

'Rob or Tom or something generic.' She shook her head. 'I don't remember. Aiden and I only chatted with him for a minute or two, but he was the polar opposite of Lamprecht. Friendly, shook our hands, seemed authentic, and joked about being shocked that Connor and Lamprecht hadn't attached the brake pads to the windshield wipers,' she said. 'My husband and I got no bad vibes off him.'

'Anything else you can tell us about the guy?' Crystal asked.

'Tall, black hair – he was good-looking – a few years older than Connor,' she said. 'I remember him saying he was from Chicago, and that his mom lived in,' Walsh thought for a long moment, 'Logan Square.'

NINE

The figure sat at the desk, alone in the pre-dawn hour, holding a sizable diamond between a forefinger and thumb. The gem, free of flaws, was of the highest elegance, its atoms arrayed in the most uncorrupted of crystals. Light reflected from every facet and dispersed through the top. They called this particular diamond a round brilliant – a full fifty-eight facets – it was the *gold standard*. Nothing interrupted the passage of light through the gemstone's facets or, perhaps more properly christened . . . *its eyes*.

Ultimately, it was the gift of a master cutter that permitted this *poetry of light* to be reflected. A poor cut loses light through the bottom – the poetry is gone.

And without poetry, it was just another trinket, like what you'd find at a strip mall.

The figure behind the desk flipped the gemstone in the air a time or two before it disappeared back inside a coat pocket. This round brilliant was kept on their person at all times. It was a reminder from where the figure had come . . . and the lengthy journey that led here.

But there were more pressing things in mind that morning than waxing poetic about gemstones. The figure reflected on Catherine Dando, and how they'd known one another a lifetime ago. Catherine had no idea what became of her son those many years ago, and though she had been the one to report her son missing, she would have great difficulty explaining how her boy continued to contact her in the months following his death.

It was a damn shame the secrets at Kankakee River State Park refused to stay buried.

But the fixer had done his job . . . and the link had been severed.

TEN

Crystal read the missing person's report on Connor Walsh. She couldn't fault Milwaukee PD. They'd been thorough in questioning neighbors, his landlord, friends, and classmates, even several of Connor's teachers as well as an ex-girlfriend – also a Marquette University student – he'd broken up with that spring. The breakup had been acrimonious, but they ruled out foul play on her part as she'd been back home in Minneapolis all summer break, living with her parents and working at their catering service. Connor's ex-girlfriend had been shocked and saddened to hear about his disappearance and helped MPD in making an extended list of Connor's MU acquaintances.

No one MPD interviewed had heard Connor say boo about an August camping trip to Mount Rushmore or Devils Tower and, from everything she'd read in the file, Crystal got the sense Connor was more city boy than boy scout. Neither of his two credit cards had been utilized since July of that year, his Visa card having last been used at a gas station in Germantown, a suburb of Milwaukee. Therefore, if Connor had gone camping, he'd have used cash; however, his bank card had last been used – sixty dollars – at a campus ATM, also in July.

All in all, the only tidbit MPD learned came from Connor's landlord. Though he'd not seen Connor since sometime in July, he informed the police that the missing student's *pride and joy* – his 1975 Ford Mustang – had sat in the apartment's parking lot for the entirety of August.

Crystal took a sip of her now cold coffee and recalled Mrs Walsh mentioning how her husband passed away five years after her son's disappearance. Crystal's fingertips danced across the keyboard. Seconds later Aiden Walsh's obituary in the *Chicago Tribune* displayed on her monitor.

> *Walsh, Aiden L. Age 52 – loving husband, father, son, brother and uncle – passed away unexpectedly on December 11. An Illinois native, Aiden was the managing partner at Walsh/Montgomery, an architectural firm in downtown Chicago whose designs include the Lakeview Tower condominiums in Glencoe and Arbor Plaza in Hyde Park, amongst numerous other buildings and structures. Survived by spouse, Viviana Walsh; mother, Doireann Walsh; sister, Cara Summers (Mark); brother-in-law, Gabriele Lanaro (Aurora); nieces, Bridget Summers, Elisa Summers; and nephew, Mattia Lanaro. Preceded in death by his father, Devlin Walsh.*

Crystal felt her heart lodge in her throat. It wasn't that Viviana Walsh hadn't listed her son Connor as either *survived by* or *preceded in death*. Crystal understood how difficult a decision like that had to have been for the newly widowed Viviana – not knowing for certain if her son was alive or dead.

No, what captured Crystal's eye was when she realized who Viviana Walsh's brother was . . . who Connor Walsh's uncle had been.

Gabriele Lanaro was her brother.

And Mattia Lanaro her nephew?
That changed everything.

ELEVEN

Viviana Walsh drove her Lexus ES past a daunting set of wrought-iron gates and steered the sedan another half-mile on a paved road that wound itself toward Lanaro manor. Her nephew and his family lived in what a casual observer might refer to as a mansion – but what Viv would term a *compound* – on the outskirts of Naperville, thirty-something miles west of Chicago's city center. Her nephew lived on sixty acres he'd inherited from his father and her brother, Gabriele Lanaro, who had passed away in his sleep four years earlier.

It was far from the only thing her nephew had inherited from his father.

The compound was several stories of light stone and curved roof tiles, the property itself surrounded by an ominously high security fence. Viv imagined some kind of patrol marched the perimeter, both day and night. She figured no one got into his estate unless her nephew wanted them in.

Viv had only been here a handful of times since her brother's funeral.

It was never a trip she'd looked forward to making.

She parked her Lexus along the circular drive, in front of the steps leading into her nephew's home. Mattia himself stood at attention in a tailored black suit on the walkway to greet her. Her nephew had short black hair, some gray about the temples, with bifocals obscuring a set of inquisitive hazel eyes. If Viv hadn't known better, she'd assume Mattia was an accountant.

Hovering nearby was a much bigger man in a less costly black suit – a man with something bulky beneath his left breast pocket.

'Aunt Viv,' her nephew said as she stepped from the Lexus.

They hugged briefly. Mattia looked in her eyes and added, 'This news about Connor breaks my soul.'

'Would you like an espresso?' Mattia asked after they entered the mansion.

'No, thank you.'

'Aunt Viv,' Mattia said, 'please have an espresso with me. I'll even make it myself as it only took me a year to figure out how the damned machine works.'

'In that case,' she replied, 'how can I refuse? Thanks, Matty.'

Mattia paused a second, and then smiled as he realized he wasn't about to instruct his only aunt to refrain from calling him *Matty* as she'd been calling him that since he was a child. No one else called him Matty – Mattia would not have tolerated it – but from Aunt Viv, he knew it was a term of endearment.

Viv sat on an upholstered bar stool on the far side of a kitchen island the size of an RV. She imagined this was where her nephew held meetings and plotted strategy – where the sausage got made. Mattia's wife had yet to be strutted out to greet her. Good, Viv thought, her nephew knew the two of them had family business and, perhaps, some unpleasantness to discuss.

She said, 'You know Connor worshiped the ground you walked on?'

'He was more of a brother to me than cousin,' Mattia replied as he worked the levers on the espresso maker. 'Did Connor tell you I'd visit him in Milwaukee whenever the White Sox played the Brewers? He and I caught a bunch of games at the old County Stadium.'

Viv nodded. 'Connor always had a good time when you were around.'

Mattia paused in making the concentrated coffee and turned her way. 'What are the police telling you?'

'Not much beyond informing me his dental records matched one of the bodies.' Viv shrugged. 'They're trying to track down another *friend* Connor had over to our house a couple weeks before he went missing.'

Mattia placed the tiny cups of espresso on saucers, walked around the island, placed them on the marble countertop, and sat on the bar stool next to his aunt. 'I hear things from CPD,' he said. 'They're pursuing an interesting avenue.'

'What?'

'Do you remember the robbery at the Crown National Bank?'

Viv shrugged again.

'It was all over the news around the time of Connor's disappearance.'

'I had other things on my mind back then.'

He nodded slowly and said, 'I caught a documentary on the robbery a year or two back. Daytime heist, crowded bank – they got away with millions. A guard was shot and killed, yet they never caught the crew that pulled it off. Not to this day.' He added, 'The whole thing's become a bit of a legend.'

'Well, whatever it was, my son got sucked into something . . . *unwise*.' Viv leaned over her cup of espresso. 'I know the two of you talked a lot back then – you know, about the family.'

Mattia sighed. 'I should have been horsewhipped for filling his mind with romanticized bullshit.'

'The thing Connor wanted most in the world was to please you.'

'I was only twenty-three when he went missing. Just two years older than he was, but I—' He stopped mid-sentence and stared down at his lap. A moment later he said, 'Please forgive me, Aunt Viv, for being so . . . fucking thoughtless.'

'I was mad at you for so long.'

Mattia pushed his cup to the side. 'I know you were.'

'But I was wrong.' She reached out and touched her nephew's forearm. 'Whatever happened to Connor was not your fault, Matty. You were just a kid yourself. I know that now.'

Mattia looked at his aunt with wet eyes.

She asked, 'Connor never came to you or Gabe with anything he might have been *involved with*, did he?'

'Of course not. If Con had, I would have talked him out of it. Whatever he got mixed up in, I would have nixed it.'

'Connor sometimes got angry with me,' she said, and waved a hand about the room, 'for not letting him be a part of this.'

Mattia shook his head. 'It was the smartest thing you and Uncle Aiden ever did.'

'Gabe wasn't upset with me?' she asked. 'I could never tell with my brother.'

'Dad never cared you *went Irish*,' Mattia said and smiled. 'He just loved giving you shit about it. And Dad couldn't have been prouder about his nephew becoming an architect.'

'All the best laid plans . . . and yet the worst thing in the world came to fruition.'

Mattia placed his hand over hers. 'I've always thought Con tripped over something that sounded good – sounded real good – and he assumed it'd be cool if he showed up after the fact and gave us our cut as though it were all some bullshit TV show,' he said. 'If only he'd come to me with whatever it was those convicts roped him into.'

'I know.'

'And if it had come to my father's attention,' he continued, 'well, you know your brother. He was not only old school – he was Old Testament – and those shitbags would have been in barrels of cement at the bottom of Lake Michigan.'

The two sat in silence a long second, before Viv asked, 'Whoever killed my son must not have known who he was.'

Mattia shook his head again. 'Dad squeezed at the time – he went scorched earth – and we got nothing from men who, believe me, would have given up anything they knew. At first Dad thought they were coming after him, but – Aunt Viv,' he said, 'Dad found out that wasn't the case. If Connor had been killed over a *family matter*, Lake Michigan wouldn't have been deep enough for everyone Dad sent there.'

'There were no leads?'

'Not a single one. Everything we squeezed took us to a dead end,' Mattia said. 'Dad tore the city apart, Aunt Viv, trying to find out what happened to Connor. Men are in barrels – multiple men, plural – and we couldn't find a thing.' He slapped the countertop with his palm. 'Not a goddamned thing. That's why Connor had to be involved with *civilians*. They had no clue as to who he was.'

Viviana posed the question she'd really come to ask. 'Where do we go from here, Matty?'

'I've thought of nothing else since you called about Connor's remains, Aunt Viv. But unlike back then – when we had nothing – we now have a thread to pull on. At least five men went into the state park that day with Connor, and we know at least one of them walked out.' Mattia took a deep breath and continued, 'Like I said, we've got ears at CPD, so we'll know what they know in real time.'

'How does that help us, though?' Viviana asked. 'Getting updates ahead of the news media?'

'I should not be sharing trade secrets with you, Aunt Viv,' Mattia said and grinned. 'I've got a man who specializes in finding people that do not want to be found. Even in this day and age, sometimes we need that skillset. The man's a hunter – and he will find whoever walked out of the state park that day.' Mattia stopped grinning. 'And when he does, there'll be no cement barrels and Lake Michigan this time. None of that,' he said. 'I will flay them alive for what they did to my cousin, and I'll use their skulls for bocce ball.'

Tears began to stream down Viviana's face. 'You have to promise me something, Matty,' she said. 'Promise me this. When this man of yours – this hunter – finds them, and when they're being made to pay for what they did to my only child . . . I need to be there.'

Mattia stared at his aunt as though seeing her in a new light. Then he slowly nodded his consent.

Neither one had touched their espressos.

PART TWO
The Soldier

The dog lives for the day, the hour, even the moment.
– Robert Falcon Scott

TWELVE

June 9, 1994

'You've got to be shitting me,' Thomas Dando said.

The guy lying in the bed could barely raise his head off the pillow. Dando spotted the empty bottle of Jack Daniel's on the floor. He could also smell it radiating off the man's shirtless torso. It stood out in the mix of foul fragrances defiling the one-room armpit of an apartment.

This was the man Lamprecht vouched for, the man he wanted Dando to meet. The man Lamprecht knew from his years at Stateville. The man Lamprecht swore cut his eyeteeth knocking over gas stations.

For Christ's sake, Dando doubted the drunk was even aware other people were in the bedroom with him. Truncated moans emanated from the man's throat in response to Lamprecht's repeated kicks at the mattress and demands that he *wake the hell up*.

Lamprecht's *associate* was to have met with them over an hour ago at a nearby Wendy's. After chewing their burgers and sucking down Cokes, the two decided to pay Lamprecht's guy a visit and see if he was home. The man had no vehicle, which was why Dando agreed to meet him in his neighborhood – at a burger place northwest of downtown Milwaukee. It took Lamprecht less than ten minutes to lead Dando to his chum's apartment. Two minutes of heated knocking conveyed zero signs of life. Dando figured the guy wasn't home, but Lamprecht turned the handle and damned if the door didn't swing inward.

Lamprecht called out for his associate as the two of them worked their way through stacks of fast-food wrappers and dirtied plates, empty beer cans and damp carpeting, a regiment of ants and what appeared to be a spurt of vomit on their journey across the living room, to the kitchen, and, finally, to the man's bedroom.

Lamprecht yanked the covers off the bed and, as the stench rose up to greet them, said, 'Aw fuck!'

Lamprecht's friend had soiled the sheets in more ways than one.

'Does he know anything?' Dando crowded Lamprecht against the brick wall of the apartment building as soon as the two men had stepped outside. He had three inches and thirty pounds on the scuzzy prick. The ex-Marine could crush the ex-con like the bug he was.

Lamprecht shook his head. 'No.'

'It's *imperative* I never lose control again,' Dando said, looking deep into Lamprecht's eyes. The man made Dando's skin crawl, a thousand maggots squirming under his flesh; unfortunately, he needed the ex-con. But he also needed the man held in check, and he knew how to speak Lamprecht's language. 'We got our asses dumped off in the middle of a sandstorm with orders to dig in. You couldn't see three feet in front of you. I'm going to town with my E-tool – that's a folding shovel – and out of fucking nowhere there's an Iraqi soldier crawling toward me. I practically tripped over the bastard.' Dando punched this next part home. '*I lost it, Lamprecht*; I couldn't stop hitting him with the shovel until there was nothing left of the guy's skull,' Dando said. 'Now if you told that drunken fuckup anything about *my business* – and I mean *anything at all* – God help me, I'm going to lose it again.'

'Jesus, Tom, take it easy, already,' Lamprecht replied, his eyes wide, message received loud and clear. 'He don't know fucking nothing.'

'It was a literal shit show. The guy was so wasted he'd crapped the bed and didn't even know it,' Dando spoke into the payphone. 'Jesus – I thought I've been hitting the firewater a bit much; looks like I've got a hell of a way to go.'

'It's a good thing we found out now he's dysfunctional,' the voice on the other end of the line replied, 'as opposed to later.'

'Yeah, but we still need a fourth guy,' Dando said. 'No way we pull it off without a fourth.'

'Any ideas?'

Dando thought for a second. 'I know a guy – he's a student at Marquette.'

THIRTEEN

'So the Marquette student is Tony Soprano's cousin?' I asked Crystal. The plot had thickened enough to stir with a canoe paddle. Two ex-cons and now the nephew of a high-level mobster inhabited the first grave Alice and Rex had sniffed out – the grave furthest from the trail – while the lone remains in the second grave had yet to be identified.

'In Chicago, the mob is called the Outfit. New York has its five families, but here there is only one – the Lanaros,' my sister said. 'After his father's death, the current head of the Lanaro crime syndicate is Mattia Lanaro. And to your point – yes – Connor Walsh is Mattia Lanaro's first cousin.'

Crystal and I stood in front of a beige bungalow in Logan Square, a neighborhood on Chicago's northwest side. Alice and Rex swirled around our legs as I glanced about the scene. My sister's Honda HR-V and a CPD squad car filled the driveway while my Silverado sat curbside. The bungalow belonged to an elderly woman by the name of Catherine Dando, whom my sister had been having a difficult time locating.

Crystal sleuthed out that Dando's twenty-four-year-old son, Thomas Dando, had been reported missing in Milwaukee by Catherine on the first day of January in 1995. Unlike Tharp and Lamprecht, Thomas Dando had not been an alumnus of Stateville penitentiary. Quite the contrary, actually, as Thomas Dando had been a decorated United States Marine who served in the first Gulf War – in both Desert Shield and Desert Storm – back in 1990 and 1991. His name had not been netted in Crystal's initial search results of those reported missing due to his residence in Milwaukee instead of Chicago as well as his reported missing date having been early 1995, not the summer of 1994.

My sister's call caught me in mid-bite as I'd returned home after morning class. She asked if I could grab the dogs and meet her at an address in Logan Square right after my afternoon class. I did Crystal one better; I mumbled ambiguously about having no additional classes today, gathered Alice and Rex, and GPS'd it to the address Crystal had provided. My sister wasn't buying that I was being entirely honest about my afternoon schedule, but she had a situation on her hands and that came first.

Crystal had been at Catherine Dando's residence since nine thirty in the morning. She had called Ms Dando's landline and cell phone yesterday afternoon to no avail; both calls went to voicemail. She repeated the effort first thing today, again to no avail. Upon arriving, my sister rang the doorbell repeatedly as well as knocked on the door with escalating strikes. Crys had gone around to the side of Ms Dando's detached garage and noted that Catherine's 2019 Camry was, in fact, parked there.

She then worked the neighbors. The woman in the house on Dando's left side said she'd not seen Catherine in several days, which was odd because Catherine was always puttering about in her yard, working on the lawn or garden. The family in the house on the right kicked the significance of Catherine's absence up to the next level. They'd not seen her, either, but had gathered Catherine's mail yesterday as it had begun to overflow from her mailbox. That neighbor had also tried her door to no avail.

'It's as though she's disappeared,' Crys had informed me over the phone. 'Just like her son.'

Crystal then contacted CPD's 14th District, which covered Logan Square, to send one of their officers over to perform a wellness check. She wanted her ducks in a row in case they had to break the locks. Then she got the number of Catherine's sister, who lived in Elmwood Park, called her, and found out the woman had a spare key. The sister promised Crystal she'd jump in her car and drive right over.

This was when I arrived. With the sister on the way with a house key, no one wanted to jimmy their way in. The police officer from the 14th District and I took the time to circle the property with Alice and Rex. Our jaunt included an average-sized front yard with a couple of trees, minimal side yards with bushes and no trees, and a small backyard as it abutted a stretch of woods that, the officer informed me, eventually emptied out above the soccer fields by one of Logan Square's high schools.

Except for a squirrel Rex felt had it coming, nothing in our orbit around Catherine Dando's abode caused my two rascals to alert.

By the time we returned to the front yard, there was a newish Kia Forte parked half in the driveway and half in the street. The passenger's door remained open. Two people stood chatting with Crystal – a mildly plump woman in a green sweatshirt, who had to be Catherine Dando's sister, and a mildly thin man with his hands deep in his trouser pockets, who had to be the sister's husband. He stood a step back from the unfolding drama.

'Do you think she's OK?' the sister asked Crystal.

'We're performing a wellness check,' my sister replied. 'None of the neighbors have seen Catherine in several days.'

'Oh my God,' the sister said as she mined through her purse for the house key. 'I spoke to Cath last week and she was doing fine.' She paused in her search and again asked, 'Do you think she's OK?'

'We'll take a peek inside and hope that everything's OK.'

The sister pointed at the garage. 'Is her car in there?'

Crystal nodded.

'Oh my God,' the sister repeated as she pulled the spare key from her purse and scrambled up the porch steps to the door.

Once the door was unlocked, the sister began to enter, but Crystal placed a hand on her shoulder and said, 'I think it would be best if we checked inside first.'

The sister backed out of the doorway.

Crystal and the police officer entered Catherine Dando's home and disappeared into the interior. Catherine's sister focused on the entryway as though she were memorizing an eye chart prior to an exam while her husband smiled down at Alice and Rex.

They get that a lot.

A minute later the officer exited the house, and a minute after that my sister did the same.

'We did not find anyone inside,' she spoke directly to Catherine's sister and held her forearm to calm her. 'That's a good thing, but I'm going to send our K-9s in just to verify, OK?'

Catherine's sister nodded her consent, eyes wide and mouth open, likely having dark thoughts of her sibling having been shoved inside a closet or stashed behind the washing machine.

I smile at the sister as Alice and Rex and I slip past her and into Catherine Dando's bungalow. It was a single story, three bedrooms and one bathroom, living room, kitchen, and washroom all on one level. I figured it couldn't be more than fourteen hundred square feet if I tacked on the front porch.

Crystal and I and the dogs had once searched a home where a killer had hidden his victim inside a box. No such luck here. Alice and Rex did not alert as we trekked through each room and checked every closet, crevice, and niche.

I came back outside, smiled again at the sister, and gave a quick thumbs up as the group stopped everything to look my way. They then went back to conversing.

'She's been retired for years,' the sister, who I soon found out was named Donna, informed Crystal. 'She had no trips planned. Outside of church and shopping, I can't think of where she'd have gone. We're in the same book club, but that doesn't meet until next Thursday.' Tears began running down Donna's face. 'I have no idea where Cath could be.'

'We're going to find your sister,' Crystal said. 'But can I ask you a few questions about your nephew?'

Donna wiped a sleeve across her face and nodded.

'Catherine reported him missing in January of 1995, right?'

Donna nodded her agreement. 'It was heartbreaking.'

'I know a lot of time has passed, but can you recall the last time you saw Tom?'

Donna glanced over at her husband.

He shrugged and said, 'I'm thinking Thanksgiving of 1994.'

A long moment passed and then Donna corrected him. 'No, only Catherine came over for Thanksgiving that year, remember, but she had spoken to Tom that morning.'

'Do you know when it was Catherine last spoke to her son?'

Donna now stared at Crystal in confusion, puzzling over what her nephew's disappearance from a lifetime ago had to do with her currently missing sister. 'I think it might have been that Thanksgiving morning. Tom had moved to Milwaukee and, unfortunately, we didn't see him much after that.' She added, 'What's all this got to do with Tom, anyway?'

Crystal shrugged. 'Evidently, nothing. I'm sorry to have troubled you.' She pointed at the policeman from the 14th District. 'I'm going to turn you over to this officer. He'll be sure to—'

'Crystal,' I cut in. 'Can I speak with you for a second?'

She shot a glance my way, finished introducing the police officer to Donna and her husband, and then cut across the front lawn with me. 'What's up, Cor?'

'There are acres of woodland behind the house,' I said and looked down at Alice and Rex. 'It goes on for a bit until it comes out at a high school.'

Crystal caught my drift. 'If Thomas Dando was running around in late 1994, wishing his mother a happy Thanksgiving, he's not connected to my case,' she said. 'But if something bad happened to Catherine Dando a few days ago . . . it'd be awfully easy to drag her into the woods.'

FOURTEEN

'Find,' I spoke the command as Alice, Rex, and I stepped from Ms Dando's backyard into the strip of forest behind her house.

I never weary of this part, of watching my dogs as they morph from the endearing goofballs they are at heart into the consummate professionals they've been trained to be. Snouts shot up as they shifted into air scenting mode. They spread apart for maximum coverage, sprinting forward as I followed along at a slower gait.

The Kankakee River State Park case remained a sticky mess. Two of the three identified in the first grave Alice and Rex had found – Kenneth Tharp and Ronald Lamprecht – had served time at Stateville penitentiary. Their sentences overlapped and, per the correctional center's records, they were in the same cellblock. It would have been unlikely for the two not to have known each other.

The third occupant in the mass grave, Connor Walsh, had no prison record at all; in fact, his record was squeaky clean. Connor had been a twenty-one-year-old college student whose father was a noted architect, and – oh, by the way – his uncle Gabriele Lanaro just so happened to be the head of the Chicago crime syndicate. And since Uncle Gabe's passing a handful of years back, the Windy City's crime syndicate mantle had fallen upon the genealogical shoulders of Connor Walsh's first cousin – Mattia Lanaro.

Nah – no big deal there.

Immediately, my mind turned to Connor's death being tied into Lanaro family business. I base this on having seen *The Godfather* and *Goodfellas* about seven times each. But if that were the case, why would Connor's mother, Viviana Walsh, have come forward to CPD after recognizing Ronald Lamprecht from his photograph in the newspaper as having been an acquaintance of her missing son? That wouldn't make any sense. If Viviana knew her son had been wacked over Lanaro family business, wouldn't she have just shot her brother in the face?

Also, Crystal mentioned no connections had been unearthed between Tharp and/or Lamprecht and the Chicago mob or the Lanaro family.

None at all.

And speaking of *no connections*, we have yet to tie any of this to the Crown National bank heist and murder of a security guard that had occurred years before I was born.

As for today's business, Crystal had tracked down some guy by the name of Thomas Dando who vanished in the latter months of 1994. Dando had moved to Milwaukee sometime after he'd parted company with the United States Marine Corps. Lamprecht lived in Milwaukee; Connor Walsh was a student at Marquette University in Milwaukee. Tom Dando's dental records had yet to be compared against the remaining unidentified body from Kankakee State Park, the remains from the second grave – the single-occupancy grave I'd seen the police dig up. Like Crystal, I doubted the records would match as Dando had been talking to his mother long after retired parole officer Chuck Sims reported Kenneth Tharp as having gone AWOL.

However, another crazy twist had reared its ugly head. Thomas Dando's mother, Catherine Dando, is nowhere to be found, which goes a long way toward explaining why I'm stumbling about in the patch of forest shrouding the back of her property.

The woodlands angled upward before leveling off and I huffed it behind Alice and Rex when I first heard the clamor. I glanced at my watch and wondered if school was out for the summer.

Whether it was an afternoon Phys Ed class or a summer league game, people were playing soccer as the sounds floated up from the high school fields on the other side of the ridge.

Rex looked back as if to say, 'Can I try out?' I pointed forward and we continued on our quest. A second later a round of cheers erupted – someone had scored a goal – and that's when Alice and Rex caught hold of the scent. The two cut back my way, downhill for several feet, came together, and zipped off as I struggled through the thickets to keep them in my line of vision.

I tripped over a tree root and went down. As I pushed myself up I spotted the marks in the topsoil. It was as if a sled had been towed along the crust of the hill, through the dirt and dead leaves. It was the trail my dogs were following. I glanced to my right, from where we'd come, and noted the marred soil angled downward, back toward Catherine Dando's bungalow.

Shit.

I climbed to my feet, my dogs now lost from sight. I listened for several seconds. No nearby commotion or flurry of activity. Just the further-off sounds of kids at play on the high school soccer fields.

Alice and Rex had ceased moving.

I hustled forward, following the markings in the dirt, cutting right around a crop of scrubs, and there they were – both dogs sitting in front of a downed limb from a shingle oak tree. Alice patted at the ground with a front paw while Rex peeked back my way, his face a perpetual grin.

At first I didn't register their discovery. I got down on all fours and inched forward through the briar-patch of prickly vegetation, brushing aside branches from the downed limb with one arm. I figured the busted branch had been recent as most of its leaves were still green. I'd lay money it came down during last week's thunderstorm. I pushed aside more foliage and peered into the fissure I'd created.

Something was indeed there, some kind of mound. I shuffled a few feet to my left, in search of a better angle, and pushed aside another clump of thorny plants. I stretched forward with my right hand and felt some kind of material, plastic or something, shrouding the mound. I crept a couple feet closer, sliding under the downed limb. I slid my iPhone from my pocket, tapped on the flashlight application, and aimed the light at the object in front of me. At first I thought it was some kind of tarp but slithered backward when I spotted the zipper.

Double-shit.

I wasn't about to open the body bag. I'd leave that for Crystal's forensic team . . . but I suspected we'd found the missing Catherine Dando.

FIFTEEN

June 12, 1994

'Chevy's answer to Ford Mustang was the Camaro,' Thomas Dando said and set down his beer. 'They based it on their Nova platform, but souped-up the shit out of the engine.'

'You'd take a Camaro over a Mustang?' Connor Walsh asked.

'The father of a friend I grew up with had this 1972 Camaro – the kind with the V-8 engine. And whenever his dad was away on a business trip, we'd sneak it out,' Dando said. 'That puppy could sail, so – yeah – I guess I've a fondness for Camaros.'

'You guys went Ferris Bueller?'

Dando chuckled. 'I guess we did, but we didn't screw it up like they did with that Ferrari.' He added, 'Don't get me wrong, Connor, I love Ford Mustangs and if yours ever goes missing, it's a good bet it was me.'

Dando had met Walsh a little over a year ago when Connor brought his prized possession into the garage he was working at with a complaint about a vibration and nerve-racking shudders at speeds over fifty miles per hour. The shop manager called Dando over and left him to talk vibrations and shudders with the shop's new customer. Dando had Connor fill out the paperwork and told him he'd give him a call as soon as he ferreted out the problem. By the end of his shift he'd had it pegged as an imbalanced driveshaft, exactly what he'd assumed it would be. A relatively easy fix, Dando had it ready for Connor early the next afternoon.

Connor paid the invoice, jumped behind the wheel, and took off.

The kid returned an hour later with a smile on his face, a song in his heart, and, in his trunk, a case of Leinenkugel's for his now-favorite auto mechanic. Dando jotted his name and phone number on the invoice, telling Connor to hunt him down if anything came up with the vehicle as he'd forgotten more about sports cars than any of the other grease monkeys at the garage had ever known.

Connor called him a week later, but not with any repairs in mind. Instead, he asked if Dando would like to come along and check out a racing festival they were throwing in Richfield that weekend.

Dando agreed and the two had been friends ever since.

Now they sat at a high-top table in a forgotten corner of Clover's on North Water Street, drinking suds and debating sports cars versus muscle cars.

After a second round had been served, and the waitress had left, Dando scratched at a cheek and said, 'Can I talk to you about something?'

'I didn't want to rush it,' Dando said into the payphone. 'I only gave him the vaguest of generalities. You know, hypothetical this and theoretical that, just to feel him out. Nothing the kid could run to the cops with.'

'How did he take it?' the voice on the other end of the line asked.

'He laughed at first, like I did with you. He didn't think I was serious,' Dando said. 'But he knows I was in the Marines and that I'm an expert driver. He settled down and listened after a few minutes.'

'And?'

'We're going to connect again and chat some more.'

'Good.'

'One thing, though – he's not a waste of flesh like the other two dipshits,' Dando said. 'He's one of us.'

'Of course.'

SIXTEEN

'Crystal,' I said, 'I'm heading out.'

The police officer from the 14th District, the cop who'd been at Catherine Dando's house since the beginning, since Crystal requested his presence for a wellness check at the Dando residence, escorted me inside the bungalow to inform my sister I was leaving unless she needed me for anything else. The officer and I had certainly gotten our ten thousand steps in for the day, what with taking arriving members of the forensics unit up the side of the wooded incline to show them where Catherine Dando had been found.

'Crys?' I said and stepped by her side. We were in a sewing room and my sister, lost in thought, stood staring at the photographs displayed along one wall. 'The dogs are in the truck and I'm heading home unless you've got something else for me.'

Once I'd staggered down the slope and raised the alarm, Crystal followed me back into the woodlands, up the ridge, and to the spot where Alice and Rex had discovered the body bag. She crawled under the branches of the busted limb, much as I had done, and hooked the hole in the zipper's pull tab with a paperclip. Crystal then unzipped the body bag a couple feet and – with the stench of decomposition released – I watched as my sister jerked her head sideways and did her best to govern her gag reflex. I knew that feeling well. A long second later Crystal turned back to the task at hand and, wearing gloves, slowly spread the plastic sheets apart.

Catherine Dando's vacant eyes stared back up at her.

That had been several hours ago, and I was now in beat-rush-hour mode.

Crystal turned to me. 'This room is a shrine to her missing son,' she said. 'All of these photos are of him.'

I glanced about the room and noted she was correct. 'Maybe this was once his bedroom.'

Crystal pointed at the wall in front of us, at eye level. 'Shouldn't there be a picture there?'

I followed Crystal's finger to the open space in the collage of photographs, then I glanced at the opposite wall where the pattern of displayed photos was similar except – yes – that wall contained a picture in the corresponding spot. 'Yeah, there's a gap.'

The bungalow was now considered a crime scene, hence the police escort to check in with my detective sister. The forensic unit was still mired in the thickets, documenting the scene and bringing down the body, but soon they would be turning their attention toward Catherine Dando's home as that was likely where the poor woman had been murdered before being dragged off into the woods.

I hoped to be miles down the road by the time forensics set up shop in the Dando residence.

Crystal stepped forward and stared at the break between the other photographs. 'There's a hole for a tiny nail to support a picture frame,' she said. 'Something had once been hanging there.'

It caught the interest of the cop from the 14th District, who stepped from the doorway and asked, 'Do you think that means something?'

My sister shrugged. 'Not sure, but I think my brother's right. This was once her son's room. I doubt she'd have given him the master bedroom, and the third room's a home office.'

I glanced at my watch. Realization sank in; I wouldn't be beating rush hour, certainly not Chi-Town's rush hour. But now I was intrigued. I knew my sister's moods, and I could tell there were thoughts bubbling to the surface. 'What's going on, Crys?'

She shrugged again. 'First, our perpetrator is a professional. Ever known of an amateur to bring their own post-mortem bag to a murder?' she said. 'Second, the timing of Catherine's death is beyond suspicious.'

I am her brother; I have an obligation to needle her. 'Aren't you the one who always says *coincidences make the world go round*?'

'Right,' Crystal said, not taking the bait. 'But I'm real curious now, Cor, and I've expedited the match on the dental records to find out if that last body in Kankakee is, in fact, Thomas Dando.'

SEVENTEEN

June 23, 1994

'You probably want an answer?' Connor Walsh said.

'Let's chow on the apps first,' Dando replied. They were back at the same high-top table at Clover's. The two were fast becoming regulars and even had the same waitress from a visit or two prior. Dando looked at his friend and added, 'You can tell me to go fuck myself, Connor. I wouldn't think any less of you.'

Connor shrugged. 'Be honest, Tom – what are the odds of us pulling something like this off?'

'I'm at ninety percent. And I'm not painting a rosy picture here. Our driver monitors the police scanner, so we're a car horn away from bailing if anything turns to shit. We've got two routes of escape in play; either one gets us on a freeway in a hair over a minute if we hit the lights. I've timed both, and I'll be behind the wheel once we're clear of the bank.' Dando took a long sip of his beer and continued, 'You'll work crowd control with one of the other guys and then help haul duffels on the way out.'

Connor stared at his beer as the waitress dropped off their order of chicken wings. After she left, he whispered, 'I'm not shooting anyone.'

'Neither am I,' Dando replied. 'We'll get steel toe shoes. A kick to the ribs will take the fight out of any bullshit.' He looked down at the food. 'It's not risk-free, but my ass'll be there with you every step of the way.'

'OK then, one last question.'

'Ask away.'

'Why are you doing this, Tom?' Connor said. 'You're a smart guy. Why the fuck are you doing this?'

Dando glanced slowly around the bar and said, 'It'll jumpstart getting my own shop where I can work on nothing but classic cars by about a decade or two.'

'That makes perfectly good sense, Tom, but I'm pretty sure it's bullshit.' He then added, 'Why are you really doing this?'

Dando finished what remained of his beer. 'This fell on me out of the blue, kind of like how I dropped it on you. But I can't get it out of my mind, and the reason I can't get the damned thing out of my mind is because . . . because I know I can do this, Con, and I know I can get away with it.' He slid his empty bottle to the edge of the table, hoping the waitress would notice and bring him another. 'Like I said, feel free to say no.'

The two men stared at the appetizer tray in silence.

Connor sighed. 'I ought to have my head examined,' he said finally. 'Count me in.'

Dando nodded and stabbed at a chicken wing with a fork. 'I know this goes without saying,' he said, 'but not a word about this to anyone.'

Connor chuckled in response. 'Hell, Tom – that's my family motto.'

Dando spoke into the payphone, 'The kid is in.'

'That took a while,' the voice on the other end of the line replied.

'A few heart-to-heart conversations and several bottles of beer.'

'How much did you tell him?'

'No specifics – he doesn't know which bank – just that we've got dates and times when the maximum cash flows in . . . when best to hit them.'

'He knows we have a source?'

'I imagine he's inferred that,' Dando said. 'I sketched him a picture, the layout – where the guards are stationed, where the manager keeps the keys, the teller windows, and the vault.'

'Jesus Christ, Tom. All before he agreed?'

'I had to prove we weren't half-assed,' Dando replied. 'The kid's not an idiot.'

'OK,' the voice said. 'Then I guess it's time to bring everyone to Chicago. It's time to *get specific*.' The voice then added, 'It's time for them to meet me.'

EIGHTEEN

Further down the block, on the opposite side of the street, a man sat behind the wheel of a Jeep Grand Cherokee. He held a small set of binoculars to his eyes. There was an anthill of activity outside the Catherine Dando residence. He counted three squad cars, an unmarked, two white vans for the forensic team, and a Honda belonging to that female detective.

Parked in the street with two of the police cars and the white vans was a Chevy Silverado whose best days were far behind it. He'd watched as a young man loaded a couple of dogs into the pickup's backseat before he and a police officer headed inside the Dando bungalow. The man figured it was the dog handler that had discovered the elderly Ms Dando up along the wooded ridge. He'd heard the dog handler was related to the lady cop, that he was her kid brother.

An unmarked SUV with darkened windows turned on to the block, came to a stop in front of the Dando residence, and sat idling in the middle of the street. *The meat wagon has arrived*, the man thought to himself. A minute later the police officer that had gone into the house with the dog handler came back outside and jumped behind the wheel of the squad car parked in the driveway. The dog handler trailed behind but veered across the yard to his pickup truck. The man watched as the cop backed his car out of the driveway and the SUV, in turn, backed into the vacated space.

Body bag or not, stuffing remains into the back of a coroner's SUV was best kept to a minimal amount of spectators. Neighborhood kids have a hard enough time drifting off to sleep during the summer months without adding something like this into the mix.

To be honest, there'd been no need for the man to venture out to Logan Square this afternoon, but he liked getting the feel of the investigation – the taste of it – even at such a distance. There was nothing he learned at Logan Square that couldn't have come from his sources inside CPD – in fact, he learned from one of his sources that the lady cop was pushing hard to compare Thomas Dando's dental records against the body that remained unidentified. Smart move. The man behind the wheel would have done exactly the same thing if he were still working cases. And were he a gambler, he'd bet everything he had in the bank – including his offshore account – that the dental records would bring back a match.

The man's major takeaway of the day was that whoever killed Mattia Lanaro's cousin thirty years ago had panicked . . . and was now in the process of tying up loose ends.

He would personally report that finding to Mr Lanaro.

The hunter slipped his Jeep Cherokee into Drive and drove slowly past the scene of the crime.

NINETEEN

It was half past eight in the evening and Crystal was nearing her limit. She'd been at Catherine Dando's house eleven hours with just a couple of energy bars from her glove compartment for lunch washed down with lukewarm gas station coffee that had been sitting in her Honda's cup holder since she'd first gassed up that morning.

She looked forward to getting home, to leashing Alice and Rex, and taking the two of them on a full-bore sprint around the neighborhood, just to excise the heebie-jeebies of an incredibly long and, quite frankly, frustrating day. After that, perhaps some real food – even Cory's idea of real food – and then the world's shortest shower before dropping into bed.

Yes, Catherine Dando had been choked to death. Crystal didn't need a forensic pathologist to tell her that. She knew it as soon as she zipped open the post-mortem bag. The abrasions circling the poor woman's throat informed Crystal of that in real time. There are three categories of strangulation: hanging, ligature strangulation, and manual strangulation. Clearly, Ms Dando did not hang herself. If she had, it would have been a hell of a Houdini-like trick to get herself inside the body bag and up the backyard hill. Based on the markings surrounding her throat, Crystal believed a manual strangulation had occurred, an assumption confirmed an hour earlier per a quick update from the coroner's office.

Unfortunately, the coroner also informed Crystal that the killer had worn some type of medical exam gloves as he used both of his hands to choke the life out of the elderly woman.

Further bad news, the forensic investigators' dusting of the post-mortem bag had unearthed no fingerprints – the body bag was clean. And the bad news gathered steam as the forensic unit's comb-through of Catherine Dando's bungalow had come up snake eyes. It was clear Ms Dando kept a tidy home. If Catherine ever placed the bungalow on the market, her realtors could arrive posthaste to take photographs or film a video tour. Floors were swept clean, carpets vacuumed, tables wiped, shelves dusted, dirty dishes parked in the dishwasher – not even a stray cup loitering in the sink – toilets were scrubbed, garbage and recycle taken out to the trash and recycle bins located along the side of the garage. And the only items investigators had found inside the Hefty garbage bags were spent coffee grounds and banana peels, eggshells, tea bags and melon husks, empty cartons, food wrappers, used napkins and paper towels. Forensics would examine the napkins and paper towels, but, Crystal figured, whatever the killer used for cleaning up the scene, he took with him . . . the man was a professional.

Though Crystal presumed the killing had occurred in the kitchen – a likely gathering point for house guests – the forensic investigators couldn't affirm that hunch with any degree of certainty.

The only decent news of the afternoon – if you could call it that – came a few minutes after Cory took off with the dogs. Crystal found no need to jump up and down when she heard the update as it was something she'd strongly suspected. Yup, dental records confirmed that Thomas Dando was, in fact, the body found in the second grave the dogs had come across at Kankakee River State Park. Upon hearing the news, Crystal's colleagues – Detectives Horton and Andreen – arrived at Catherine Dando's Logan Square cottage so fast you'd have thought they'd been shot from a cannon. The two detectives had been holding palaver with the forensic unit in the kitchen before figuring they'd best get their asses up the hillside, to inspect the spot where Ms Dando had been discovered, before the sun went down.

Patrol officers had spent the afternoon canvassing the neighborhood, going door to door, asking questions. Unfortunately, no one on Catherine's block had witnessed any suspicious activity – no screams for help emanating from the Dando household, no stranger dragging what might appear as a lump inside a sleeping bag into the backyard woods, no unfamiliar cars parked in the driveway. Crystal knew from her years on the force that people who spent their days auditing vehicles in their neighbors' driveways were few and far between. However, Crystal also knew from her years on the force that many a crime has been solved with the aid of the neighborhood busybody.

Crystal closed her eyes and contemplated how she'd have pulled it off.

After the deed was done, and Ms Dando was dead and in the post-mortem bag, she would have shut the curtains to the sliding glass door leading out on to the backyard deck. Then, she'd place the body bag in front of the glass door as there would be less ground to cover from the back deck to the woods at the edge of Catherine's property than from Catherine's side door. Using the side door would be stupid; it would be absurd. She'd be exposed to the street; any cars driving past might wonder what the hell they'd just seen. But the backyard – Crystal would only be exposed to the adjacent neighbors for all of maybe the four seconds it took to drag the body bag off the deck and into the thickets.

Crystal figured she'd also wait until nightfall, and the cover of darkness, to make that four-second trek across the back lawn.

Waiting for sundown would provide Crystal all the time in the world necessary to wipe down the cottage. She would even be able to leave Catherine's home and – hell, depending on what time of the day Catherine had been killed – could grab lunch or dinner. Then she'd head over to the high school campus on the other side of the wooded hillside. Crystal had, in fact, driven there several hours earlier, left her Honda, and walked the periphery of the activity fields the campus had to offer. She got the lay of the land and discovered a crumbling blacktop, big enough for two people to hike side by side, that cut between two of the soccer fields and up into the woodlands. The trail wound about for nearly a mile before emptying out on the opposite side of the high school.

Crystal had stepped off the blacktop near the top of the ridge and worked crossways through the strip of forest, toward the forensic unit still working the crime scene. She figured the killer completed a similar recon during the day of the murder, in order to find the best place to dump the body in the hope that no one would trip over it for a considerable chunk of time. And the killer had discovered the downed limb from a shingle oak tree and found it to be the perfect spot. Then, he likely scouted the best trajectory for him to take to the downed limb from Catherine Dando's backyard.

Hell, the killer probably counted the exact number of steps needed to drag the post-mortem bag into the woods before veering leftward. That knowledge and a penlight to illuminate the route once the sun dipped over the horizon would assist him on his journey.

Ten minutes of cardio and a quick shove under the downed limb would do the trick.

Then, before the killer returned to whatever rock he lived under, he'd chuck his shoes or boots in an apartment or fast-food dumpster.

Crystal opened her eyes and returned to the sewing room, to Catherine's shrine to her lost son. She found herself again staring at the wall of photographs, the side of the room that appeared to have a missing picture frame. Crystal shrugged as she looked at the wall. So what, she thought for the tenth time. It's not as though this room was part of the Louvre. Occam's razor – the simplest explanation is often the best – would dictate that a missing picture frame only meant Catherine Dando ran out of photographs of her only son and this wall took the hit.

Crystal glanced about the room. Along with the photographs of Thomas Dando posing with friends and family members were several old yearbooks, the thinner paperback ones they made for students in junior high. In the room's only closet, and hung in a dry-cleaning bag, was Thomas's blue dress uniform from his days in the United States Marine Corps. In another dry-cleaning bag hung Thomas's combat utility uniform.

There were no other clothes stored there.

Crystal peeked down at a floor vent, and then scanned about the wall space near the ceiling for any return air vents. One was located near the entry door, so Crystal dragged the sewing machine chair to that section of the wall. She pressed against the back of the chair to gauge its sturdiness, to make sure it was strong enough to hold her weight. The chair appeared solid, and Crystal stepped on to it and gazed into the vent.

She spotted nothing.

Though there'd been no indication Thomas Dando dealt drugs, dealers had been known to hide their stash and/or cash inside air vents. As such, these were among the places searched when serving a warrant.

Crystal dug about in her coat pocket for her mini screwdriver kit. It came with four basic screwdriver tips; the entire unit could fit in the palm of her hand. She popped in the flathead and removed the two screws holding the vent in place. She stepped off the chair, crossed the room, and set the vent and screws on the sewing table. Crystal returned to the chair, stepped back up, and gazed inside the air duct. Again, she spotted nothing, but stuck a hand inside, fumbling her fingertips along the top of the vent, both sides, and finally along the bottom. The tips of her fingers grazed against the tips of something metal that stood an inch out from the HVAC duct. It wasn't natural; it didn't belong there, so Crystal stood on tiptoes and stretched her hand further down inside the venting unit. She felt three prongs pointing upward, thin as toothpicks, forming some kind of clip or clasp, and she inched her fingers further downward. About a half-inch under the prongs, there appeared to be a wad of paper or stack of cards or something held in place.

What the hell, she thought. Not really where you'd store your HVAC warranty.

Crystal pressed herself against the side of the wall, forcing her hand even deeper into the vent until she came to the bottom of the makeshift clip or clasp. She held her breath as her fingers clawed inward, grasping ahold of the hidden packet and, fearful of dropping whatever it was into the depths of the ductwork, she took her time working it to the surface.

Crystal took a lungful of air as she stepped off the sewing room chair and looked at what she had fished out of the air vent.

A Crown National bank strap of one-hundred-dollar bills.

TWENTY

July 26, 1994

'As soon as I drop you off, go to your landlord,' Thomas Dando said. He and Connor were in Dando's Chevy Impala, cruising I-94, hitting the outer suburbs of Milwaukee. 'Ask about their pet policy. Tell him you want a dog, and then act all sad and rejected when he says they're not allowed.'

Connor stared at the interstate ahead of them and slowly nodded.

'Then go to the campus library, check out a couple of books, and flirt like hell with the librarian. Pour it on thick so she'll remember you.'

Connor nodded again.

Dando had a *Semper Fi* sticker on the Impala's rear bumper; the cruise control was set to the speed limit, not a mile faster. No way would they get pulled over unless they'd fucked up.

Unfortunately, Dando already knew . . . they had fucked up . . . and fucked up bad.

The two drove on in silence, as they had for most of the trip back from Chicago, since the crew had split apart to head their separate ways. Finally, Connor said, 'So we're not even going to talk about it, are we?' He added, 'What that fucking psycho did at the bank?'

Dando glanced over at Connor a long second before turning back to the road. 'I'll take care of Lamprecht.'

'Jesus Christ!' Connor twisted sideways in his seat. 'Yeah, sure, the guard gave him the stink eye – he gave all of us the stink eye – but the guy's hands were cuffed. He didn't *break free*, and he wasn't *making a move* or *going for it* like Lamprecht said.'

'I know.'

Connor's eyes were wet. 'The fucking psycho aimed his gun at the guard's face, he let the poor guy know what was coming . . . and then he pulled the trigger.'

'I know,' Dando said again. 'It was intentional; it was first degree.'

'I almost shot him on the spot,' Connor said. 'He sensed it coming and turned his gun my way right as you rushed us out of there. If you hadn't come along—' Connor's voice trembled; he stopped mid-sentence, stared at the dashboard, and cleared his throat. 'What do you mean you'll take care of Lamprecht?'

'You know what I mean.'

Connor digested that tidbit and then asked, 'What about Tharp?'

'Tharp, too.'

Connor stared at Dando as they drove another mile in silence. 'You going to be taking care of me, too, Tom?' he asked. 'Am I on your *to-do list*?'

'Jesus, Connor.' Dando glanced again at his friend. 'No more bullshit thoughts, OK? Nothing's going to happen to you.' Dando's eyes returned to the road. 'Lamprecht and Tharp were never walking away. Those two dipshits will get caught for something else, and then they'd use what happened today to bring us all down.'

'Did you know Lamprecht was a fucking monster?'

'No,' Dando replied. 'He'd done time for armed robbery, not murder.'

Connor shook his head. 'I never got why you had the asshole help me with my brake pads.'

'You both were going to be in charge of guards and customers and the entryway. I wanted the two of you to be in sync.'

'Hell of a team-building exercise,' Connor said. 'I was up all night making sure he didn't take my parents' silverware.'

'You won't have to worry about him anymore.'

'So this thing ends with half the bank crew dead . . . and I just sit back, scratch my ass, and trust you?' Connor settled back into the car seat and faced forward. 'I am a fucking idiot.'

Dando took the Impala out of cruise control and said, 'You know how I never mention my time in the Marine Corps?'

Connor nodded.

'Remember when you asked me about the *Semper Fi* bumper sticker and I blew you off?'

'Yeah,' Connor said, still facing forward. 'I figured it was a sensitive issue.'

'Well, I don't talk about it, not only because it would bore the living shit out of you, but because there's a dicey part I hate bringing up,' Dando said. 'In fact it pains me to bring it up, but let me give you a little taste, OK?'

Connor turned and studied his friend's profile. 'OK.'

Dando nodded, took a deep breath, and began, 'My immediate unit consisted of three Marines and myself. I was a corporal; I was their team leader. When shit hit the fan – in January of ninety-one – we got orders to dig in outside a crappy little airport in northern Kuwait, to make fighting holes. They dumped us off a truck – four units – right in the middle of a sandstorm. It was crazy, Connor; you could barely see your hand in front of your face. You could barely hear a goddamned thing, either. It was fucking insane.' The memory poured through Dando as though it had occurred yesterday. 'And to make matters worse, they dumped our asses off damn near on top of a beehive of Republican Guard soldiers – Saddam Hussein's elite troops.' Dando shook his head. 'I shit you not.'

'Jesus, Tom.'

'Yup – the working definition of a clusterfuck. We started digging in before we realized what had occurred. The only reason I'm here telling you this today is because the Iraqi soldiers were just as blind and deaf and screwed as we were.' Dando hesitated a moment and then dove back in, 'I killed four Iraqis that day, Connor. Four soldiers . . . four men. I got their blood all over me. And I only used my sidearm on the last one – that's how *intimate* the fighting had become. But throughout the skirmish, the only thought pounding through my head was getting my unit the hell out of there, getting my three guys back to base safe and sound. That's all that mattered to me.' Dando checked his rearview mirror and changed lanes. They drove in silence several seconds before he continued, 'We fell back and were lucky to escape. There were three dead from the other units – one of them was a corporal, like me, and a good friend of mine. Four others were shot to shit but somehow managed to pull through. It was later that night – Lord knows I couldn't sleep – when I made the decision. When the time came, I would not re-up . . . which is why you found me working on car transmissions in Brew City.' Dando took another deep breath. 'Anyway, Connor, to make a long story short – you're a part of my unit now.' He then added, 'Trust me, kid. You'll be coming home.'

Traffic picked up as they headed into the heart of Milwaukee.

Dando absentmindedly adjusted the Impala's speed, lost in memories of days gone by.

Connor finally said, 'Lamprecht will be on high alert. You know that?'

Dando nodded.

'I'm sure he's had some thoughts of his own, of helping himself to all those duffel bags of cash. And I bet he's been whispering in Tharp's ear, too,' Connor said. 'This could turn into the O.K. Corral.'

Dando nodded again. 'Doesn't involve you, Connor. Trust me – you don't want any part of what's coming.'

'It's a bit too late for that, Tom. I'm neck deep in this. And if I don't hear back from you, what happens then? I spend my days peeking over my shoulder,' he said. 'You'll need strength in numbers.' Connor tapped lightly on the dashboard with the fingertips of one hand. 'Where is this taking place?'

'Kankakee River State Park,' Dando said. 'That's where we're divvying up the money.'

'OK – you and your friend go Wyatt Earp when the time comes, but until then I'll be on Lamprecht like a fly on shit. If he sneezes wrong, I'll pin his ass to the ground.'

Dando glanced over at his friend. 'You got my back?'

'Yeah,' Connor said. 'I got your back.'

TWENTY-ONE

'I knew it!' Chuck Sims said over Crystal's speakerphone. 'I knew that mouse-faced little shit Tharp was involved in this!'

The exuberance in Sims's voice rubbed off on Rex. My springer spaniel darted downstairs, snatched his knotted sock from his doggie bed, flew back up to the main level, and tried to find where the retired parole officer was hiding before bringing his favorite toy to me. He wanted to throw down with the sock, but I made a settle motion with my hand and whispered, 'Don't make me call you a dingo, Rex.'

He took his prized sock and slouched behind the couch.

'You called it, Chuck,' Crystal said. It was nearly one o'clock in the morning. Crystal had woken me up to share her discovery. Then, due to the lateness of the hour, she'd texted Sims so he could read about it first thing in the morning. However, ten seconds later her cell phone rang. Sure enough, it was Sims; he'd been awake. 'Great instincts,' she added. 'It just took a few decades to get the evidence.'

Crystal was famished. She stood at the kitchen island, finishing the Chinese takeout I'd picked up hours earlier. No chopsticks tonight, just shoveling it in with a fork. I sat on the sofa and listened as the two discussed the breakthrough in the case.

'They stole nearly four million dollars in cash, but this Dando guy sticks ten grand in the air vent in his old bedroom,' Sims said. 'Why the hell would he do that?'

'I have no idea,' Crystal replied. 'A hundred hundred-dollar bills in a Crown National bill strap. That's a lot of currency to hide in there. I don't know what Dando was trying to tell us.'

'*Tell us?*' I said.

'Well, what Dando's trying to tell whoever found his hidden band of cash.'

'OK, Detective Pratt – let's noodle this out,' Sims said, full of energy for such a late hour. 'Dando could be saying: *hey, I may be in trouble here* or *if you find this wad of dough, it means I'm dead* or *if I'm dead, it's because of the bank heist.*'

Though Sims couldn't see Crystal over her speakerphone, my sister nodded along. 'Being a detective may have been your true calling, Chuck.'

'Ah, you've got to be pretty cagey to keep on top of ex-cons,' Sims replied. He paused a second, and then added, 'Dando's mother's murder means whoever was left of the bank crew – the last man standing – is still alive. Clearly, he's still active. He caught the news about the bodies surfacing at Kankakee, got real skittish, and knew he had to eliminate anyone who could connect him to Thomas Dando.'

Crystal tossed her fork in the sink. 'In the context of her son's involvement in the Crown National robbery, as opposed to the old narrative of his having gone missing,' she said, laying out the logic, 'Catherine Dando had information, whether she knew it or not, that could have pointed us in the killer's direction. The killer could not allow her to be questioned.'

'Right, he's in a lethal cover-your-ass mode,' Sims said. 'So what happens now?'

'The FBI is back in the mix. Todd Surratt, the special agent in charge of the Chicago Field Office, called a meeting for eleven o'clock this morning. And I think you should be there, Chuck,' Crystal said. 'Surratt would want you there as well. I can have them leave a visitor's badge for you in the lobby if you can make it.'

'Hey, I'm retired – my schedule's wide open.'

Crystal turned my way as she dropped the empty carton of Kung Pao chicken into the kitchen bin. 'Guess what, Cory? Surratt wants you there as well.'

'Me?' I said.

'Yup, he's getting the band back together.'

'But I'm going to computer school.' I'd been sucked into an FBI task force last fall. To be honest – it hadn't gone well . . . not well at all. 'Why the hell does he want me there?'

'Surratt mentioned you'd say that, and he told me what to tell you.'

'What?'

'He said, quote, "Tell that scrawny-ass brother of yours we wouldn't have these meetings if he'd stop tripping over dead bodies every time he goes out to get the mail," unquote.'

I sat and stewed as Chuck Sims chuckled over the speakerphone.

TWENTY-TWO

Since I had to hit Harper for my afternoon class, I drove separately to the FBI's Chicago Field Office on West Roosevelt Road. I made it with three minutes to spare and found Crystal waiting for me in the lobby. An agent tossed visitor lanyards our way and hustled us to the same eighth-floor conference room used in last fall's task force meetings – large and windowless, dark blue carpeting, multiple tables set in the same rectangular shape. I could feel my blood pressure start to rise as we entered the room and took two of the few remaining chairs. Special Agent in Charge Todd Surratt was once again the only person inside the rectangle of tables, same dark gray suit, crisp white shirt, and red tie. He leaned back against a table, square jaw and hawk-like nose, his arms folded across his chest as he waited for the minute hand on the clock to hit twelve in order to commence the meeting. Surratt nodded as we took our seats.

I wasn't sure if I belonged at Harper Community College, but I sure as hell knew I didn't want to be here.

Bad memories.

I glanced about the room and spotted Crystal's new partner, a round man – round face, round shoulders, rounding middle – named Mark Lahlum. Crystal's previous partner had been killed by a nightmare of a man late last year, and she'd been reassigned to Detective Lahlum in December. I've met him on a couple of occasions, and he seemed like a good enough guy. Crystal likes working with Lahlum though she's commented on more than one occasion how he's trying his damnedest to tuck his livelihood as a CPD investigator into an unassuming nine-to-five vocation.

Lahlum caught me gawking and nodded. I nodded back.

In the chair next to Crystal's partner sat Chuck Sims. The retired parole officer was hard to miss on account of his being a third bigger than the next largest man in the room. Sims's head appeared freshly shaven and, unlike my get-up in black jeans, tennis shoes, and a polo shirt, he'd dressed for the occasion in a brown suit and white shirt. Sims smiled my way. I could be wrong, but I got the sense he was enjoying the day's field trip. Perhaps it was a tad less tedious than whiling away the hours in retirement.

My sister whispered in my ear that the two men at the table next to Lahlum and Sims were Detectives Horton and Andreen, and that the older of the duo, white-haired Detective Horton, was taking lead in the investigation, even as it had evolved from multiple homicides to missing persons to, now, bank robbery. I did not envy the man.

Rounding out the room were a couple more tables of police detectives – I assumed from both Bourbonnais and Milwaukee – and then another dozen or so federal agents that reported to SAC Surratt.

Surratt looked at the clock on the wall and said, 'OK, let's begin.' The head of the Chicago division of the FBI then provided a barebones overview of the Crown National bank robbery that had occurred in late July of 1994. Likely, Surratt expected the attendees to have done their homework in regard to the bank heist. He then glanced my way and gave a quick summary of the four sets of human remains unearthed at Kankakee River State Park. Then he looked at Crystal and said, 'Now I'd like to have Detective Pratt shine some light inside the crypt and bring you up to date on her latest find – on the reason we are all sitting here today.'

Crystal spoke for a minute on what she'd discovered inside the air vent in Thomas Dando's old bedroom at his mother's bungalow in Logan Square. Then she nodded at an agent working a laptop that was wired into the conference room's flat-screen TV mounted on one of the room's side walls. A large image filled the screen with what appeared to be a stack of hundred-dollar bills secured in a bank strap. If you tilted your head sideways, you could make out Crown National stamped across the strap.

Crystal said, 'Please advance to the next image.'

The next picture allowed us attendees to un-crimp our collective necks as it now displayed the stack of hundreds vertically, allowing us to read the bank's name from left to right.

'Next image, please,' my sister said.

The next photograph was an extreme close-up of the previous picture. Only now we could see what appeared to be light markings, some initials or an acronym, on the bill strap below the Crown National stamp.

'Can everyone see that?' Crystal asked.

Heads nodded, affirmatives were mumbled, and an FBI agent asked, 'What does it spell?'

Crystal turned toward Detective Horton, who stood and said, 'It's pencil on a waxy bank strap, but we believe it reads *A1* – as in the number one – or *AI* – with a capital i – or *Al* – with a lowercase l.'

'But what does it stand for?' the same agent asked.

'I met with the bank manager at Crown National first thing this morning,' Horton said. 'He wasn't with Crown National thirty years ago, but he said they've not marked bank straps in this manner in the dozen years he's been running the bank.

However, his theory is that it had a certain meaning or significance to one of the retail businesses where the bank's armored trucks went to pick up or deliver cash.' Horton shrugged. 'He told me if that's the case, it could be something as simple as a stacking notation.'

SAC Surratt said, 'If it's *A1*, that often stands for an excellent rating or top quality.'

I didn't bring up my favorite steak sauce. Instead, I asked, 'Would *AI* mean anything? Artificial intelligence?'

'Outside of a few *Star Trek* episodes or sci-fi books, *AI* didn't have the mass appeal in 1994 as it does today,' Horton replied. 'Certainly not in the context of bill straps or armored trucks.'

A female agent said, 'Could it be an acronym for *AL*? Allowance list or acceptance limit, an accounting term or something like that?'

'Hard to say, but I tend to agree with the bank manager that it's some kind of notation from one of the retail businesses where a pickup had been made,' Horton said, and shrugged again. 'It's a barely legible scribbling on a bill strap that sat in, basically, an air tunnel for three decades.'

Something occurred to me. 'Can you bring in a handwriting expert?' I asked. 'To see if it's Dando's handwriting?'

'We are looking for samples of Dando's handwriting, but as you can see this isn't cursive,' Horton said. 'It's only four lines – three to form the A and one to form the letter I or L or the numeral one. Quite frankly, it looks a lot like my chicken scratching.' Horton turned toward my sister. 'Detective Pratt will now provide us with a deeper dive into Thomas Dando's background, his curriculum vitae.'

Crystal cleared her throat, glanced from Horton to Surratt, and began. 'Thomas Dando was a veteran; he had been a corporal in the United States Marine Corps. Dando served four years on active duty and was still on call as a reservist when he was reported missing by his mother, Catherine Dando, on January 1st of 1995. He served in both phases of the First Gulf War – Operation Desert Shield and Operation Desert Storm. In fact, Dando saw combat in Desert Storm.' Crystal glanced down at her notes. 'He returned home in 1992 and much of the following information comes from his aunt, Catherine Dando's sister, who, quite frankly, was a mess when we talked, but her husband helped fill in many of the details. Dando stayed with his mother in those first few months after leaving the Marines. It was obvious he had changed. He was quiet and more morose than his usual can-do self. Dando likely suffered from PTSD, but he sought no treatment. Instead, he self-medicated – anesthetized might be a better word – with alcohol. Catherine did her best to get her son into counseling, especially after nights when he woke the household screaming in his sleep, but her efforts served to irritate him, and Dando ultimately moved to Milwaukee where he got a job at an auto repair shop working on cars.'

'Can you back up a little, Crystal?' Surratt said. 'Where was Dando's father during this time period?'

'His father had been out of the picture for quite some time.' Crystal looked again at her notes. 'Catherine and Lawrence Dando got divorced in 1975. According to Catherine's sister, Lawrence cheated on Catherine with a colleague from work. Lawrence then married the woman he'd had the affair with and, soon after, they relocated to Missouri and started a new family. Lawrence paid child support for a couple years after the divorce before ceasing payments altogether. Catherine could have gone after him, but, by then, she worked fulltime as a real estate agent and made enough money to raise Thomas by herself,' Crystal said. 'Dando's uncle told me it was best for all involved as Lawrence had a *nasty temper* and *would get a little slappy* if his wife or son so much as looked at him wrong. Dando's uncle said they never heard from Lawrence again, and, as far as he knew, Thomas never went looking for his father.'

Horton raised a hand and said, 'Tell them about the mystery, Crystal.'

My sister looked toward Sims as she collected her thoughts. 'Parole Officer Chuck Sims reported Kenneth Tharp to the court in early August of 1994 after Tharp failed to check in with him. In regard to ex-con Ronald Lamprecht, no one reported him missing; however, a credit report from October of 1994 indicates Lamprecht ditched out on his apartment lease. Rental situations take several months to resolve, so we believe Lamprecht disappeared in July or August of 1994 as well. Viviana Walsh and her husband last saw their son, Connor Walsh, in July of 1994, and reported him as missing to the Milwaukee Police Department in early September of 1994.' My sister took a breath and continued, 'These dates paint a fairly clear picture of when the incident – the killings – at Kankakee River State Park took place; yet, in Thomas Dando's case, his mother didn't report him missing until January of 1995 as she'd not heard from her son since he called her on Thanksgiving Day of 1994.'

The room digested that nugget of information for a second and then Horton added, 'The forensic pathologist is unable to determine whether the remains found in Kankakee were murdered in July of 1994 or post-Thanksgiving of 1994. Three decades is too much for them to determine the exact time of death. Even though Thomas Dando was placed in a separate grave from the other three bodies, we do not believe there were two separate incidents in Kankakee State Park. Especially when you consider how hard the ground would be in late November or early December.'

It was then Chuck Sims spoke for the first time. 'Ken Tharp had a cabbage-level IQ. He spent most of his free time hanging out in bars, hoping to get drunk or get lucky. There is no way in hell Tharp would have gone undetected all of these years had he not been taking a lengthy dirt nap. Quite frankly, I doubt Tharp would have made it to Thanksgiving.'

'So if Dando is killed with the others in late July or early August, how can he be talking to his mother in late November?' Surratt asked. 'Anyone have some thoughts?'

'Catherine's sister and brother-in-law reference Thomas calling his mother through Thanksgiving,' Crystal said. 'They believe their nephew was having conversations with her. But in Catherine's missing person's report with Milwaukee PD, she limits it to having received numerous voice messages from Thomas left on her answering machine. In fact, Catherine didn't recall the last time she'd spoken directly with her son.'

Sims then said, 'Something like that wouldn't be too hard to pull off; you wouldn't need artificial intelligence to fake it. I had a VHS film recorder back in the day to videotape the kids. I also had an answering machine at home to record incoming calls. They had audio editing software back then as well.' Sims then glanced around the conference room. 'Say I'm the killer. I've known Dando for years. Dando believes I'm his friend, but, in the end, it turns out I'm anything but. Now, say I've filmed Dando farting around on videotape. Say I've also got him taped on my answering machine with a bunch of generic *how are ya doin'* messages. Say Dando leaves me a message saying: *Hey, Chuck, Tom here calling to see what you're up to. I'll try again later. Have a great day.* So I nuke the *Hey, Chuck* piece but play the rest of his recording into his mother's answering machine at a time I know she's at work or shopping or away from her house,' Sims said. 'Not fucking hard at all.'

'I agree with Chuck,' Crystal said. 'The killer strings Catherine along; he gaslights her for months on end, so Catherine thinks her son is still alive and kicking.'

'But why would the killer do that?' another agent in a black suit asked.

'To create a different narrative, a different reality, a different chain of events,' Crystal said. 'To keep Catherine from reporting her son as missing, to throw off the timeline and push his disappearance further out from the bank heist. Even though the killer didn't think the bodies of his bank crew would ever be found, he didn't want Dando's disappearance lumped in with the others, to form any kind of pattern for the investigators.'

Sims added, 'And once the bodies surfaced, the killer had to get rid of Catherine Dando because she'd be questioned about whom Tom hung out with in the summer of 1994, or about those mysterious phone calls and who would have been close enough to her son to have made recordings of him.' Sims leaned back in his chair. 'Catherine Dando knew her son's killer – that's for shit sure.'

'But if Thomas Dando's disappearance got pushed back to 1995,' a female agent said, 'wouldn't he have a broken lease like Lamprecht had? Or wouldn't he have disappeared from his auto repair shop?'

Detective Horton stood again and fielded this query. 'Thirty years is a hell of a cold trail, but as far as we can tell Dando didn't jump his lease. And the car shop where Dando worked is owned by the same family that owned it back then.' Horton turned to his partner. 'Detective Andreen tracked down the now retired garage manager that Dando reported to.'

Detective Andreen remained in his seat and said, 'He remembered Dando, thought he was not only a great mechanic, but was their go-to guy for any work on classic or foreign cars. The manager was sorry to see Dando put in his notice and recalls him saying something about moving to California or Arizona or some other warmer pasture.'

'Which would make sense,' I said. 'If Dando planned the bank heist, he wouldn't want to leave any loose ends pointing back his way.'

'So why then would he leave ten thousand dollars in the air vent?' another agent from one of the FBI tables asked.

'The obvious reason, which makes no sense, is that he was skimming off the top,' Crystal replied. 'A less obvious reason is that Dando got spooked toward the end . . . and he left it there as a message in case anything bad happened to him.' My sister looked at Detective Horton and lowered her voice, 'Do you want to tell them about the curve ball?'

Horton stood a final time. 'Connor Walsh shared the mass grave with the two ex-cons,' he said. 'Connor was heading into his senior year at Marquette University. Now Connor's father, Aiden Walsh, was a well-known and well-respected Chicago architect, but Connor's mother, Viviana Walsh, well – Viviana's maiden name is Lanaro. Yes,' Horton said to the conference room, 'Connor's uncle was Gabriele Lanaro . . . and his cousin is Mattia Lanaro.'

You could have heard a pin drop as all eyes snapped toward the CPD detective.

TWENTY-THREE

July 28, 1994

'How come in the movies it's a piece of cake. They're able to dig a grave in like twenty minutes?'

''Cause they're not a lazy butt like you,' Thomas Dando said. Currently, the hole they'd been hacking away at was six feet in length, but only two in depth. 'Use the digging fork before shoveling. It'll go quicker.'

'Isn't it your turn yet?'

'What – I do forty minutes to your ten?'

The two had taken mountain bikes off the trail, heading northwest across the forest floor, until they found the perfect spot – a bleak and isolated crook of Kankakee River State Park. They'd brought a single garden shovel with a round head and a digging fork for loosening soil. They'd have brought along more tools, but Dando didn't want any eyebrows raised amongst the hikers and bikers they'd pass along the trail. As it was, Dando had strapped the gardening tools together inside a green tarp and attached them to his backpack. A casual glance would look as if he were lugging a tent of some kind. Dando wished they'd packed another shovel as the job would be nearly done by now.

At least he wouldn't have to haul the shovel and digging fork out of the park after they finished digging the hole today. They'd be leaving the gardening tools here overnight as they'd need them again tomorrow – after it was over – when they plugged the hole with dirt.

Dando's friend leaned on the shovel and said, 'Do you trust this Walsh kid?'

Dando chuckled. 'Only enough to talk him into robbing a bank.'

'But how well do you know him?'

'Don't get jealous – you're still my oldest and dearest friend.'

'Right, 'cause you know how jealous I get,' his friend fired back. 'Seriously, though – the kid's OK?'

'Connor's solid; like I said, he's one of us,' Dando replied. 'Lamprecht's the goddamned nutjob; Tharp's got his head up his tailpipe, but the two served time together – and you know damn well they've been chatting.'

'Four million dollars will give scum like them a lot to chat about.' Dando's friend returned to shoveling. 'And Lamprecht got bent out of shape when we didn't split the money on the spot, even though our plan called for later.'

'Yeah, I read his face. He was weighing his options and realized he wouldn't survive three against two.'

Dando's friend tossed a shovelful of dirt on top a growing pile. 'I know you had qualms over this part, Tom, what has to be done – dealing with Lamprecht and Tharp.'

'Not anymore,' Dando said.

At first, when his old friend had shown up in Milwaukee and

taken him out for dinner and drinks, he thought his friend had gotten a wild hair and that it was some kind of practical joke. But as both the evening and the drinks wore on, his friend laid out the particulars of the plan, the specifics . . . and, though he'd had too much to drink, Dando had to concede – it was not a shoddy plan.

Not shoddy at all.

Nevertheless, he'd said no.

Of course he did.

He couldn't believe his friend was serious. Robbing a bank in the heart of downtown Chicago for Christ's sake? His friend had never been accused of having the greatest sense of humor, but his friend clearly had something else. His friend had someone on the inside, a source with information and insight into all things Crown National, from the layout of the bank to the positions of the security guards, to where the managers kept their keys, to the vault where the money was shuffled about, and, most importantly – so they wouldn't go through all this insane bullshit only to pocket a couple grand – the armored truck schedules.

They knew exactly when to hit Crown National in order to abscond with the maximum amount of cash.

Dando had slept on it for a week – quite frankly, it was all he thought about at work – and then he'd driven to Chicago to determine if his old friend was, in fact, serious. The two talked more; the two drank more. Though refusing to cough up the identity of the inside man, his friend explained how the source was wired into Crown National, and how the bank information was on the up and up as well as up to date. They discussed the smartest way the theft could be accomplished, and how they'd need three additional men in order to pull it off. They talked into the wee hours of the morning about how exactly one recruits for a bank robbery, whom one recruits, and afterwards . . . how to deal with those recruited.

It was at this point Dando's friend mentioned it might not bode well for their *future well-being* if *those recruited* were each given half a million dollars and sent on their merry way.

That's when the lightbulb clicked on over Dando's head, when he realized why his friend had approached him with this outrageous scheme. His friend knew Dando had served in the United States Marine Corps, knew that Dando had seen combat in Desert

Storm . . . and knew that Dando had killed men . . . had killed them up close and personal.

Dando got pissed off, big time, stormed from his friend's apartment, jumped into his Impala, and tore ass out of Chicago as the sun crept its way over the horizon. Perhaps his mother was right – perhaps he needed to see a shrink. Jesus. Dando figured they should attach that Jaws of Life rescue tool to his underside and use it to flip him inside out so he could disappear into his own asshole.

What the fuck had he been thinking?

However, as the days slowly passed, the idea of the bank heist gnawed away at him. Like a sliver, it had worked its way under his skin, becoming all but impossible to dislodge. It scratched at his consciousness, a challenge he couldn't resist, until, ultimately, Dando came to the conclusion that – goddammit! . . . they could pull it off.

Two weeks later – in the last week of April – he contacted his friend, who, in turn, jumped in a car and drove to Milwaukee, straight to Dando's apartment. It was after midnight, and after a six-pack of beer and a large sausage pizza, that they agreed to see who exactly they could recruit to their cause – they needed undesirable men with a desirable skillset – and, once the bank heist was complete, that was when the two would decide the *next part of the plan*.

Within a week, surprisingly, Dando's friend came to him with a list of ex-cons living in the Milwaukee area. His friend had burned through several days at the Chicago Public Library, scanning old newspapers in both microfiche and on optical disc – focusing on police reports – in search of felons convicted of robbery whose prison sentences would have elapsed by this point in time. Then his friend crossed-checked those names against court records and white pages and, in some instances, contacted directory assistance service – that is, dialing 411.

'That had to suck,' Dando said as he glanced at the short list of names and addresses.

'It sucked out loud,' his friend had replied.

A few days later, Dando struck out with the first name on the felon list. He'd followed the former inmate into a dive bar, ordered a beer, and noted the man sitting alone at a table, staring into his mixed drink as though it were a crystal ball. Dando stepped over and sat opposite him.

'Fuck do you want?' the ex-con said.

Dando addressed him by his name and asked if he had a few minutes to talk.

'Nope, because either you're a cop dicking with me,' he told Dando, 'or, if not, well, the last time someone came to me with a job, I got seven years in Pontiac.' He took a sip from his glass. 'Leave me alone or the bartender calls the police.'

'You don't want to hear me out?'

The former inmate looked toward the bar and hollered, 'Benny!'

Dando left a nearly full mug of Budweiser on the table as he promptly exited the tavern.

The second name on the list was one Ronald Lamprecht. This time Dando spent his after-work hours following Lamprecht around Metcalfe Park, where the ex-con lived, getting a sense of the man before finally approaching him. Of course Lamprecht had a favorite watering hole, of course Lamprecht was A-OK when a stranger struck up a conversation about the Milwaukee Brewers, of course he was A-OK when the stranger bought a pitcher of beer for them to share, and – though Dando kept things intentionally vague – of course Lamprecht was interested in hearing about a *job opportunity*.

You could say Ronald Lamprecht was a thousand percent more receptive than the first name on the felon list. And, ultimately, Lamprecht led him to Kenny Tharp.

But, in terms of the *next part of the plan*, Lamprecht's execution of the Crown National security guard had sealed both ex-cons' fates.

Ronald Lamprecht and Kenny Tharp were living on borrowed time.

And the *next part of the plan* could not come soon enough for Dando.

'All right,' he said. 'Get your lazy butt up out of that hole.'

'But it's still my turn?'

'Yeah, something tells me if I leave the digging to you, Al,' Dando told his old friend, 'we'll be here all week.'

TWENTY-FOUR

'Because *my family* had nothing to do with Connor's disappearance or murder,' Viviana Walsh said, standing, her hand on her hips, terse . . . not happy with the turn the line of questioning had taken.

Crystal and Detective Horton sat at a glass table on the tile floor adjacent to Viviana's kitchen. Horton had requested Crystal come along since she'd been the one to read the genealogy leaves and discover who else nested in the Walsh family tree – that Gabriele Lanaro had been Viviana's brother and Mattia Lanaro was her nephew. Detective Andreen and SAC Surratt had sought to come along for today's *visit*, but a decision had been made they not attend. Detective Horton did not want Viviana intimidated or spooked into requesting counsel be present.

It was a moot point, Crystal thought, as Viviana Walsh did not seem the type prone to intimidation, quite the opposite, actually.

'We just wish, Mrs Walsh,' Horton said, delicately, 'that you'd made us aware of your family connections when you came to see us the other day.'

'Why?' Viviana asked. 'If your car is stolen, do you provide your mother-in-law's name?'

'I'm not sure my mother-in-law knows how to drive a stick shift,' Horton said and smiled weakly, attempting to lighten the mood.

It fell flat.

At least they'd achieved their primary objective. Viviana scrutinized the photos of Thomas Dando as though she were a bald eagle scouring a field for mice – several pictures from Catherine Dando's shrine to her son as well as Dando's photograph from his Wisconsin driver's license, taken when he'd moved to Milwaukee – and told the detectives she was ninety-nine percent certain the pictures were of the man who'd shown up to ensure the repairs on Connor's Mustang had been performed correctly. At that point Horton informed Viviana that Thomas Dando was indeed the fourth and final set of remains identified at Kankakee River State Park.

Viviana nodded slightly but did not appear surprised.

Crystal said, 'We don't mean to be crass, Mrs Walsh, but we would not be doing our job if we didn't look into what happened to your son from every possible angle, especially in light of recent events.'

Viviana sat down at the glass table, taking the corner opposite the two detectives as though she were an opposing prizefighter. 'Then you would know that *my side of the family* does not rob banks,' she said. 'You would also know that Dando and Tharp and Lamprecht have no connection to my side of the family.' She added, 'In fact, if that Lamprecht ghoul had been associated with my side of the family, he would have treated my husband and me with the utmost respect when he stayed here overnight.'

Crystal cleared her throat. 'Did your brother and nephew help look for Connor when he went missing?'

'Yes.'

'Do you know what that entailed?'

Viviana shrugged. 'They talked to people. They looked into anyone that may have had a conflict with the family to see if it was related to Connor's disappearance.'

'And they found nothing?'

'They did not.'

'You're aware of the Crown National bank robbery,' Horton said, 'where a security guard was shot and killed by one of the thieves?'

Viviana looked down at the table. 'I've read the news accounts of what happened. I feel horrible about the guard, but there is *no way* my son shot him,' she said. 'You know Connor's record was squeaky clean? You know that, right?'

Both detectives nodded.

'Neither your son or Thomas Dando had criminal records,' Crystal said and thought of the late Catherine Dando, and how these two women had more in common than met the eye. Living solitary lives in lonesome dwellings, haunted by memories . . . the years stretch past but refuse to lighten the heartache.

Viviana mentioned upon their arrival, as salutations were exchanged, how her late husband, the architect, had designed their Winnetka home, and it was a brilliant house from all that Crystal could see. But it was a little like *Humpty Dumpty*, she thought, and all the entry halls and libraries and fireplaces, the double-digit rooms, and the butler pantries and wine closets couldn't put Viviana Walsh back together again.

'Why do you think Connor became involved with these men?' Crystal asked.

Viviana sighed. 'My son got sucked into this nightmare by a snake in the grass. And I now know the snake wasn't Lamprecht or Tharp. Those two were ghouls and creeps. Connor would have never hitched his horse to their wagon,' she said and pointed to the pictures littered about the table. 'There's the snake.' Her eyes were misty; her voice shook. 'Thomas Dando got my boy killed.'

Crystal followed Viviana's thought process. Lamprecht was most certainly a creep, but Dando was someone her son had bonded with, likely over their appreciation of classic cars. And Crystal knew it was all but impossible for Viviana or her nephew, Mattia Lanaro, to have been aware of Connor's Kankakee connection with Thomas Dando as CPD identified Dando as the fourth and final victim in the park's two graves *after* Catherine Dando's body had been discovered.

If that were not the case, Crystal would be looking into them for Catherine's murder.

Viviana looked at the detectives and continued, 'Though we were not part of my family's world, Connor was certainly aware of it, of its *mystique*. I imagine my son had thoughts in his head of – after it was over – letting Gabriele and Mattia know what he'd accomplished.' She added, 'And it was all for nothing . . . it only served to get him killed.'

TWENTY-FIVE

'The guy was homecoming king and captain of the football team,' I said, paging through the Joseph W. Fifer High School yearbook Crystal handed me. It was from the year Thomas Dando graduated high school.

'Don't forget pitcher on the baseball team,' Crystal added. 'He ran with the popular crowd . . . Dando was the popular crowd.'

I flipped through the senior pictures until I found Dando's photo and, in the margins alongside the portraits, I read his senior quotes. 'He references the sports he competed in, "Rickie's Party Cabin," "Speeding with Dave," and something about a girl named "Livvy."'

'Olivia Burke – Livvy – was Dando's girlfriend for a good chunk of his senior year. She was heavily involved in drama at Fifer and sucked him into acting in a couple of school plays.'

'You talk to her?'

'Yes. Turns out Livvy Burke got married back when she was in medical school. Livvy – I should call her Dr Griffith – is a dermatologist at the Mayo Clinic in Rochester, Minnesota,' Crystal said. 'She's not seen or talked to Dando since high school. Their relationship ended badly, a breakup right before graduation. Evidently, Dando may have stepped out on her with a girl in the sophomore class.'

'Did you track that girl down?'

'Yeah, but she swears she and Tom only started dating after he and Livvy broke up,' Crystal replied. 'I get the feeling Dando had no problem finding dates.'

'A lot like me, huh?'

'Yeah, he's exactly like you,' Crystal said. 'Actually, I dated a guy like Dando in high school.'

'Did I ever meet him?' My sister is six and a half years older than I am and, if memory serves correctly, she had a revolving door of dates and boyfriends while growing up and had attended every school dance from junior high school on up through prom of her senior year. I, on the other hand, watched a lot of television.

'You remember the guy that held you upside down?'

'That was him?' I said. 'He gave me swirlies, too – held me upside down over the toilet and threatened to flush.'

'He was quite mature for his age.'

'I loved that guy, Crys,' I said and kind of meant it. 'I was laughing so hard over the swirlies I almost peed my pants.'

'He was a BMOC – big man on campus. A senior while I was a sophomore, although I told Mom and Dad he was a junior so they wouldn't freak out.'

'Really?'

Crystal nodded. 'I bumped into him at a restaurant a couple years ago. He'd beefed up a bit and was as bald as an egg shell.'

'Doesn't matter – you should have married the guy.'

It was nearly eleven o'clock at night. The pack and I heard Crystal arrive home, so we headed upstairs to greet her. Currently, she was dipping deli meat into a jar of Dijon mustard for dinner while filling me in on her day. My sister looked beat, but whenever Crys works a case, she's more dogged than my canines.

She had spent the better part of her afternoon at Joseph W. Fifer High School. Fifer was the high school on the opposite side of the wooded ridge where Alice and Rex found Catherine Dando, the school with the soccer fields. There were no high school yearbooks in Thomas Dando's old bedroom, just the paperback ones they sold to students in junior high. Summer school was in session at Fifer, so Crystal had an administrator hunt down a yearbook from Dando's senior year.

'Have you contacted any of his jock friends?'

Crystal nodded and pointed at her pocket-sized notepad lying open on the kitchen island. 'Four of his teammates, including Rick Jensen of "Rickie's Party Cabin."'

I glanced down and read the names of the teammates she'd spoken with: Rick Jensen, Chris Merrill, Dave Albertson, and Keith Jacobs. If Rick had the party cabin – likely his parents' cabin, of course – then Dave was probably the buddy, per Dando's senior quotes, he'd gone speeding or racing cars with.

Crystal continued, 'They all loved Dando back in high school. Hanging with him made their stock rise in the popularity department, which translated into girlfriends and parties – fun times. But none of them did much with him once he returned home after leaving the Marine Corps. Evidently, Catherine had a welcome home party for her son and his buddies all came, but each one said Tom wasn't the guy they'd grown up with. He was reserved and quiet and a bit on the sullen side,' she said. 'They all made plans to hit the bars, but whenever they set something up, Dando never returned their calls.'

'What did they think happened when he fell off the face of the earth?'

'The consensus was that Tom had gone through some horrible-scary shit in the Gulf War, and he left Chicago so he wouldn't bump into any old friends and get reminded of how life once was,' she said. 'They're all stunned by what they've read in the newspapers this past week, but Rick Jensen put it best, "Tom's been away so long it's like he died years ago."'

I set the Joseph W. Fifer yearbook next to Crystal's notepad and grabbed the bag of miniature pretzels. Immediately, Alice and Rex were at my feet. Between stuffing my face, I flicked individual pretzels off my thumb so the two took turns chasing after them. If my pups had gone to high school, Alice would have been the class valedictorian. Rex, however, would have been a good-natured class clown.

'It doesn't make sense.'

'Which part?' Crystal asked.

'There's no way a guy's an Adonis in high school – a freaking sports god – adored by all, can date anyone he bumps into, and he decides not to order any yearbooks. I mean Dando's practically on every other page.'

'I know, especially since he'd bought those chintzy ones they sell in junior high,' Crystal replied. 'But maybe by that point he thought he was too cool for school.'

'Well,' I said, 'even with all the shit that happened to me in high school, I'm glad I picked up the yearbooks.'

'I had to force you to order those.'

I nodded and said, 'I'm glad you did.' Mom and Dad died my junior year. I was a hot mess; I spent most waking hours flipping my middle finger at anyone and everything that crossed my path. In retrospect, I was projecting – the middle finger had been meant for me. 'I'd been with a lot of those folks since kindergarten. The yearbooks, especially the senior one, kind of encompass that era,' I said. 'And I wasn't even homecoming king or super jock or God's gift to women.' I looked at Crystal. 'You think the killer stole a picture off the wall in Dando's old bedroom. And now you've got missing high school yearbooks. Whoever killed Catherine and took the picture off the wall may have also grabbed his yearbooks.'

'That crossed my mind,' she said and dipped another clump of ham into the jar of Dijon. 'The only difference between the ones I picked up at Fifer today and the ones Dando may have purchased back then would be what his friends and classmates wrote in them.'

'Right – that whole *sign-my-yearbook* thingy. I doubt if any of his old football buddies would have written: "Can't wait until we knock over Crown National in a few years." But I bet there were some handwritten notes on what *great pals* we were and *best friends forever*,' I said. 'The kind of notes that might point toward a friend who wouldn't walk away after a few unreturned phone calls.'

Crystal set down the jar of mustard. 'Catherine is killed because she could have told us who hung out with her son during those last few months of his life, even though he's all sullen and despondent and stand-offish.' My sister swallowed a final piece of ham and added, 'It's like what Chuck Sims said – Catherine knew her son's killer.'

'Definitely,' I agreed.

'But I can't box myself into Dando's high school years,' she said. 'I can't exclude other aspects of the guy's life.'

'Yeah, what about any fellow soldiers he knew from the Marine Corps? Catherine might have met a few of them. Maybe one of them came to visit Dando during that last summer?'

Crystal nodded.

'Or maybe Catherine knew one of her son's friends from his time in Milwaukee, you know – a mechanic or gearhead buddy he hung out with?'

Crystal said, 'A list of possibilities.' Whether it was the long day or the late hour, my sister looked as though she were ready to hibernate for a week.

I filled a glass with water, took a step toward the staircase leading down to my domain, but then turned and asked, 'Where do you go from here?'

'I'll keep looking at Joseph W. Fifer,' she replied. 'There were over five hundred students in Dando's graduating class. The guy was on varsity in everything by his sophomore year, so if the killer is a Fifer grad, he could be a couple years older or even younger.' Crystal shrugged. 'I guess I'll start by finding out if any of his old teammates have criminal records.'

TWENTY-SIX

July 29, 1994
8:00 A.M.

'There she goes,' Dando said. 'Like clockwork.'

He and Connor sat in the used Ford F-150, sipping coffee, parked several doors down from his mother's house in Logan Square. Four battered mountain bikes sat in the truck bed, bikes Dando had picked up for cash at a neighborhood garage sale. The pickup's cab was big enough to seat Tharp and Lamprecht in the back as they'd be picking the two ex-cons up at a Denny's in less than an hour, and on from there to Kankakee River State Park in order to divide and disperse the duffel bags stuffed with cash into six equal shares.

In actuality, however, something entirely different would be meted out at Kankakee.

Something entirely different.

Dando had a flask filled with vodka in the glove compartment. He'd toss it in the backseat when they picked up the two men in the hope that Tharp and Lamprecht would get a little lubed on the drive toward their final resting place. There were no duffel bags in the F-150, so he and Connor shouldn't have to fear Lamprecht on the journey to the state park.

Once they were there, though, all bets were off.

Al was already at Kankakee, prepping for what was to come.

Dando had appropriated the F-150 from the auto repair shop he'd recently quit. He'd raced there from Kankakee late yesterday afternoon, arriving at the garage right as they were closing for the day. He brought with him a case of Miller High Life and a bullshit story about moving out west the following morning. The owner and a handful of mechanics hung around, likely more out of free beer than friendship. As they gabbed and joked about, Dando feigned interest in what vehicles the shop was currently working on. He glanced through the work orders long enough to note an F-150 was waiting on an air conditioning compressor in the overflow lot. He palmed the key to the pickup and was back sipping beer with the gang a moment later.

At dusk, Connor dropped him off at the overflow lot. A half-hour later the two of them were in the F-150, taking I-94 back to Chicago. With a little luck, Dando figured he'd have the pickup wiped down and back in the overflow lot before anyone knew it was missing.

'Why'd we have to wait until she left?'

'I don't know about your mom, Connor, but if we go in there, she'll insist on making us breakfast and gab for an hour, trying to figure out how I've been doing.'

'You're leaving a note?'

'Let her know I've quit my job, that I'm taking a trip out west to find work.' He shrugged. 'Tell her I love her.'

Dando hated lying to Connor. He was not there to leave his mother a note.

Once inside the bungalow, Dando went straight to his old bedroom. He slid a desk chair over to the air vent by the entry door and unscrewed the cover. He had earlier picked up a clip that would meet his needs as well as a tube of superglue at a hardware store. He squirted a glob of glue on to the back of the clip and pressed it against the galvanized steel of the ductwork for an entire minute before releasing.

Dando then went back to the desk and grabbed a pencil. He jotted a couple letters on the bank strap, got pissed, and cussed at how the strap's waxy texture fuzzed up his writing. Screw it, the Crown National band would be enough to set off fire alarms – it would have to do. Besides, he'd be back tomorrow – to chat with his mother in person – and retrieve the hidden band of cash.

That fucking Lamprecht.

Executing a bank guard.

And the bank guard had a name – Andy Benson. And the bank guard had a family – a wife and kids and grandkids.

Jesus Christ.

Dando wanted to strangle the ex-con with his bare hands, to see the light slowly dissipate from the bastard's eyes. He knew what was coming up at the state park was going to be tricky. He also knew Tharp would back whatever play Lamprecht had in mind, but what he and Al and Connor had in store would take those two shitbags out of play damned near immediately.

The plan Al brought to him had skidded horribly sideways. He shook his head. For fuck's sake – a dead security guard . . . they were all murderers now.

Dando couldn't shake this feeling of dread. It ate away at the next-to-nothing sleep he'd gotten since the bank heist.

What if something – if anything else – went wrong?

That was the four-million-dollar question.

As a kid, Dando got pissed when he caught his mom eating a bunch of his Halloween candy. So the next Halloween he took out all the hard candy and other crap he hated and set that in a bag in the kitchen for the two of them to share, but then he got all James Bond-ish and hid the good stuff in the air vent in his bedroom. He had his stash of sweets in a bag tied off with a string, and with the excess string tied to the air vent cover to keep it from plummeting into the depths of the HVAC.

After he'd gnawed through his bag of goodies – and his mom complained of the lame stuff left for her in the kitchen – he'd confessed. It had been a huge pain in the ass retrieving the bag every time he wanted to eat a Snickers bar, but Dando was kind of proud of himself, so he'd let his mom in on his secret. In following years he'd joked with her about how he kept his drugs and porn hidden in there as well.

So, Dando figured, if he turned up dead, the cops might toss his room and find a certain something that could point them in the right direction. And there was no straighter arrow than his mother, no one more honest, and, if something happened to him, she might remember his joshing about and peek in the air vent, which, again, might point the powers that be in the right direction.

None of this mattered, of course, as Dando would be retrieving the band of cash first thing tomorrow morning.

And, in the evening, he'd take his mother out to the restaurant of her choice; price would be of no object. And he'd tell her how much he loved her, in person, as well as let her know he'd be going away on a lengthy trip – of discovery or some other such crap – in order to figure out what he wanted to do next with his life.

TWENTY-SEVEN

The fixer sat in a guest chair across the cherry wood desk from his client. His legs were crossed, and he had a hand in a side pocket of his jacket. Though he appeared the picture of tranquility – peaceful and serene – his fingers had been wrapped around a Kimber Micro 9 since his client's personal assistant led him from the entrance hall to the home study. Lightweight, at four inches in length, the Kimber was tailor-made for concealed carry – the perfect pocket pistol. If you were a client of his . . . well, by that very definition you were not to be trusted.

And the person on the opposite end of the cherry wood was the least trustworthy of any of those that appeared on his client list, both past and present.

'CPD found Catherine Dando's body the same day they showed up to question her,' his client spoke with no sense of urgency or excitement, or, quite frankly, any sense of emotion, as though reading instructions from an outdated user guide to a vacant classroom.

'The detective brought in cadaver dogs to search her house as well as the woodland behind her house,' the fixer replied. 'That's not normal; it was unexpected. I figured we had a few weeks before some kids found her, after the leaves died on the branch covering the bag she was in.'

'Suddenly, it's a full-blown murder investigation. Suddenly, they're able to link her son Tom to the Crown National bank robbery,' his client stated, again reading from the user guide. 'This is the exact opposite of what I wanted.'

The fixer paid strict attention to his client's movements. Any sudden changes and the Kimber would come into play. From what he had been told, but mostly from what he'd figured out on his own . . . his client's hands were bloody.

And no matter what happened today, the fixer's blood would not be added to the mix.

'CPD's being cagey with the news media, not telling them what they found, which is smart,' he said. 'I tore through the house and spotted nothing from Crown National – for Christ's sake, you never brought up Crown National. I wasn't privy to that; it wasn't on my radar. Rather, I collected the picture, the yearbooks, and the old letters you were worried about.' He uncrossed his legs. 'Catherine Dando is out of the picture; she can no longer implicate you. I have no idea what her son hid in the rafters or under the floorboards thirty years ago,' the fixer's voice grew cold, 'but you never brought that up, either. If you had,' he said, 'I would have razed the fucking house to the ground.'

The fixer was angry. He didn't like being angry, but it washed over him, a high tide at night, as he put voice to the pivotal information his client had withheld from him. In his line of work – for him to do his job with any level of competency – nothing could be kept back from him.

It was as simple as that.

His client leaned back in the leather office chair and sighed. 'I have no idea what Tom planted in his mother's house. I had no idea he planted anything at all.' For the first time there was an emotional cadence – perhaps stress, perhaps fatigue – in his client's voice.

'Whatever he hid can't come back at you because if it could,' he said, 'it would have already happened.'

'Thank God for small favors.' His client shrugged. 'What do we do now?'

The fixer stood to leave, his hand remaining inside his jacket pocket. 'We sit back and watch.'

TWENTY-EIGHT

July 29, 1994
10:30 A.M.

'Why do we have to ride these fucking bikes?' Lamprecht said. 'Let's carve up the loot in the truck here. No one's looking.'

Dando had pulled the F-150 into Kankakee River State Park's main entrance and parked in the less crowded section of the lot, on the side adjacent to the Smith Cemetery, a boneyard dating back to the dawn of the twentieth century. Dando issued a mountain bike to each of the three men and took the last one for himself. The four of them slow-rode the trailbikes to the pathway leading up to the restrooms and a log-cabin-style concession stand. From there the pathway led to a variety of trails and, ultimately, the river.

'Because the *loot* is not here.' Dando glanced back at Kankakee's parking lot. It was half full with hikers and bikers and picnickers and nature enthusiasts both entering and coming down off the pathway. 'Plus, we've got to be careful,' he lowered his voice, 'because some asshole shot a bank guard and now we're wanted for murder.'

Lamprecht snapped back, 'I told you he was making a move.'

'Jesus Christ, Lamprecht – if you ever got an enema, you'd weigh all of three pounds.' Dando then added, 'Let's haul ass. I don't want to be here any longer than you do.'

The drive to Kankakee State Park had been uneventful. Connor rode shotgun but sat sidesaddle in order to keep an eye on the two felons in the backseat. Dando realized that, unlike himself, Connor was a smooth operator. Any *discord* between Lamprecht and Connor over what went down at Crown National was long since forgotten. Velvety and unthreatening, the college senior whiled away the trip making small talk about Cubbies baseball, *Sports Illustrated* swimsuit models, July's current heatwave, and what the two men were planning to do with their share of the cut.

In smooth-operator mode, Dando figured, Connor could tell you to go fuck yourself, and you'd catch yourself smiling as you attempted to perform the act.

'Cops have prosecutorial discretion,' Connor told the group at one point. 'Of course they do. Why do you think pretty girls get off with a warning while us guys get the speeding tickets?'

Tharp laughed and sipped again from the flask of vodka. For most of the drive Tharp chatted with Connor as Dando and Lamprecht kept to themselves, except when Lamprecht volunteered exactly what he'd like to do with those swimsuit models Connor brought up. Dando was pleased to see Tharp go after the flask like a bee to pollen. Perfect, he thought to himself, keep tossing back that hair of the dog.

But about halfway to Kankakee, Lamprecht tore the flask from Tharp's grip and flipped it at Connor. 'No more,' Lamprecht barked, glaring at Tharp. 'It's not even fucking noon.'

You wouldn't need a fortune teller to see what Tharp would be doing with his slice of the pie, Dando thought, though a fortune teller might think to warn the ex-con he wouldn't be receiving one. Dando adjusted the rearview mirror so he could help Connor keep an eye on the two men in the backseat of the pickup truck. And he caught the look Lamprecht gave Tharp as he chastised the man about drinking so early in the day. Lamprecht wasn't the least concerned about Tharp's budding alcoholism, but he shot daggers Tharp's way, and Tharp gave his friend a quick nod in return.

'Turn on the air,' Lamprecht ordered at one point. 'We're roasting back here.'

'It's on the fritz,' Dando replied. 'Just leave your window down.' Unlike the alleged *move* the Crown National bank guard was attempting to make, these two dickheads were indeed going to try something. If the duffel bags full of cash had been in the pickup, there'd have already been a shootout. Both men were packing; Dando could tell by the bulges under their shirts when he picked the two up at Denny's.

But so were he and Connor. In fact, as Connor made small talk, his hand was beneath his shirt, resting on his inside the waistband holster. And when they reached their final destination, Al would be armed as well.

'What do you mean we leave the blacktop?' Lamprecht said as they came to a stop in the northwest-most corner of the park, the point at which the trail curved away in a different direction. 'We can divvy it up on one of these park benches.'

'Real bright, Lamprecht,' Dando said. 'Then a Boy Scout troop hikes past and sees us counting up the cash – but, hey, that's not suspicious, not at all.'

Lamprecht's hand inched toward his waist. 'I've had a bellyful of your shit.'

Dando's own hand dropped to his belt as he spotted Connor – who, per the plan, had been bringing up the rear – lift his shirt and reach for his holster. 'You won't have much more to take. In fact, when we're done, I'll drop you two at Bourbonnais, ten minutes from here,' he said. 'Better yet, the mountain bikes are a gift from me to you. You can take them to Bourbonnais.'

'Fine by me,' Lamprecht replied. 'As soon as I get my eight hundred grand, I'm out the fucking door.'

'Eight hundred?' Dando said. 'It's a six-way cut – you'll be getting six sixty.'

Lamprecht looked as if he'd been slapped in the face. 'What do you mean *six-way*?'

'The inside man,' Dando replied. 'That's where we got the intel.'

'Yeah, but why should he get the same amount if he wasn't in the bank? His ass wasn't on the line.'

Dando sighed. 'I'll give you an extra twenty from my cut if you'll just *shut the fuck up* for once and let us get on with it.'

Lamprecht and Tharp glared at Dando. If this were a prison yard, the shivs would be out. But if the two thought to glance behind them, they'd notice that smooth-talking, non-threatening kid from the passenger seat had his pistol halfway out of his holster.

The ex-cons then turned toward each other and shared another knowing glance.

Yup, Dando thought . . . a storm was brewing.

The four men turned off the blacktop and cut into the woods. The best thing about mountain bikes is their thick tires allow for off-roading. Bumps and crevasses and divots and sticks and rocks and tree roots won't pop tires or bend spokes as they might a traditional 10-speed. Plus, you could cover a great deal of ground in a small amount of time, which was what Dando had in mind. He wanted Lamprecht and Tharp deep into the woodlands before any red flags went up.

Nonetheless, Lamprecht coasted to a stop three minutes into the forest ride. 'This is far enough,' he said, his voice dry. 'Where's my fucking money?'

Dando stopped. He noted Lamprecht had one hand on the handlebars, but his other was now underneath his shirt. Tharp had stopped, too, one hand down by his side. Behind them, though, was Connor. His arm was hidden behind his back, his pistol already out.

'It's just up ahead.'

Lamprecht stared at Dando, embers burning in his eyes. 'Prove it.'

Dando shrugged and shouted, 'Hey, Al – you up there?!'

A second later came a muffled response, something that might have been 'What?' Off in the distance a figure stepped into the clearing, out between a set of smaller trees and saplings, and waved a hand in the air.

Dando turned to Lamprecht. 'Good enough?'

Lamprecht responded by getting back on his bike seat and pedaling toward the figure in the murky light of the forest canopy.

Dando rode along next to him. 'You ever do much camping?'

Lamprecht said nothing.

'We don't want any nearby tents,' Dando lied as no one was communing with nature in this forgotten section of Kankakee State Park. 'No busybody campers.'

As the quartet closed in on Dando's old friend, they spotted three backpacks sitting in a row on the forest floor. Two packs were zipped shut, stuffed full, clearly bulging. A third backpack sat upright and unzipped, the top flush with Crown National straps of hundred-dollar bills. At least twenty lay in plain sight, with plenty more crammed inside the swollen backpack.

It was a sight to behold as the four men came to a stop.

And that's when Dando slammed his fist into the side of Lamprecht's head. The ex-con, mountain bike and all, dropped hard to the ground. Dando had to hand it to Lamprecht as the man went for his sidearm. Even in intense agony, some feral part of the felon's brain warned him it was kill or be killed time. But he never had a chance, not even close. Dando stepped from his bike, stamped on Lamprecht's gun hand, and kicked the pistol away. Then Dando stepped on Lamprecht's mountain bike, pinning the man to the forest floor. He then stuck his Beretta M9 in the ex-con's face and said, 'Here's your cut of the loot,' and squeezed the trigger.

Simultaneously, Tharp panicked. He'd been white around the gills – vodka and biking are never a good mix – but he pawed at his waistline. Connor kicked sideways at Tharp's bike, tipping the ex-con over and sending his firearm sliding across dirt and dead leaves. Dando's old friend marched over, Beretta in hand. And though Dando had worked with Al at the gun range over the summer, at this distance it didn't matter.

Tharp's scream was stifled in its infancy as Al shot him through the forehead.

Dando breathed a sigh of relief.

It had gone as planned – hit the ex-cons at their most vulnerable, while straddling their bicycles. Dando glanced down at the dead men – clearly no need for double taps – and, though the grave they'd dug was another forty yards or so away, hidden from view so Lamprecht and Tharp wouldn't spot it, he looked toward where they'd soon be dragging the bodies. It was still July, Dando thought; if anyone on the outer reaches of the park heard gunshots, they'd think kids and firecrackers, and a minute later, after they'd returned about their business, they'd have forgotten they'd heard anything at all.

When Dando glanced back, his old friend now pointed the Beretta at Connor.

Connor's jaw had dropped, his eyes wide open. And the poor kid stumbled over his own bike as he turned to flee.

A third shot rang out in the Kankakee woodland.

TWENTY-NINE

Catherine Dando's funeral took place at Wicker Park Lutheran Church. Once again I leapt at the opportunity to play hooky and skip my afternoon class. Crystal drove while I navigated per parroting the voice on my Maps app until we arrived at the corner of Hoyne Avenue and Le Moyne Street. I tapped End Route blocks before my sister found us a spot to dump her Honda as I'd spotted the church's two towers a half-mile out. Wicker Park Lutheran had that rectangular-basilica thing going and Crystal and I were ushered into the nave right as the service began. The church was nearly packed – evidently, per the funeral pamphlet, Catherine had been a member for decades – and we found two open seats in a rear pew.

Catherine's closed casket sat sideways in front of the altar as the pastor stood before the congregation and cleared his throat. I saw Catherine's sister and her husband in the front pew. Surrounding them were mourners I took to be part of their immediate family, their children and grandchildren. I glanced about the church and spotted Detectives Horton and Andreen tucked inside a pew halfway up the aisle. Like my sister, their heads swiveled as they surveyed those in attendance. The detectives were here to people watch, looking for anyone in their mid-fifties that Catherine's son may have known from his high school or military days.

One of the inspectors, most likely my sister, would be snapping photographs of the signatory pages in the memorial guest book before departing today.

I also noticed several men and a woman in black suits not unlike those worn by the FBI agents at SAC Surratt's task force meeting or, perhaps, they were simply mourners here to grieve an old friend. I myself looked equally stylish in my navy-blue wool – the only suit I own – which I'd picked up at a factory outlet super sale. I glanced behind me and saw Crystal's partner, Mark Lahlum, leaning against the back wall, the perfect perch from which to observe attendees as they both entered or vacated the house of worship.

The melancholia hanging over Wicker Park Lutheran was as thick as drying cement when the pastor began to speak. It's hard to hold a celebration of life when that particular life had been violently snuffed out. In this case, long-term parishioner Catherine Dando had been murdered and, per recent news reports, Catherine's long-missing son, Thomas, had been identified as one of the four sets of human remains unearthed at Kankakee River State Park, and had been linked, along with the other three remains, to the Crown National bank robbery from over a generation ago.

That was a lot for the congregation at Wicker Park Lutheran Church to process . . . and even more for them to grieve.

But the pastor did as best he could under the circumstances. He spoke of how the sudden death of Catherine Dando has left the church reeling, feeling as if their world has been turned upside down by an act of senseless violence. He spoke of how the loss of Catherine in such a manner is a paralyzing tragedy, with many dear friends and fellow worshipers finding it difficult to imagine a future without her. He spoke of how we needed to support each other in times like these, and to give our hearts over to God so He may guide and direct us through this time of sorrow and despair.

The microphone was then passed around as friends and fellow parishioners as well as old colleagues were invited to say a few words about Catherine. An underlying theme was how they were humbled and touched by her time spent with them, and how quick Catherine was to welcome new people into her friend group, and how she had always been a kind and caring person who never turned down the opportunity to meet others or to be on hand whenever someone was in need of help. Catherine's positivity – considering the misfortune and heartbreak that had befallen her – had been an inspiration for everyone in Catherine's orb.

Ms Dando sounded like an amazing human being. And I only wished I could shake the flashback of Crystal zipping open the body bag in the stretch of woods behind Catherine's Logan Square bungalow.

As with many memorials, lunch was served in the church basement following the service. Crystal and I sat silently and watched as funeral attendees left Wicker Park Lutheran to get on with their day or head toward the staircase or elevator. After the flock had dispersed, Crystal and I headed downstairs ourselves. The line for the ham sandwiches, macaroni salad, and potato chips was lengthy, so I advanced on the urns of coffee and other refreshments, leaving the four CPD investigators to share their observations in private. I tore open several packets of cream, dumped the powder into my Styrofoam cup, whisked it in with one of those miniature red stirrers, and then backed out of the way so others could have their shot at the drink table.

I stood off against a side wall and watched the room. Eventually, Crystal meandered my way, stopping briefly for a cup of java herself.

'Anything up?' I asked.

'Just going to talk with anyone that seems of Thomas's age,' she said.

I sipped at my lukewarm coffee and then spotted a woman I swore I knew. An attractive fifty-something with sandy hair, medium cut, who stood about five-seven in her black pumps. 'Hey, Crys,' I said, 'how do we know that woman getting lemonade?'

Crystal glanced toward the refreshment table. 'She does have a familiar look.' My sister tossed her cup, coffee and all, in a nearby bin. 'Shall we?'

'Excuse me,' Crystal said as we approached. 'Sorry to intrude, but we both feel as though we know you from somewhere.'

'Oh no, not again,' the woman said and smiled. 'Please tell me you've not seen any TV commercials for Quinn Chevrolet.'

'Bingo,' I said. My eyes lit up. 'I knew it was you, I knew it . . . and I am so sorry to hear about your husband's passing. I loved his car ads.'

'Well, Paul certainly had a blast making them. To be honest, he liked making those spots more than actually selling the cars.'

'I bet they reeled in a ton of people, though,' I said. I'd once driven out to Paul Quinn's auto dealership, not to purchase a new vehicle – couldn't come close to affording one – but to see if the place embraced the circus-like atmosphere as witnessed on television. It did – balloons and flags and popcorn and peanuts, a miniature Ferris wheel and multiple ball pits and enclosed trampolines for the little ones. 'You remember the one where he did a handstand on the hood of a truck for the entire commercial?'

She nodded at the memory. 'I hate to kill the illusion, but there may have been some special effects involved in a few of those scenes.'

Her late husband, Paul Quinn of Quinn Chevrolet, passed away from a heart attack or heart disease or heart something or other a couple of years ago. He'd attained a certain local celebrityhood due to his energetic and fun – or witty and madcap – advertising campaign for his car dealership. Paul Quinn himself, we're told, either wrote or ad-libbed many of the TV spots. Sure, the commercials were over the top and tongue in cheek; nevertheless they were highly entertaining. Props included gymnastic tricks, yo-yos – Paul was a master – a unicycle, a trapeze, and, my personal favorite, a talking skunk.

'If I remember right,' I said, 'you took over doing the commercials.'

'After Paul died, the gang at the dealership conned me into doing a couple of spots.' She took a small sip of her lemonade. 'Biggest mistake I ever made – cringe inducing, and don't bring up the pom-poms.'

I chuckled. 'No way, those were fun.'

'They're forbidden to run either of those commercials ever again,' she said. 'I'm not an extrovert like my husband. Now they just have me sit at the desk and say, "Get a Great Deal at Quinn Chevrolet."'

I got a little excited and blurted, 'I drive a Silverado.'

'Well, cheers.' She tipped her Styrofoam of lemonade in my direction. 'If you ever want to trade it in, tell them I sent you.'

'Really?' I said, and then felt Crystal's palm on my forearm, nudging me out of the picture. It was for the best, though, as I was just about to tell Mrs Quinn I'd have to pay them to take Dad's antiquated pickup off my hands.

Crystal said, 'I'm also sorry to hear about your husband.'

'Thank you,' Mrs Quinn replied as she turned her attention toward my sister. 'Paul was a good man.' She smiled again, bittersweet this time. 'He may have had a screw loose, but boy could he make me laugh . . . and take me away from the world.'

My sister let that sink in a moment and then dove in. 'My name is Crystal Pratt. I'm a detective with the Chicago Police Department. I'm hoping to chat with people who knew either Catherine or her son, Thomas.'

'Well then, you came to the right place,' Mrs Quinn said. 'Why don't we grab a seat and you can ask me anything you want.'

We settled into folding chairs on one side of an empty table before Crystal asked, 'How long have you known the Dandos?'

Mrs Quinn smiled again, her teeth perfect and white. I couldn't help but think of pom-poms.

'Catherine was my second mother,' she said. 'My parents were fascists about not having any dessert or snacks in our house, so I'd sneak over to Tom's as Catherine made the best cupcakes.' She added, 'Sometimes, she let me make them with her.'

'When did you first meet Tom?'

'A million years ago to be exact – elementary school.'

'The two of you were friends?'

'Only since kindergarten,' she replied. 'We climbed trees and played tag, had rock fights – yes, ouch! – and went trick or treating every year.' Mrs Quinn glanced across the room at nothing in particular. 'We even played kissy face once in seventh grade, but we both started giggling because it seemed so weird, like making out with a family member.'

I looked at Crystal and laughed.

'Tom was popular at school, right?'

Mrs Quinn nodded. 'He was smart and funny, excellent at all sports . . . and a hunk – everyone loved Tom. I may have been first to play kissy face with him, but Tom went on to play it with a few other girls.'

Crystal then asked, 'Did you stay in touch after high school?'

'I wrote to him when he was in the Marines, but he never wrote back.' Quinn's face turned somber. 'And I was at the party Catherine threw when he came home.'

'How did that go?'

'Well, by then Tom wasn't Tom anymore.' She swirled her cup of lemonade. 'I think everyone you talk to will say something to that effect. Tom sucked down beer after beer. He'd checked out and only nodded along with whatever anyone was saying,' she said. 'Catherine warned us he'd been through a nasty ordeal in Desert Storm.'

'Did you keep in touch after the party?'

'I tried making Saturday a movie night for us to catch a show and grab a bite. I forced it on the poor guy for a month or two, but it felt like work, and we both let it dwindle away.' She thought for a second and continued, 'I did try setting him up with a friend of mine, but he blew it off. He told me he wasn't ready to start dating.' She shook her head. 'Like I said, Tom wasn't the Tom we used to know.'

'Did you see him after he moved to Milwaukee?'

'A couple of times. He came home one weekend, and we went to a car show,' she said. 'Tom loved cars. He would have gotten a kick out of my husband's dealership.'

'Did you keep in touch with Catherine?'

'Maybe a few phone calls back in the day.' Her eyes grew moist. 'I moved on with my life and, to be honest, I didn't give *my second mother* a second thought until I read about what happened, you know, about her death.' She blinked back tears. 'Then I sat down and wept.'

'Don't beat yourself up.' I passed her a coffee-stained napkin. 'It sounds like you did quite a bit.'

Crystal paused as Mrs Quinn dabbed at her eyes, and then asked, 'Are you in touch with any of Tom's high school friends?'

'I may have spotted a few upstairs during the service.' She shrugged. 'Frankly, I only see the old gang at class reunions.'

'There had to be talk, right, at the reunions?' Crystal said. 'I mean here's a guy who practically owned the high school, and then he just goes away as though none of it really mattered.'

'We were all so young when Tom came home. We didn't understand PTSD at the time, but knew he'd been through a lot and was having *difficulties* settling back in. To your point, though, most everyone at the reunions thought Tom moved out west to start over, to get away from anything that reminded him of his past,' she said. 'I liked picturing Tom out west all of these years, starting over, a brand-new life. I Googled him now and again and could never find anything, but a lot of people don't have an online presence.' She dabbed again at her eyes with the napkin. 'Of course we now know Tom never made it out west; there wasn't a new life for him.'

Crystal nodded slowly and asked a final question. 'Is there anything else you can think of that might be of help in the investigation?'

'Well, I loved Tom, and I'm finding it impossible to believe what's been coming out in the news,' she said. 'First, it's heartbreaking to hear he's been dead this entire time. And what they're suggesting, the bank robbery – well, that breaks reality. But if it's true, it wasn't the Tom I grew up with that was involved . . . it was Broken Tom – the man who came back from the Gulf War.'

We sat in silence a moment before Crystal reached out her hand and said, 'I can't thank you enough for speaking with us. You've been incredibly helpful, Mrs Quinn.'

'Glad to be of assistance and, for crying out loud, don't call me Mrs Quinn – that's my mother-in-law,' she told Crystal as she shook her hand. 'Call me Alaine,' she said. 'My friends call me Al.'

PART THREE

The Inside Man

The gift which I am sending you is called a dog, and is in fact the most precious and valuable possession of mankind.
— Theodorus Gaza

THIRTY

July 29, 1994
11:12 A.M.

Dando was on Alaine in an instant. He twisted the gun from her hand, tearing flesh, and smashed Alaine's Beretta M9 against the side of her head. Like Lamprecht, she hit the ground hard, and gazed back up at Dando, stunned, like a bird that had flown into a clear glass window.

Dando stuck the barrel of the Beretta against her cheekbone. 'I should fucking kill you.'

Instead, he turned, took the open backpack by its shoulder strap, and flipped it upside down; bands of cash and the phone books packed inside tumbled to the ground in his dash toward Connor.

'It's OK,' he said as he folded the backpack in half and pressed it against his friend's shoulder blade, where he'd been shot. 'It's going to be OK, Connor.'

'She . . . shot me,' Connor mumbled into the dirt, sinking into shock.

As gently as possible, Dando rolled his friend over. 'It's not that bad,' he said. 'I'll get you out of here, kiddo, and a quick ambulance ride to Bourbonnais.'

'Why'd she . . . shoot me?' Connor struggled with his words.

''Cause she's a greedy fucking pig.'

'You don't even know who he is, Tom,' Alaine spoke for the first time. She leaned upright on an elbow, her free hand pressed against the side of her head.

Dando said nothing. Connor's wound was more serious than he was letting on. Beretta M9s at point blank tend to do that. No way could Dando get Connor up on a bike by himself and he didn't think he could fumble-fuck it out of the park with the two of them riding one bike.

So it boiled down to the fireman's carry.

'Tell him who your uncle is,' Alaine said.

Dando caught the look on Connor's face, something else mixed in with the shock and pain.

Alaine waited a long moment and then continued, 'His uncle is the head of the Chicago mob.'

'I don't care if his uncle's the King of Siam.'

'Tom,' Alaine said, slowly moving into a sitting position, blood dripping down the side of her face. 'His uncle will have us killed.'

'No,' Connor said, looking up at Dando, a sheen of sweat across his face. 'Uh-uh.'

'If he shows his uncle a million dollars, we'll be dead in a day.'

'No,' Connor said, still holding Dando's eye. 'This was never about . . . my uncle, Tom.'

'He's suddenly a millionaire, but they'd never piece together Crown National and the dead guard?' she said. 'Tom – we'd be killed in a day.'

Connor gripped Dando's hand. 'No – I'd never give . . . names.'

Dando squeezed back at his friend's hand. 'Don't worry about it, kid,' he said. 'I know you wouldn't.'

'Jesus Christ, Tom – you've always been the practical one,' Alaine said and pointed at Connor. 'His uncle would have our names out of him in twenty seconds flat.'

Dando knew he had to move. He lifted Connor into a sitting position and got ready for what would be the Guinness World Record of firemen carries, all the way back to the park's main entrance.

'If Connor leaves here, Tom,' Alaine said, 'we're dead.'

There was something in Alaine's voice, a sturdier timbre, and that raised the hair on the back of Dando's neck. He glanced her way. Alaine had slid across in the dirt and picked up Tharp's firearm. She pointed it directly at them.

'You fucking—'

Alaine fired. The bullet punched a hole through Connor Walsh's left eye.

THIRTY-ONE

There was a light knock on the French doors of Alaine Quinn's home study before one side opened inward. Quinn's executive admin stood in the entryway. Teresa Schorr was not only Quinn's Girl Friday and jack of all trades – though Teresa drew the line at dishes and laundry – but the person who made the trains run on time, which explained the current disruption.

'Just a reminder, Alaine, you've got a two o'clock conference call with the people from Lithia Motors, which is in forty minutes.'

Alaine's eyes shot to the mid-century grandfather clock adjacent to the gas fireplace. 'Thank you, Teresa,' she said. 'We'll be finished by then.'

Schorr bowed slightly and shut the office door, leaving the fixer and Quinn to continue with their meeting.

Once again the fixer sat in a guest chair opposite his client. His hand had since exited the side pocket of his jacket as today's topic piqued his curiosity and served to tamp down his instinctual distrust. However, he was surprised at whom Quinn had in line for an upcoming Zoom call. 'Lithia Motors?' he said.

'We are in the early stages of selling the Chevrolet dealership,' she replied. 'I'll be meeting with several automotive groups in the coming weeks.'

'Paul's kids good with that?' Years back, the fixer had removed some frustrating roadblocks for Paul Quinn. It was how he had first met Alaine.

She shook her head. 'They have never warmed toward me. Understandable – they were in college when Paul and I tied the knot.' Alaine held his eye. 'We've not been on speaking terms since they contested the will.'

'Wouldn't it be simpler if they bought you out?'

'Paul's son made noises to that effect through his attorney. I made an offer that was millions less than I expect to receive from one of the automotive groups, but there's been no follow through.'

She shrugged. 'They would need to find investors, and that would require initiative. They've never been known for their initiative.'

'If you're handed everything on a silver platter,' the fixer commented, 'you're lucky if you even know how to spell *initiative*.'

'Don't worry,' Alaine said, 'they'll get theirs, all right. Paul would have wanted that.'

From the manner in which she spoke, the fixer doubted Paul's kids would be getting *theirs*, much less a tenth of what their father would have desired to go their way. The clock was ticking, and he returned his attention to the issue at hand. 'Alarms went off when you gave them your nickname?'

'Detective Pratt was eating out of the palm of my hand,' Alaine replied, 'but when I asked her to call me "Al," it was like I flipped a light switch or something. Suddenly, she starts grilling me about my going by "Al." Even her idiot brother got all wide-eyed a few seconds into the inquiry.'

'What did you say?'

'I knew I'd stepped on a landmine, so I told Pratt I'd gone by Ally in high school, especially since Ally Sheedy from the Brat Pack was in vogue back then. I told her my college roommate kept introducing me as "Al" and by the time I graduated from Northwestern, the damage was done; it was set in cement.'

'Did she buy it?'

'At first she wanted to know if Tom called me "Al." I said he may have once or twice, but just as a shortcut for Ally.'

'Did you ask why this mattered?'

'Yes, but she ducked the question and started asking if there was anyone else I knew named Al or Alan that Tom may have known.'

'Let's back up a moment,' the fixer said. 'Why did you go to the funeral in the first place?'

'The police were going to get around to asking me questions about Tom *eventually*,' Alaine replied. 'I figured it'd be better to get it done at a crowded memorial service.'

The fixer studied his client as he continued, 'The news indicates they found cash from the bank robbery in Tom's old bedroom. Clearly, CPD is holding something back.'

Alaine sighed. 'That's what I'm afraid of.'

'But if Tom left an incriminating note, wouldn't it be formal, like "Alaine Quinn did it?"'

'White.'

'What?'

'My maiden name was White. I was Alaine White back then,' she said. 'And, yes, if Tom hid a confession in his room, I'd be screwed.'

'What did you tell Pratt about *other Alans*?'

'I brought up Alan Recksiedler, who was lead in most of the school plays. He was King Arthur to Tom's Lancelot in *Camelot*.'

'A high school that size must have had a dozen guys named Alan.'

She nodded. 'Our senior yearbook has fourteen Alans in grades ninth through twelfth, and if you count a couple grades ahead of us, there'll be more.' A humorless smile spread across Alaine's features. 'But let's talk last names, because I think we got lucky. One of Tom's oldest friends is "Dave Albertson." Dave was a big guy. He played linebacker on the football team, and he was a complete toady when it came to his pal Thomas Dando,' Alaine said. 'Seriously, if Tom bought galoshes, Dave would have five pairs the following day.'

'Has Albertson been living in Chicago all these years?'

'Yes, Dave never left the city, but there's even better news. He was known on the football team as "Big Albert." A pun off the old cartoon "Fat Albert," only Dave was "Big Albert."'

'Was he also called "Al" or "Big Al?"'

'Mostly it was "Big Albert."'

'Well, hell, close enough,' the fixer said. 'Was Albertson married back in ninety-four?'

Alaine shrugged. 'I don't believe so. Dave was still single at the five-year reunion but showed up married at the tenth. Divorced by the twenty-year, though,' she said. 'I remember sitting at a table with the old gang at that one. Dave had been drinking all evening. Knowing him, he may have started earlier, before the class reunion began, and at one point he called his ex-wife a *fucking bitch* – the guy practically screamed it.'

'OK, issues with alcohol fall in the plus column,' he said. 'Is Albertson smart or not smart?'

'Dave was fortunate to inherit his father's landscaping business, and he acts like he's Howard Hughes at all the reunions, so he gets by and earns a living, but Dave was always a C-student.' She added, 'No, he's not bright at all.'

'Good – I can work with that.'

'What are you thinking?'

The fixer said, 'I'm thinking in two days you won't have a thing to worry about.'

'No worries in two days?'

'Three if I've lost my magic touch.'

Alaine glanced again at the grandfather clock. There was still time left before her two o'clock call. 'One last thing,' she said. 'Detective Pratt was all over Catherine's house from the get-go, she brought in the dogs, and I suspect she is the one that found whatever cash or whatnot Tom had hidey-holed away in his room.' Alaine then stressed, 'Detective Pratt's grilling gave me goose-bumps on the back of my neck. The woman is not to be underestimated.'

The fixer stared at her across the table and spoke in a hushed tone, 'Nothing happens to the detective. It would rain hell on the investigation.'

'I understand,' Alaine replied. 'But what if something happens that makes her take, say, a leave of absence?' Alaine cupped her hands on the cherry wood desk. 'Perhaps something to do with her brother.'

THIRTY-TWO

July 29, 1994
11:22 A.M.

Dando didn't register flying across the forest floor or swatting aside Alaine's pistol as if it were a gnat hovering about his head. He was on her in an instant, fingers wrapped about her throat, choking the life from her. His old friend's eyes bulged as she lay on the dirt, staring up at him, offering no resistance.

Somehow Dando stopped himself at the last second, before it was too late. It took all he could muster, but he rolled off her and sat upright.

Time passed as Alaine massaged her neck and gulped air as though through a straw.

'What happens now?' she said finally, her voice a gravel truck.

Dando stood, shook empty another backpack of phone books, and used it to collect the handguns strewn about the forest floor. 'What happens now is you're going to drag Tharp and Lamprecht to the grave we dug for them.'

'What about—' Alaine didn't finish, but Dando read her mind.

'Connor won't be sharing a hole with those two scumbags.'

'We're going to dig another one?'

Dando shook his head. 'I will be digging another one, not you,' he said. 'Make sure you empty all their pockets,' he pointed toward the dead felons, 'before you roll them in. Then wipe the blood off the side of your face,' he said and added, 'because you've now got three bikes to ditch.'

Without another word, Dando strode toward the open grave where he retrieved the digging fork and shovel. He passed Alaine as she dragged Tharp toward his final resting place by the hem of his blue jeans.

'Look, Tom,' Alaine said as he walked past, but Dando kept moving.

He scanned about the woodlands, realizing there'd be no scenic spot out here to bury his friend – no view of a nearby lake, no rolling hills, no sun beating down – and settled for another site where, like yesterday, the digging would be easier.

Dando dropped the backpack of firearms and began working the shovel. As he dug, he heard Alaine grunt as she dragged Lamprecht's body to the first grave. He stomped down on the shovel, lifted dirt, and threw it off to the side. He wished there was something he could do to make this second grave more appealing, then cursed himself for having such a dumbass notion. Stomp and throw, stomp and throw – robotic, no wasted effort – and he brought the digging fork into play whenever he hit hardened soil.

Somewhere along the line Alaine rode past on her mountain bike. She had one hand on the left side of her handlebars while her other hand cupped the middle of the handlebars on a second bike. Alaine would bring the second bike back to the blacktop, follow the trail a minute or two, and then cut off track and head down to the river. Once there, she'd toss the bike in, as far as she could, where it'd likely stay submerged for a year or three or ten.

Or perhaps a kid would find it or perhaps . . . whatever, it wouldn't matter by that point.

Dando made surprisingly good progress by the time Alaine returned from dumping the third bike. The hole in the forest floor was an open mouth; it even looked like a coffin. He just needed to go deeper, so it'd stand the test of time.

Alaine got off her bike and sat on the ground next to him. Dando glanced her way. She wore a baseball cap that kept a tangle of medium-length hair over her ear, covering her wound and most of the dried blood. He spotted the redness around her throat where she'd been strangled, but he felt nothing.

'Did anybody see you?'

'A couple of hikers, but I just smiled and flew past.'

'No one saw you chuck the bikes in the river?'

'No,' she replied. 'I was able to shove them a good ten feet in, all submerged.'

Dando nodded.

'What now, Tom?'

He glanced around. 'Get that backpack,' he pointed at the bloated one that'd been left untouched, 'and all the phone books and the other shit back to your car,' he said. 'When we leave, I don't want so much as a toothpick left behind.'

Dando resumed shoveling as Alaine set the backpack and phone books and other odds and ends inside a heavy-duty construction bag. It might look a bit silly her riding back to the entrance with a garbage bag propped up on her lap, but park employees would assume litter from a picnic.

Alaine set a bottle of water next to Dando's pile of dirt before, once again, riding off to the trail. As soon as she was out of sight, Dando twisted the cap off and pounded the entire bottle in ten seconds. He hadn't realized how thirsty he'd become.

Of course, he'd not anticipated having to dig another grave.

Dando leaned against the shovel. He'd known Alaine since

they'd first met in kindergarten. They'd climbed trees together, took swim class at the YMCA together, played ding-dong ditch, read comic books, and made countless candy runs to a nearby drugstore together. The two had been inseparable. Once, they'd even made out until it dawned on both simultaneously that it was like kissing a sibling.

And somewhere along the line, he'd nicknamed her 'Al.'

Out of all the people Dando had grown up with . . . Alaine was the only one he loved.

Al had been his best friend.

But none of that mattered anymore, because she'd crossed a line you don't come back from.

Alaine was going into the grave with Tharp and Lamprecht.

Connor was his friend; Connor had his back. Though he was no longer a soldier, Connor had become part of his unit. Dando had been so concerned with the threat that was named Ronald Lamprecht . . . he'd not seen the real threat coming.

And it cost Connor his life.

Alaine had not been acting her normal self lately. Robbing a major bank in broad daylight in downtown Chicago tends to weed back the lighthearted and frivolous shit. He'd become paranoid lately, but, quite frankly, he didn't think Alaine had it in her to take out Tharp once he'd removed Lamprecht from the equation. He'd been ready to step in, as had Connor, but he'd underestimated Al . . . had he ever.

Dando went back to digging. Stomp and throw, stomp and throw, rinse and repeat. Deeper, and deeper still. His face and neck were red, his armpits and chest a gloss of perspiration. A chunk of time passed and right when he began wondering if Alaine would ever return, there she was, cruising back on her mountain bike, stepping off, using the kickstand and, as though reading his mind, she handed him another bottle of water.

He twisted the cap, drank most of the water in a single serving, held his head back, and poured the rest over his face. It was then he realized Alaine was standing behind him, in his blind spot. The hair rose on the back of his neck.

'Fuck.'

'What?'

He leaned against the shovel. 'You had another gun in the car?'

'Yes,' Alaine said. 'You made sure we were well armed, Tom. Driving those packets of cash around, I stuck the extra SIG Sauer in my glove compartment just to be safe.'

Dando nodded slowly. 'Smart move.'

Alaine said nothing.

Dando tossed the empty bottle of water near the other one. The digging had caused the Beretta M9 in his waistband holster to grow uncomfortable, to strafe against his abdomen, so he'd taken it off and set it down next to the backpack containing the other handguns.

There was no way he'd make the Beretta in time.

But Dando had the shovel at his fingertips . . . and he'd used a shovel once before.

'Can I ask you something, Al?'

'You can ask me anything, Tom.'

'Was there ever a scenario where I'd be leaving here today?'

Alaine said nothing.

Dando grabbed the shovel and began to spin around.

A final shot rang out in Kankakee River State Park.

THIRTY-THREE

I was in hibernation mode when Crystal trudged home last night – I didn't even hear her come in – but we were both up and huddled about the coffee maker by six in the morning. My sister wanted to head back to the precinct ASAP, but I conned her into taking a walk around the block with Alice and Rex. A chance for her, after a trying week at work, to relax and smell the roses – well, at least the roses the pups hadn't lifted a leg to.

'There were several *Alans* at Joseph W. Fifer during Dando's high school years,' Crystal said. 'It's a huge pain in the ass, like tracking down guys named *Steve* or *Mike*.'

We paused as Rex stuffed his upper torso under a juniper shrub while Alice sat back and observed. I figured a rabbit had nested under there sometime in the past millennium. My springer spaniel got excited; his tail beat against the retractable leash as though he were strumming a banjo chord.

'Come on, Rex,' I said and tugged gently at his leash, but he'd caught on to a scent and didn't want to leave. If he had his way, we'd be here for hours. 'Come on, boy – there's no need to build a religion around it.' I turned to Crystal. 'Wasn't there an Alan something or other in the shows Dando's girlfriend had him try out for?'

'Alan Recksiedler,' my sister replied. 'Interesting fellow; I talked to him for an hour last night. He studied drama at the Theater School at DePaul. He told me he came out to his family after college – was more difficult back then – and his parents had major issues with it. So he up and moved to California in 1993 and has only been back for his mother's funeral.' She added, 'Recksiedler was Ariel in *The Tempest* at an LA playhouse when Crown National was robbed. I checked the dates; it would have been impossible for him to have been in Chicago during the production's run.'

'Did he have anything to say about Dando?'

'Said he thought the world of Tom, but they only hung out during the duration of the play, though, as they ran in different social circles,' she said. 'He told me Dando was the perfect Sir Lancelot, not because he was much of an actor but because he had similar traits to Lancelot – courage, strength, gentleness – or *a hidden gentleness* as Recksiedler put it.'

'Well, I suppose if Lancelot bailed on the Round Table and took to robbing banks.'

Crystal shrugged. 'Like everyone else, Recksiedler said he couldn't believe what he'd seen in the news lately. And he's heartbroken to know his *Camelot* costar has been dead all these years.' She added, 'He broke down a little on the phone.'

Rex reversed out from under the bush and allowed us to continue on our journey down the sidewalk, from scent to scent, fire hydrant to mailbox post.

'Pretty cool Recksiedler made good in acting.'

'Actually, he runs a real estate office in San Diego,' Crystal said. 'He appeared in productions at middling venues and got parts in a few commercials, even got to speak in a Wrigley's gum ad, but he grew weary of waiting tables to cover the rent and, eventually, tossed in the towel.'

A squirrel bolted toward a maple tree in the middle of a neighbor's yard. Alice and Rex both looked my way, but I shook my head. 'So what about last names? Wasn't there a guy Dando went *speeding* with in high school named Alberts or something?'

'That was Dave *Albertson*.'

'If I had a buddy named Albertson, I'd call him Al.'

'Guess what, Cor? He was nicknamed *Big Albert* on the football team.'

I stopped to look at Crystal. 'Well, there you have it.'

'He runs a landscaping business out of a storage warehouse on the edge of Bucktown. I dropped by yesterday for a chat, and he said an assistant coach pushed the nickname on him during football season due to his size. Albertson liked it well enough, but his friends were used to calling him Dave as he only started bulking up sophomore year,' she said. 'He put on forty pounds to play varsity as a junior.'

'OK,' I said. My sister once complimented me for being such an excellent sounding board as she noodled her way through a difficult investigation. That's a lot to dump on a guy. It forced me to up my game. No way could I be *Sherlock Holmes*, but perhaps the dimmer of the two *Hardy Boys* or a cut-rate *Encyclopedia Brown*. So I racked my brain as we sauntered down the boulevard until, finally, something occurred to me. 'What about all that Crown National money? Isn't landscaping something you can float a million bucks through, here and there? Pretend to sell or buy materials or equipment? Fake a bunch of projects? Or fake a bunch of invoices.' Clearly, my knowledge of money laundering came from old episodes of *CSI*.

'Albertson inherited the business from his father years after the robbery,' Crystal said. 'I drove by his house, also in Bucktown – a two-story, looked middle class, nothing extravagant. He told me he dropped out of college after a year of partying too much, and then worked as a landscaper and laborer for his father until he became manager and, eventually, took over the operation.'

'OK,' I said again. 'Maybe the guy is on the up and up?'

'Well, Albertson has two DUIs from his early twenties. He even lost his driver's license for a year. He also had a restraining order filed against him from an ex-girlfriend when he was twenty-six – stalking, harassment, that kind of crap.'

'Isn't it a bit of a leap from being a garden-variety a-hole – DUIs, harassing exes – to becoming John Dillinger and casing banks?'

Crystal shrugged again. 'There was a domestic 911 call right before Albertson and his wife got divorced. Evidently, they were screaming at each other at the top of their lungs. It was summer and the windows were open, and a neighbor finally called the police. There was no physical altercation involved and no charges were filed. The two were just told to keep the noise level down.'

'Sounds like a real Romeo,' I said. 'Did he mention anything about Dando?'

'He said he loved Tom. Said they were best buds since junior high, after a minor fistfight in a back hallway which neither won. Albertson also confirmed that, yes, he and Tom got a little reckless now and again while driving cars at night.' Crystal continued, 'He also stated that everything in the newspaper about Tom and the bank robbery was pure bullshit.'

'Did you ask him if he hung with Dando that summer?'

'Albertson said he never saw Tom again after Catherine threw the welcome home party. He told me he tried to get the guy to go out and party a few times, but Tom refused or never called him back,' Crystal said. 'Albertson also told me Catherine was an angel, and that her house was always the gathering point for the old gang.'

We crossed the road to head back home and I tossed in my two cents. 'I know you've been focusing on Dando's childhood and high school years, which makes sense, but what about any Alans he may have known from his time in the Marine Corps. I love those guys, but let's be honest here, Crys, they'd be way more capable of pulling off a bank heist than any of Dando's high school wingmen.' I added, 'Maybe Catherine could have pointed the finger at a fellow soldier her son hung out with that summer.'

Crystal nodded. 'Horton and Andreen are covering the military angle.'

My sister's phone must have been set to vibrate as she fished it out of her pocket, glanced at the screen, and then stabbed at the green circle to answer. The hounds and I moved on to the next sniff and pee – a black lamppost – in order to give her some privacy. Even though we were ten yards further down the sidewalk, I heard a *What?* followed by a *You're kidding me.*

A few seconds later, my sister caught up with us. 'Speak of the devil,' she said. 'CPD got a hit on their TipSubmit line. Dave Albertson's SUV was seen near Catherine Dando's house on the night of her murder. With that and the possibility of *Al* on the Crown National bank strap standing for *Big Albert*, Horton's going for a search warrant on both Albertson's home and office.'

THIRTY-FOUR

The tip had been submitted overnight – anonymously – through the Chicago Police Department's TipSubmit form which appears online on CPD's website. Tips submitted anonymously from this web app are sent directly to the Crime Prevention and Information Center, or CPIC, where they are first analyzed and, if deemed legitimate, forwarded on to the appropriate police unit. As such, Horton spotted the TipSubmit message as soon as he booted up his laptop. The detective read the tip three times before his first pot of coffee had completed brewing.

I've never met Catherine Dando, but I live two blocks away from her Logan Square residence. As a neighbor I've been following this story in the news and noted the date of Ms Dando's unfortunate demise as provided by the medical examiner.

I work fifty-hour weeks, but when the kids are getting ready for bed, I make time for my nightly jog. I often take the pathway through the woods behind Joseph W. Fifer High School, and I ran this route on the date referenced by your medical examiner.

When I came out between the athletic fields, I noticed a black Ford Explorer XLT (I once owned one myself) parked in the nearby lot. It was dusk. There were no games that evening, and no other vehicles were in the parking lot. I don't recall the entire license plate number, but the last five digits were '99924.' I also noticed a minor dent in the passenger's side front panel.

I assumed the Ford Explorer was parked there by another

jogger or that some teens had left it there while they wandered into the woods to smoke something they didn't want lingering in their parents' SUV. Either way, I wanted to bring this to your attention.

If this helps with anything, excellent! If not, sorry to have wasted your time.

'Why the hell do they have to tow my car?'

'The Explorer is listed in the warrant,' Crystal said. She stood with Dave Albertson, aka Big Albert, in the front yard of his two-story in Bucktown. She'd come along with the posse as Detectives Horton and Andreen served the warrant and wound up babysitting Albertson as the process played itself out.

It had been a big production. Once Horton got a judge to sign off on the search warrant, he and Andreen served it on a stunned Albertson at his landscaping office-slash-warehouse at eleven o'clock. The warrant included both Albertson's office and home, so as several investigators began riffling about his warehouse, Albertson agreed to accompany the detectives to his Bucktown residence in order to voluntarily unlock his front door.

Crystal counted two squad cars parked on the street along with her Honda HR-V. In the driveway sat an unmarked police car as well as a white forensic van as a forensic unit had arrived in order to assist with evidence collection. Albertson's driveway was wide enough for three vehicles, so the tow truck operator was able to get at Albertson's SUV without interrupting the investigators inside Albertson's house. Once the Ford Explorer had been towed out from Albertson's garage, Detective Andreen had the driver stop and he then began taking pictures of the Explorer's right front panel.

'Why's he taking pictures of the dent?' Albertson asked.

Crystal knew, but she shrugged and kept quiet.

'I bumped into a pallet of landscaping blocks last year,' he said. 'What's the big deal?'

'He's just being thorough.'

Dave Albertson was still a large man. All these years later and his football moniker remained apropos. Though he now sported a gut the dimensions of a mid-sized beach ball, his biceps and chest were massive, and Crystal assumed Albertson spent a chunk of his free time pumping iron at a local gym. He had the look of a bouncer in some seedy and forgotten strip club. Since Crystal had questioned Albertson the day before, Horton thought it best if she'd stay with him while they searched his home – kept him out of the way, kept him out of trouble. However, due to Albertson's size as well as his potential involvement in Catherine Dando's murder, a police officer of a mildly larger body mass hovered a few feet away from the two of them.

'How long is this going to take?'

Crystal peeked at her watch. 'Search times vary, but they've finished at your warehouse.' She added, 'If you'd like, please feel free to contact your attorney.'

'I'm not paying for an attorney,' Albertson said. 'I didn't do anything.' The man's face was beet red; could be too much sun or rosacea, but more likely a result of his current predicament. The redness held a harsh contrast against Albertson's medium-cut salt-and-pepper hair. 'Jesus – it's hot out here.'

'Would you like to sit in the squad car?' Crystal asked. 'It has air conditioning.'

'No, I don't want to sit in a squad car.' Albertson glanced around the street. 'Christ – the neighbors are going to think I'm a drug dealer.'

Crystal watched as the tow truck left with Albertson's Ford Explorer and noticed several kids on both sides of the block were sitting on the grass and staring their way. She imagined more than a few neighbors were doing something similar, only behind shades or curtains or drapes.

Albertson was right – the neighbors would certainly be thinking he'd been up to something.

If Dave Albertson had been involved in the Crown National bank robbery, and if Albertson had been the one to walk out of Kankakee River State Park that day, then, once news came out that the bodies had been discovered, Albertson had no choice but to kill Catherine Dando in order to keep her quiet. Otherwise, Crystal figured, Catherine would have told the police something to the effect of, 'Of course Dave and Tom hung out that summer. They were thick as thieves. I saw Dave more that summer than I did when the two of them were kids.'

Catherine might also have acknowledged that Albertson could

have had tape recordings of Thomas that could have been played into her answering machine in order to trick her into believing her son was still alive several months after he'd been shot in the chest and dumped in a grave.

Detective Horton appeared in the front entryway. He held two bags in one hand and waved Crystal over with his other.

'Please stay here,' Crystal said to Albertson. 'I'll be right back.'

He replied, 'Where the hell would I go?'

When Crystal reached the stoop, Horton held up one of the evidence bags and whispered, 'We've got three of Thomas Dando's yearbooks, from tenth grade through twelfth.'

Inside the evidence bag appeared to be the yearbook from Dando's senior year of high school. 'Where did you find them?'

'Albertson had them stuffed between the mattress and the box spring in the master bedroom,' Horton said. 'A ton of classmates signed the books, and the notes are all addressed to Tom, not to Albertson.'

'That explains why the books weren't in Tom's old bedroom at Catherine's house.'

'Yup – and we found Albertson's own high school yearbooks stacked on a shelf in his home office.' The detective continued, 'One other thing, remember you thought a picture frame was missing off a wall in Dando's old room?'

Crystal nodded.

Horton held up the second evidence bag. This one contained a picture frame but no photograph. 'Does this frame look familiar?'

Crystal took out her iPhone and tapped the Camera app. She browsed through the pictures she'd snapped in Dando's old room at his mother's house. When she hit a picture of the wall of photographs, she expanded it with a thumb and forefinger. Both investigators looked at the picture frames in the photo and then glanced at the one in the evidence bag. It was the same type of picture frame.

'Where did you find that?'

'It was under his bed. Have no idea what he did with the photograph, probably burned it,' Horton said and caught Crystal's eye. 'I'm going to arrest Albertson and bring him in for questioning.'

Crystal nodded.

Thirty seconds later the sizable policeman was cuffing Albertson as Horton read him his Miranda rights. As they led Albertson toward the back of a squad car, he stared at Crystal, eyes wide. 'I didn't kill Catherine – that's insane,' he said, his face wet with tears, a string of saliva hanging from his top lip. 'And I didn't rob any fucking bank.'

THIRTY-FIVE

I tossed the Frisbee, this time angling it to the right so Rex would have a chance at fetching it first. The pair tore off after it; Rex won by a whisker, and scampered back to me, disc in his mouth. I'd not come home for lunch, so after the pups had taken care of their personal business, I wanted to wear them out with backyard Frisbee.

It had been a good day, a very good day, and not only because it sounded like they had a major break in Crystal's case, but because – yes – I had lunch with a classmate, and a female classmate at that. And though my heart pounded as if it'd hammer through my chest as I gnawed on my Jimmy John's – I don't think she heard it – and though I got a bit tongue-tied and awkward on a couple of occasions . . . I had a blast.

OK, some details – her name is Brielle. Like me, Brielle's a fulltime student at Harper Community College who's taking a couple of summer classes in order to leapfrog ahead. She's in my UNIX class – her father is a system administrator at Civis Analytics – and I've seen her around in the hallways. Well, seeing *her around in the hallways* is a bit of an understatement as Brielle's kind of hard to miss on account of that girl-next-door with the can-do smile thing she's got going.

Brielle missed yesterday's class and, after today's class ended, she had the audacity to stop me in the hallway and ask if she could crib my notes. I stared back at her, a deer caught in the headlights, and I damn near fled, but then she added, 'We could grab a bite to eat.'

Who was I to refuse? I figured Alice and Rex would not only understand my truancy but wholeheartedly approve.

It took Brielle all of eight seconds to copy any notes she needed – my brilliant insights – and then we sipped Cokes, ate subway sandwiches, and gabbed. Somehow she pried out of me how I was thinking of dropping out of Harper, that programming might not be my cup of tea.

'You should give it awhile longer, maybe through fall semester and see where you're at then,' she said. 'And, hey, if you need a study partner, give me a call.'

Had I a tail, it would have wagged.

It was closing in on five, so the pups and I migrated inside. I took a frozen burrito out of the freezer, tossed it in the microwave, and then peeked in the fridge. Crystal must have finished the last few cans of Rolling Rock – so that's what she's been doing when she gets home late at night – but she'd replaced them with a six-pack of Rolling Rock in bottles. About dang time. My sister runs a deficit in the picking-up-the-beer department. I had the cap off a bottle and took a healthy swig before the buzzer rang on my supper.

I tossed the burrito on a paper plate, drowned it in salsa, and then caught Alice and Rex staring up at me, looking all crushed and hangdog, so I polished off the beer as I readied their dinner buffet. Once done, I reached for a second Rolling Rock before I sat down to eat.

I wondered if Brielle liked Rolling Rock.

I wondered if Brielle liked me.

I'd had a serious relationship in high school, but that cratered along with everything else that cratered the night my parents died. Since then I've been out on a handful of blind dates, set up by friends who meant well or felt sorry for me, but they never went anywhere . . . which, I admit, was a hundred percent on me.

I wasn't ready.

I'm not sure I'm ready now.

But lunch with Brielle today felt different. I felt some kind of connection – an emotional connection – something I've not felt in years. Butterflies. Brielle gave me butterflies; she made me all nervous and scared inside. We weren't even dating, had just *officially* met today, yet I'm acting all giddy and weird and dork-like.

To be honest, though, I'd be shocked if Brielle didn't already have a boyfriend.

However . . . I could be her study partner.

Yup, just lying in the weeds until her boyfriend screwed up.

Because that's how I roll.

The burrito was passable, the beer was better. I'd yet to finish my second bottle, but I'd already gotten a buzz off it. I stood to put the paper plate in the trash bin, and then settled back down in my chair. I felt dizzy. Maybe I stood up too fast. OK, I sat there and sipped at the beer. I'm not sure how much time had passed, but I found myself with my head resting on my forearms atop the mess that was my paper plate. I needed hydration and glanced toward the sink, but after a Shrek-sized yawn, I stared at the couch in the living room . . . and then I stared at it some more.

I needed a nap.

It was imperative I sleep.

It had been a long-ass day and . . . and . . . and I think I met someone today.

Something had occurred, it had, and I'd remember what it was if I could just shut my eyes for a little while and get some sleep.

I slid out of my chair on to the floor, my muscles refusing to obey, so I slithered toward the couch, was elated when I crossed from tile to carpeting – a major accomplishment – and at that point I lay on my side, my head on the matting . . . and wondered about someone that may have been somewhere . . . maybe something happened today at school.

THIRTY-SIX

It worked like a charm.

The fixer sat in the back of the Amazon Prime van on the outskirts of the Target store nearest the Cory and Crystal Pratt residence in Buffalo Grove and watched the drama play out on his smartphone app via the miniature camera he'd planted in Pratt's kitchen, concealed in an overly full and chipped utensil holder on the far side of the oven. He watched as Pratt kept nodding off on to his dinner plate before sliding to the floor and then attempting to swim to the safety of the living room as though he'd been dumped in Lake Michigan. Though Pratt's upper torso was now blocked from view, his ass and legs remained on the kitchen tile as his two dogs wandered curious circles about their master.

Nope – Cory Pratt was going nowhere soon.

The fixer had used Rohypnol. Tasteless and odorless when mixed in a drink, Rohypnol is a central nervous system depressant from the benzodiazepine family. Recognized as a date rape drug, Rohypnol was powerful, known to cause blackouts and amnesia or, in Cory Pratt's case, extreme sedation when mixed with alcohol.

'It's time,' the fixer said to the man behind the wheel of the van, the man who went by *Derek*, even though it was not his real name. And Derek didn't know the fixer's name, either, which, quite frankly, worked out best for all involved.

Derek was a professional thief and a master lock pick. When they'd first swung by the Pratt residence at ten that morning – after Cory decamped for school, long after his cop-sister had left for work – the fixer, dressed in the blue and black Amazon flex vest and cap, stood by the van in the driveway, a medium-sized box at his feet, and stared into his phone app as though he were studying for the bar exam. It was pure theater as Derek, also dressed as a delivery driver, had already slipped around the side of the house. Within ten seconds Derek had made it inside the garage and, a minute later, had made it inside the house.

Derek knew how the two-story was laid out, and he knew there would be dogs. In one hand he held a canister of dog repellent spray, the type used by the US Postal Service – it had to be tried and true. In his other hand he held an open bag of bacon strip dog treats. Derek had been breaking into homes since the age of twelve and his lack of a criminal record testified to the fact that he moved like a ghost. Fortunately, the dogs were in the basement – it must be where they loafed or slept during the day – and he nearly made it to the downstairs doorway when he heard them hear him. Derek spotted a bloodhound bounding up the steps, followed by what might be a springer spaniel. He tossed the bacon strips into the stairway and slammed the door shut an instant before the bloodhound hit the top step.

A cacophony of barks and yaps commenced. The dogs knew something was afoot.

Derek opened the front door for the fixer and said, 'They don't have a doorbell camera.'

Grateful a giant elm tree blocked Pratt's entryway from the street, the fixer nodded and stepped quickly into the house. He handed Derek the Amazon Prime box he'd been using as a prop. 'Dogs under control?'

'Stuck in the basement.'

He nodded. 'Give me a second.'

The fixer headed straight to the kitchen and opened the refrigerator. Good – it was exactly what he expected, what with Pratt being a guy in his early twenties. He returned to the front door and handed the few cans that remained inside a twelve-pack box of Rolling Rock to Derek, who then placed the carton of beer inside the Amazon box.

'I'll need a six-pack of Rolling Rock in bottles,' he told the professional thief.

'Back in twenty.'

The fixer used the twenty minutes wisely. He began by snooping about the upper level first. Detective Pratt must have the master bedroom as both the drawers and the medicine cabinet in the master bathroom contained feminine products; the various shoes and outfits in the walk-in closet indicated likewise. It made sense since the kid and the dogs probably got stuck with the basement.

The endless chorus of yelps and growls grew tiring as the fixer hid the camera amongst the spatulas and wooden spoons and whisks in the utensil holder, and verified it was in working order. He did his best to tune out the canine clamor and actually smiled when he hit pay dirt in one of the kitchen drawers. It contained expired coupons for Subway and Arby's; however, laying underneath were a couple of backup car keys for the household's vehicles. Good to know he had a key to Pratt's Chevy Silverado, but the fixer would still fish the one out of Pratt's pocket as the poor kid had a date this evening with an antiquated pickup truck.

A date in an enclosed garage.

The truck was from the late nineties, hell, the pickup was a year or two older than Pratt himself. It was perfect for what needed to be done as newer models tend to emit lower levels of carbon monoxide.

The kid would be at peace in less than an hour.

And the fixer's job would be done.

THIRTY-SEVEN

The two men followed the same strategy from earlier in the day, where the man who went by Derek slipped around the side of the house and got inside Pratt's garage while the fixer removed a mid-sized box and worked his iPhone as though he were personally contacting Jeff Bezos.

Once inside Pratt's house, Derek held up his right palm in a calming gesture while his left covered the canister of dog repellent spray clipped to his belt. Part of Derek's livelihood was dealing with pups left to roam the household while their owners were at work. 'Settle,' Derek said softly as he approached. 'Cory's going to be OK,' he said. 'Settle – Cory's going to be OK.'

It was essential he not act in an aggressive or threatening manner, and he removed a couple of the bacon snacks from his breast pocket and set them down on the floor as he knelt beside Pratt. He held out his hand for the dogs to sniff. 'Let me check on Cory, OK?' he said. 'I'll check on Cory.'

Derek gently patted Pratt on the shoulder and reached for a pillow from the couch and slid it under Pratt's head.

The disruption caused Pratt to curl into a fetal position and mumble something to the effect of, 'Orgladoram.'

'See,' Derek said. 'Cory's OK. Cory's just sleeping.'

Derek stood and backed quietly into the open doorway leading down the basement steps. 'Let's *go outside*,' he said. 'Time to *go outside*.'

He hoped the words would act as a command; after all, the dogs were trained. The springer spaniel, having gobbled up one of the bacon treats, headed in his direction. The bloodhound continued licking at Pratt's face, causing its dazed master to mumble something that sounded like, 'Whistlecaster.'

'*Come*,' Derek tried that command. He said it again louder, '*Come!*'

The springer spaniel stepped forward and sniffed again at Derek's hand. Then Derek tossed the rest of the bacon treats down the stairs, which was enough to get the spaniel into the staircase, but the bloodhound approached cautiously, growling lightly as she came toward the landing . . . the verdict still out on Derek's intentions.

'Let's go outside, girl,' Derek said. 'Come.'

The bloodhound inched closer and that was all Derek needed. His left hand shot to the back of the dog's neck, grabbed a scruff of skin and fistful of collar, and yanked the pooch into the staircase. The bloodhound tumbled several steps, awkwardly, but spun around, a tornado hitting full force, the springer spaniel on her heels, but Derek was quick, and the stairway door slammed shut behind him.

Yapping and howling commenced immediately, much higher in resonance than it had been that morning.

The dogs were not happy . . . not happy at all.

'Do whatever you have to do as fast as possible.' Derek opened the front door for the fixer to step inside. 'That fucking bloodhound's clairvoyant,' he said. 'I'm getting bad vibes.'

The fixer nodded and said, 'I need you for one more second.'

Wearing thin leather gloves, the fixer took a single sheet of paper from the Amazon Prime box he'd brought inside and dropped it on the carpeting next to Pratt. Then he entered the kitchen, took what remained of the tampered six-pack from the refrigerator as well as retrieved the two bottles Pratt had polished off. Derek held open the Amazon Prime box as the fixer placed the bottles of beer inside. The fixer thought a second, and then fished the two bottle caps out from the recycle bin underneath the sink and tossed them in the box. Finally, he grabbed the camera hidden in the utensil holder, tossed it in the carton as well, and said, 'Don't go far – I'll text you in ten.'

Derek shut the Amazon box and headed out to the delivery van. A smile on his face as he scanned for any neighbors who might be watching as it was just another day in the blissful life of a delivery driver. He spotted no one and, seconds later, the Amazon Prime van was heading down the street; a minute later Derek was at a nearby gas station buying a Pepsi and a bag of potato chips.

Derek's job was done; Derek would not be involved in the closing act of Cory Pratt's fate.

And the man who went by Derek was smart enough not to ask any questions.

THIRTY-EIGHT

The fixer again opened what appeared to be the Pratt family key drawer. He'd watched on his phone app as Cory Pratt arrived home from school and proceeded to drop both his wallet and keys inside the kitchen drawer the fixer had noted earlier. This made it much easier, and less intimate, than fishing the keys out of Pratt's front pocket as he lay halfway on the carpet of the living room floor and halfway on the kitchen tile. The fixer headed out to the attached garage. The Chevy Silverado was parked on the far side of the two-car garage; what a generous soul Pratt was, leaving the closest stall for his sister. He went over and verified the side garage door was locked. Yup, Derek was nothing but a consummate professional. The fixer then folded the doormat laying there in two and used it to block the slight gap beneath the bottom of the door and the frame's threshold.

Then he swung open the door to the Silverado, stepped up into the driver's seat, started the engine, and rolled down all of the windows.

He doubted Sister Pratt would demand an autopsy. There would be no evidence of foul play. His enquiry into Cory and Crystal Pratt's history had informed him of their parents passing in a car accident when Cory Pratt was still in high school. The poor kid – a thing like that could mess with anyone's head. It didn't seem like Pratt had much of a social life, either – just him and his two pups against a cold and unforgiving world. Sure, the kid had been running a dog obedience school, possibly more out of respect for his departed father who helped him set it up to begin with than out of any kind of professional calling.

And now the poor schmuck was going to programming school . . . snooze.

On a scale of one to ten in the spectrum of savoring life at an age when you should be out painting the town, the fixer gave Pratt a two.

Yes, Cory was a troubled young man, his parents dying in that awful car wreck, not many friends, certainly no girlfriend in the picture, and – for Christ's sake – the guy was living with his sister. However, if Detective Pratt did push for an autopsy to be performed on her younger brother, that in itself would eat up another month. It was Chicago after all, get in line. And by then, after taking time off to deal with this personal tragedy, to plan her brother's funeral . . . the world would have moved on . . . and Big Albert, Dando's old pigskin-playing friend, would be looking at thirty years to life.

And Detective Pratt would be on to her next case . . . again, it was Chicago after all.

Besides, what would it matter if a blood or hair follicle test indicated the presence of Rohypnol? A troubled soul like Cory Pratt would certainly want to take some type of sedation as he set about wrapping up his life.

Back in the living room, the fixer knelt next to Pratt. He took Pratt's right hand and pressed his fingers and thumb against the typed-out suicide note that would be left for his sister to discover.

Pratt lifted his head an inch off the pillow and mumbled either 'convertible' or 'comfortable.'

The fixer waited until Pratt settled back down and then repeated the same process with Pratt's left hand. He brought the note to the kitchen table, frowned as he placed Pratt's paper dinner plate in the trash bin beneath the sink, and laid the note in its stead. He walked to an end table in the living room and picked up the picture he'd noticed earlier that morning. It was of Cory Pratt, who appeared to be in his single digits, with Sister Pratt, in her teenage years, along with their mother and father, facing the camera – smiles all around – with Mount Rushmore in the background.

Happier times.

The fixer got Pratt's fingerprints on the picture frame and then set it next to the note on the kitchen table.

A nice touch.

He knew the picture would sell it.

The fixer wished the dogs would shut the hell up as he contemplated whether anything else was out of place. The six-pack of *tainted* beer was gone. Check. It'd been a cake walk twisting the caps off the bottles of Rolling Rock, mixing in the CNS depressant, and then twisting the caps back on. The camera had been removed as well. Check. The suicide note and family picture were laid out – lovingly, he had to admit – on the kitchen table, awaiting Pratt's detective sister. Check. All that remained was to carry Pratt out to his pickup truck and set him in the driver's seat, behind the wheel, and let nature – and carbon monoxide – take its course.

Originally, he tried talking Alaine Quinn out of this *undertaking*. The woman had not only been adamant, but she, he had to admit, had a point. Detective Pratt had already screwed up the timeline by bringing in the cadaver dogs and finding where he'd stuffed Catherine Dando's remains so soon after the elderly woman's demise. No great sin there; just shows Crystal Pratt was on her A-game. Then Detective Pratt somehow sinks her teeth into the nickname 'Al' as if it signifies a person of interest in a case long gone cold. Then, damned if the fixer didn't find out that Crystal Pratt was, in fact, the CPD detective that had both tracked and – literally – taken down the *Dead Night Killer* last fall in one of Chicago's most notorious cases.

Quinn had a valid point; Detective Pratt was not to be underestimated.

The fixer worked the pillow out from under Pratt's head and flipped it back on to the living room sofa. In one swift motion, he hoisted the young man into the fireman's carry. This caused Pratt to lift his head and mumble something sounding like, 'Sniggledeemer.'

'It's all a dream, Cory,' the fixer whispered quietly, carrying him past the kitchen, heading toward the hallway leading to the garage. 'Life is but a dream.'

The dogs got louder, more deafening, as he stepped past the door to the basement. He heard claws scratching on wood and thanked God the door was shut.

'What's thaaa—?' Pratt raised his head a long second and finally said, 'Alice.'

The mutts heard Pratt's voice and got further crazed. The fixer picked up his pace. He swung open the door to the garage and turned sideways to jockey Pratt's body through the entryway, and . . . that's when he noticed the silence. His head snapped back in the direction he'd just come; his jaw dropped; his heart caught in his chest.

The dogs had broken free of their subterranean vault and charged the hallway toward him like the Furies escaping hell.

The fixer panicked. He stumbled sideways into the garage, hoping to shut the door on the two beasts, but the bloodhound defied gravity, sailing through the air and latching on to his wrist. He screamed in fear and pain. The other dog sank its teeth into his pant leg, tripping him up, and they all tumbled ass over teakettle, down the stoop and on to the garage floor. The fall shook free both canines and the fixer was up and across the stoop in a flash. He seized the door's handle, opened it wide enough for him to slip through, and got the damned thing closed right as the bloodhound rebounded for a second attack.

Jesus Christ!

The fixer sank to the hallway floor, coughed a lungful of exhaust, and tried to get a heart-pounding sense of terror under control. Then he pawed at his injured wrist. The bloodhound's teeth had broken skin; he was bleeding. Not bad enough to drip on to the floor. He lucked out wearing the long-sleeved uniform. The last thing he needed was to paint Pratt's house with his own DNA.

Goddammit!

The fixer clung to his injured wrist, worked to slow his breathing, and thought through the predicament. This was salvageable; in fact, it was a push. Cory was a troubled young man, in a bad place mentally; he had been for a long time, and in his messed-up state of mind, he took the dogs – his best friends – with him on his final journey. It wasn't that big a leap, the fixer thought. Suicides were hardly known for thinking straight. Perhaps Pratt wanted to sit and hug his only friends as the carbon monoxide overtook them? Or perhaps Pratt regretted his decision to include the dogs and was in the act of letting them back inside the house when the exhaust got the best of him?

It didn't matter.
It would all be over in half an hour.
The fixer dug out his iPhone and texted Derek.
Come get me now!

THIRTY-NINE

When Alice heard Cory speak her name, she pawed at the lever handle. The house was forty years old; the door was oak with a hollow core, the latch flimsy. There'd been a gathering a few years back where she and Rex had been confined to the basement. Their whimpers ignored, Alice pawed at the handle, patting it downward. Seconds later she marched triumphantly into the living room, Rex at her heels, to find Cory and Crystal seated – along with several others whose scents she recognized as *the visitors* that now and again swung by – while one of the smaller visitors pulled a box out from underneath a lighted tree.

Alice got confused as Cory and Crystal called her 'Houdini' for several days before returning to her real name.

Alice had repeated the trick several times since that evening, mostly if Cory or Crystal inadvertently shut her in the basement. Today, the door opened the sixth time Alice pawed at the lever handle, and she and Rex spilled out on to the landing.

A split second later the two tore ass down the hallway, after the stranger carrying Cory.

I lay on the carpet what seemed an eternity, neither awake nor asleep. Alice and Rex paced about me – nudging me with wet noses, licking at my face – but when I tried raising my head, the room spun in circles, a Tilt-A-Whirl ride at the state fair. I felt nauseous and set my head back down on the carpeting to keep from throwing up.

A hundred years later a man arrived, dressed in some type of uniform – a paramedic? – and patted my shoulder and set a cushion under my head and talked to my dogs though I couldn't understand what he was telling them. I lay there in a kind of detached oblivion, as though I were a thousand miles away, and wondered if I'd had a stroke. Suddenly, Alice and Rex were gone, but a swelling of howls and growls and yaps came from somewhere nearby. What these howls and growls and yaps told me cut through my brain fog and wooziness.

My dogs were trying to warn me.

Danger!

I lifted my head off the pillow the paramedic had provided me. My temples beat like a kettledrum, and I lay back down and rolled on to my back. That simple motion took everything I had, and I needed to sleep, and the paramedic had been so nice to give me a cushion for my head and . . . and I found it impossible to collect my thoughts.

I forgot what I'd been so worked up about, if anything at all.

A different paramedic took over and tried making me hold a piece of paper. He wanted me to read an insurance form or something. Then it seemed really important that the paramedic show me an old picture taken at Mount Rushmore. I tried telling the man that was me in the picture, that it was taken years ago, that I was older now, but I couldn't form any words or syllables, and I couldn't make him understand. I set my head back down on the pillow for another year until the paramedic came back and lifted me into the air.

I swallowed bile, doing my best not to vomit on the man's shirt, and it came to me what I'd been thinking a hundred years ago – the dogs were frightened and barking . . . they were warning me of something.

Danger!

'What's thaaa—?' I tried to say as I floated above the floor, but my mind was fuzzy, and I settled for, 'Alice.'

Then I floated down the hallway, an out of body experience, a dream of flight turned turbulent as we passed through some kind of doorway. The Tilt-A-Whirl came untethered. I spun downward, free falling, smashing my elbow and forehead on an unforgiving floor.

I threw up, vomiting whatever I'd eaten, then came liquid and sourness.

I felt better for a second and leaned on my good arm, but I was shrouded in darkness, lost in a haunted house. There was a muffled sound I tried to place, something nearby, but then Alice and Rex were upon me, licking at my face as I settled back on to the hard ground.

Another hundred years passed, and the dogs were barking and snarling, right in my ear – fearful, and warning me again.

Danger!

I lifted my head and began coughing as though to clear my throat. I felt my bladder release, warm and wet, and heaved more bile on to what had to be cement. I began to lay my head back down when a flash of pain exploded in my hand. Alice had bitten my palm.

Why would she do that? It made no sense.

The barking continued, the warning finally sinking in.

Danger!

I rolled on to my side and spotted a light above me and I somehow knew that light, and I somehow knew I was in the garage. I slipped over the cement stoop, shuffled up to the door, and then gripped at the trim around the frame, somehow got a knee beneath me, waited out a wave of seasickness, and pulled myself up to the doorknob.

It was locked and I tried to tell Alice and Rex that it was locked, as though they somehow held the key, but I'm not sure if any words came out.

Their barking was unrelenting; it spurred me on.

I threw up a final time, a tablespoon of green bitterness sprayed on to the door, and it dawned on me the sound that had been droning on this entire time was my pickup truck idling.

Why hadn't I turned the damned thing off when I'd come home?

I used the doorknob to pull myself upward, higher still, and leaned into the doorframe for support. The light I'd spotted was attached to the wall, now six inches from my cheek. It took a decade for me to figure out it came from the garage door opener switch.

I wasn't sure I could let go of the doorknob and frame without tumbling, so I pressed my forehead against the switch and, as our double garage door began to lift open, I sank down to the stoop and passed out.

Another hundred years later and someone was shaking my

arm. My eyes fluttered open and Mr Reule from next door stood over me, an archangel in gym shorts, a dress shirt, work boots, and dress socks. That apparel could mean only one thing – it was lawn mowing night for Mr Reule.

'Cory!' Reule said, continuing to shake my arm. 'Wake up!'

I stared at him, wanting to ask if this were a dream, but I couldn't make words work.

'Your dogs wouldn't stop barking, so I came over and your truck was running.' His eyes were wide, his face a smear of shock. 'Why was your truck running, Cory?'

I still couldn't find words, but by then Mr Reule had dug out his cell phone and tapped in 911.

FORTY

February 28, 1994

'It's beautiful,' Alaine White said after the tour of her former employer's executive townhouse in Hinsdale. The two had returned to the kitchen, where Taleggio lasagna waited in the oven. 'I think you'll be very happy here.'

'It'll have to do. James got the house, and I'm sure he'll be quite happy there with *her*. Being regional bank manager was never good enough for him – he's gunning for bank president,' Alaine's ex-employer said, 'and he'll need the place for entertaining the VIPs.' The woman thought for a moment. 'I won't miss the entertaining.'

Alaine nodded. She'd only heard about their divorce recently, at Christmastime, when she'd received a card and short note from her former boss, the woman whose children she'd nannied on summer breaks during her final two years of college. Evidently, their marriage had ended last fall, and her ex-husband had gotten remarried in January to a woman who'd worked at one of the Crown National banks. 'Will the children be coming over?'

'Not tonight,' her ex-boss replied. 'I felt the need for a little *girlfriend time*. I've always liked you, Alaine. To be honest, I see a bit of me in you, a couple of peas in a pod.'

'Thank you,' Alaine said. She wasn't sure what to add but felt more was called for. 'I've always enjoyed your company, as well, and you know how much I love Jordan and Patrick. In fact, I plan on kidnapping the two of them once I get settled in.'

'Speaking of getting settled in,' her former employer said, taking the lasagna out of the oven, 'how is that job of yours going?'

Alaine didn't want to talk about her current *occupation*, if you could even call it that. She'd received a business degree with nearly a four-point-oh GPA and – here it was two years later – she was selling coffee to business facilities. Alaine received a pittance as a base salary and relied primarily on commissions, like something out of an Arthur Miller play. A typical nine-to-fiver included equal parts doors being shut in her face and phone calls being hung up.

'It's fine,' she said.

'Only fine?' Alaine's old boss took the Endive salad out of the refrigerator.

'Well, it has its . . . challenges.'

'Do you mind if I speak frankly?'

'Always.'

Alaine's former employer set the loaf of sourdough in the oven, just for a few minutes, to make it warm. Then she turned to Alaine and said, 'It sounds hideous.'

'No,' Alaine replied. 'It's just that I'm still acclimating to the—' Alaine stopped herself midsentence and smiled weakly. 'You're right – it's hideous, awful – but I'm only doing it until I find something else,' she said. 'Business degrees are worthless; MBAs steal all the good jobs.'

'Have you considered going back to school and getting an MBA?'

Alaine shrugged. She didn't want to talk anymore about either work or going back to school.

'Well, in that case – might I recommend a second glass of the Sauvignon while I get the meal plated?'

Two glasses of Sauvignon later, dinner had been consumed, and they were now working on crème brûlée. Alaine's former boss had opened a bottle of Tawny Port.

'How did you find the food?'

'I am reminded of how excellent a chef you are.'

'The lasagna wasn't overdone?'

'Not in the least.' Alaine sniffed at her wine glass and said, 'There's a good chance I'll be sleeping on your couch tonight.'

'I've already made up the bed in the guest room.'

Alaine took a long sip of the Tawny Port, and then asked, 'How have the kids handled the transition of the past year?'

'A lot of tears,' her former boss said. 'I stayed in Hinsdale so they could remain at the same school and be around their friends. Jordan's in second grade now. Patrick's in fourth. It wouldn't be right to rip them away from all that.'

'Do they live with you?'

'We have joint custody, but, yes, they're primarily with me.' Alaine's former employer set down her empty glass of wine and sighed. 'Please forgive me, Alaine, but tonight's invite was not entirely a social one. I've wanted to chat with you about something that's been on my mind a lot lately. I wanted to hear your take on the matter once we've consumed enough alcohol, of course.'

Alaine was puzzled; her curiosity was piqued. 'What's on your mind?'

'Do you remember the last summer you watched the children?'

Alaine nodded.

'Do you remember that one night you stayed over?'

Alaine nodded again. 'If I recall correctly, we'd consumed a bit of wine that night as well.'

'James was working late – though, in retrospect, I suspect he was with her.'

Alaine said nothing and her former boss continued, 'I remember us giggling into the wee hours of the morning as though we were at a slumber party. At one point we were laughing so hard we woke Patrick. He came downstairs, all sleepy-eyed, and told us to pipe down.' She stared at Alaine a long moment. 'Do you remember what we were laughing so hard about?'

'To be honest, that night's a bit of a blur.'

The woman reached for the bottle of Tawny Port. 'I told you how James let me share his home computer for budgeting and cooking recipes and school stuff for the children?'

Alaine nodded along, trying to recall that long-ago evening.

'It was easy-peasy because James set his password to his

birthdate,' she said. 'Anyway, I told you how his computer contained *sensitive data* from Crown National because he brought stuff home on a floppy or disk drive so he could work on it in the study?'

'Oh, yes.' Alaine smiled as the night slowly returned to her. 'You said he had security information on his PC, the kind a thief would kill for. And we giggled about how we could use it to rip off the bank.'

'Yes,' her former employer said. 'We laughed a lot that night as we thought about how it might be done.'

'We were a regular Bonnie and Clyde.'

'Perhaps a more cultured version of Bonnie and Clyde, anyway.' Alaine's former employer topped off her wine glass and continued. 'James has not changed his password since those days.'

Alaine raised her eyebrows; she leaned forward in her chair. 'How do you know that?'

'Oh, I have free reign whenever I stop by to pick up the kids. You know how those little devils are never ready when you want them to be. But James and his *new wife* have dinners and affairs to attend, and they can't be tardy,' she said. 'It happened last week. I stood at the bottom of the steps, calling for the kids to hurry up, when it dawned on me. I wandered into James's study – into *our old study* – and, after a few taps on the keyboard . . . open sesame.'

Quiet now, motionless, thoughts of finishing her dessert or glass of wine had been forgotten. Alaine stared at her former employer.

'Here's the thing about the situation I find myself in. All of my *physical* needs are met, Alaine. I will not want for comfort.' She tossed a hand in the air, indicating her new townhome. 'However, there remain certain *psychological* and *emotional* considerations at play, psychological and emotional needs that have not come close to being fulfilled. Not by a long shot,' she said calmly, matter-of-factly. 'Now this may be small of me, Alaine – in fact, it *is* small of me – but there is no way James and that *bank teller whore* of his ride off into the sunset unscathed. There's no way James wins.' Her former employer stared unblinkingly at Alaine. 'And there is no way he will ever become bank president.' She added, 'I'm going to take that from him.'

FORTY-ONE

I slowly opened my eyes.

The first thing I noticed was the needle stuck in the top of my hand. I almost jerked my hand away before realizing it was connected to some kind of flexible tubing leading up to some kind of drip. That's when I realized I was in a hospital. The room was dark, light shone off a muted television bracketed to the wall opposite my bed. It appeared set to a weather channel, though the map the weather girl faced didn't appear to be Chicago or anywhere else in Illinois. The door to my room was mostly shut; a small ray of light crept in off a quiet corridor. The clock on the wall beside the TV read five o'clock, which I took to be in the morning.

What in the holy-effin' hell?

I glanced to my left. A lone figure sat scrunched and rumpled in a guest chair, a purse lay sideways at her feet. It was my sister. Her head down, hands settled in her lap, partially obscuring a box of Kleenex.

Oh shit.

I'm in a hospital bed. I have no idea how I got here, what I'm doing here, and my sister has, evidently, been sitting next to me all night sponging up tears.

What kind of diagnosis would cause that?

Cancer?

Did Crystal come home and find me passed out? Did she call an ambulance and have me whisked here – possibly Glenbrook Hospital as that's kind of near the house? My forehead ached and I brought my left hand – my free hand – up to my brow and felt the bandage.

Had there been an operation of some kind?

A brain tumor?

I'd heard stories about brain tumors, some the size of tennis balls. That could explain my collapsing and Crystal getting me here, and then a Glenbrook MD spots the tumor in a CAT or PET scan, and they're forced to perform emergency surgery . . . and Crystal's here because they didn't expect me to pull through. Or maybe she's been informed I have a half-year at the outside.

Crystal's head nodded up, her eyes focused on me. 'Cor,' she said. 'You're awake.'

'What did the doctor say?'

She sat up in the guest chair and shook off any vestiges of sleep. 'Why, Cory?' she said softly. 'Why did you do it?'

I was confused. 'I can't help it if they found a tumor.'

'A tumor?' She studied me a long moment. 'What the hell are you talking about?'

Now I was really confused. 'What the hell are you talking about?'

'For Christ's sake, Cory – you tried to kill yourself.' She wiped at her eyes with a tissue. 'When you're well enough to stand up, we're getting you placed in a seventy-two-hour psych hold.'

'A psych ward?!'

'They can do an eval . . . and talk about depression.'

'Crystal.'

'I don't know how you could do this,' she stressed. 'You knew it'd kill me.'

'Crystal.'

She settled back in the guest chair. 'What?'

'I didn't try to kill myself.'

My sister continued staring at me and said, 'Mr Reule found you in the garage. Your truck was running, and the dogs were going apeshit.'

I had a vision of our next-door neighbor staring down at me. I thought it was a dream or hallucination. 'I didn't try to kill myself,' I repeated.

'You left a note for me, Cor.' Crystal began ruffling through her purse. She took out a folded sheet of paper, handed it to me, and flipped on some kind of lamp behind my head.

I held up the note.

* * *

> *Crystal,*
> *I am so sorry. I can't pretend anymore.*
> *I miss Mom and Dad so much.*
> *This is not your fault.*
> *Cory*

I sat upright in the hospital bed, which caused an immediate thumping in my forehead. 'I did not write this.'

'It was on the kitchen table next to a picture of our trip to South Dakota.'

'I don't care where it was – I didn't write this.' I crumpled the note into a ball and tossed it toward the bin next to the door. It missed. 'I'm not suicidal.'

Crystal retrieved the note, placed it back in her purse, and then sat back down. 'I moved home after Mom and Dad died not only so you could stay there to finish high school, but so I could keep an eye on you.'

I sighed. 'I know you did, Crys. The thought did cross my mind back then, but I chose to hate myself instead.' I had spent years blaming myself for our parents' death. 'But I didn't write that thing,' I said and leaned back down on the pillow. 'And why the hell would I type a suicide note, anyway?'

'No one writes anymore,' Crystal replied, but I could tell I was getting through to her. 'You've got a printer for the dog stuff and another dozen printers you could use at Harper's.'

'I'm not suicidal,' I repeated and closed my eyes, hoping my head would cease pounding. 'I did not write that note, and I did not try to kill myself.'

My sister took her notepad and a pen from her purse. 'What do you remember then?'

That was the million-dollar question. It was all cloudy and foggy and dream-like. 'I didn't come home at lunch, so I ran the hell out of Alice and Rex in the backyard with the Frisbee.'

'What else?'

'I think I ate dinner,' I said. 'If you're not home, I normally eat around that time.'

'But you don't recall?'

'No,' I said and opened my eyes. 'How did Reule get the garage door open?'

'He didn't. Reule said when he was getting the mower ready, he heard the dogs barking up a blue storm. Then, when he started mowing, he noticed the door go up, and then the dogs came out on to the driveway and wouldn't stop yapping until he came over.'

'I sort of remember the pups making a racket.' I glanced down at my hand with the IV in it. There was also a bandage covering my palm to the back of my hand. 'Did Alice bite me?'

'Yes, she did,' Crystal said. 'In fact, I think Alice and Rex saved your life, forced you to open the garage door.'

I seized on that. 'Even if I was suicidal, Crys – you know me – I would never hurt Alice or Rex.'

Crystal scribbled something in her notepad and said, 'I know, but if someone is suffering from mental health issues or clinical depression, it's hard to get inside their thought process.'

'I would never hurt the dogs,' I stressed and then touched the dressing on my forehead. 'What the hell happened here?'

'You've got a concussion,' she replied. 'My assumption is you fell on the garage floor.'

'Is that why I'm having trouble remembering last night?'

Crystal said nothing.

I caught my sister's eye. She was holding something back. 'Is that why I'm having trouble remembering what happened last night?'

Crystal shrugged. 'If the note was planted to make your death look like a suicide, then you were not in the house alone.' She added, 'I'm thinking you may have been . . . drugged.'

'What?!'

'Someone slipped you a Mickey Finn, Cor, to get you into the garage,' she said. 'You may have been roofied.'

I steamed and shook my head, which only served to intensify the throbbing inside my skull. 'Oh that's just fucking great.'

'Rohypnol would explain the blackouts and amnesia.'

'Of course,' I said. 'Well – get the rape kit.'

'Not funny, Cor.'

'I'm not laughing,' I said. 'I'm scared; I'm creeped out. Who the hell would do this to me?'

'Do you remember drinking anything last night? Anything with dinner, anything at all?'

'Probably had a beer,' I said, and caught a flash of a beer bottle. 'You bought a six-pack of Rolling Rock in bottles for us.'

'What?'

'You brought home Rolling Rock in bottles to replace the cans you drank.'

'I didn't bring any beer home,' Crystal said, scribbling again in her notebook. 'You get the beer and the fast food, and I get the groceries – you know, the healthy stuff.'

'But I always buy cans 'cause I dropped a bottle once and the clean-up sucked,' I said. 'I thought you'd finished off the cans and replenished with bottles.'

'I didn't bring any beer home,' Crystal was adamant. 'Look, Cory, we're going to get a blood sample for toxicology, OK? I need to run home and let the dogs out, but I'll get those bottles and have them tested as well.'

I shut my eyes again, the pounding in my forehead mildly subsiding, as Crystal got ready to leave. I finally said, 'There was a lot of barking – a lot of it. At one point it felt like I was floating above the room.' My eyes opened and I looked at my sister. 'I was being carried by a paramedic.'

'Carried by a paramedic?'

'I got it in my mind that a paramedic was carrying me out to an ambulance . . . and Alice and Rex were howling.'

'There were no paramedics at our house, Cor. You were attacked by one or more assailants. You were carried or dragged out to the garage.' Crystal stood at the side of the hospital bed, purse slung over a shoulder, key fob for her HR-V in one hand. 'Why would someone do this to you?'

I shrugged. 'No professor's going to kill me because I skipped out of their class,' I said. 'I've had to hound a few deadbeats to pay up for training their dogs, but this seems a bit excessive to duck out of paying a hundred bucks.'

'Anybody new in your life lately?'

I almost smiled. 'I had lunch with a girl yesterday.'

'You did?'

'Don't act so surprised.'

'Was it a date?'

'I wish,' I said. 'I'm sure she's got a boyfriend.'

'Did you just meet her yesterday?'

'Formally, but she's been in my UNIX class.' I knew where Crystal was heading with this, coincidental timing and all. 'And I noticed her around the college last spring. Brielle's a classmate, not some plant as though this were a *Jason Bourne* movie.'

Crystal smiled and twirled her key fob. 'So her name's Brielle, huh?'

I felt myself begin to blush. I should have known Crystal would give me shit. 'I'm a part-time dog trainer and a part-time college student. No one's going to go to this absurd level of trouble to take me out,' I said. 'It's not like I'm a cop like you.' Something spread across Crystal's features. I'd seen that look before. 'What are you thinking?'

'I'm thinking about cops like me.'

FORTY-TWO

April 29, 1994

'You love him, don't you?'

'Only since grade school,' Alaine admitted. She'd attained a higher level of candor with her former employer over the past two months than she'd had with any person in her life, including the man they currently spoke of . . . Thomas Dando.

'Does he know?'

Alaine sighed. 'If he gave it any thought at all, I imagine he does. He doesn't feel the same way, though.' The two again sat at the table in the kitchen of her former employer's Hinsdale executive townhome. This time they sipped bottles of sparkling water instead of wine. It was a conversation that called for sobriety. 'We *connected* for a few minutes once upon a time, but Tom pulled back. He started laughing, saying it was like kissing an aunt or a sister. I giggled along as though I agreed.' She then commented, 'But I didn't agree.'

The host stared at her old nanny several moments before saying, 'Personally, I think the man is out of his mind. I almost didn't hire you because of how attractive you are. Intuitively, I might have suspected my husband of being the mouse-turd he turned out to be.'

Alaine remembered how her former employer's husband, James, had come home early one afternoon during the final summer she'd watched Jordan and Patrick. The three of them were at play in the shallow end of the backyard pool, Alaine teaching Jordan how to float on her back while Patrick tried to see how long he could hold his breath underwater. James settled into a chaise lounge on the pool deck, under the shade of a patio umbrella, and watched as the kids floated and splashed. However, Alaine noticed, and practically felt, as his eyes wandered away from his children and roamed up and down her bikini-clad body as though a Xerox machine making photocopies.

Though nothing improper had been voiced that sunlit afternoon and nothing had come of it, it made for an uncomfortable half-hour before Alaine cut short the swim lesson and brought the kids inside.

'He might be out of his mind for agreeing to help us,' Alaine said.

Her former employer had come clean, confessing she recalled Alaine telling her about Thomas Dando back then, how he'd been her dear old friend, a smart guy and an excellent athlete. And how he'd turned soldier after high school graduation, and how he'd served with honor in the Marine Corps during the Gulf War. At the time, Alaine had casually told her employer that her friend was returning home, that his mother was throwing a welcome home party, and how much Alaine looked forward to seeing him.

Alaine's former employer also confessed to thinking about Alaine's soldier friend when she began reflecting on the wrong that had been done to her by a certain regional bank manager of an ex-husband of hers, and what that adulterous bastard had put her through . . . and how there was no way in hell he'd be allowed to dance away as though the last decade had meant nothing, nothing at all.

Soon after their get-together in late February, she'd laid her cards on the table, informing Alaine she was in need of what one would call a *general contractor*. Someone capable of leading a *complex project*, someone capable of thinking on their feet, of recruiting the appropriate *subcontractors*, and of following the project through to a successful completion – but it was imperative they find someone to navigate these turbulent waters who was himself a force to be reckoned with . . . and a man like Thomas Dando certainly seemed to fit the bill.

Onboarding Tom had been hit or miss.

First, it took Alaine an hour to convince her childhood friend she was not putting him on, that he needn't look around the room for a hidden film crew as if it were all some unaired segment from *Candid Camera*. After that, he questioned Alaine's sanity. Later still, after Alaine laid out the specifics, how she had a friend on the inside that was willing to bankroll the operation, Tom smirked and shook his head.

It was a hard no.

A week later, Tom surprised her by coming to Chicago for further discussion. They talked all night; every aspect of the plan was placed under a microscope. It was in the wee hours of the morning that Alaine committed a tactical error. She brought up one of her former employer's primary concerns – once the bank heist was over, how would they deal with the criminals recruited to help with the robbery? Could she and Tom trust their future well-being once the recruits were handed hundreds of thousands of dollars, sent on their merry way, and left to their own devices?

Tom got angry. Major-league pissed off was more like it. He told Alaine in no uncertain terms she could *Go Fuck Herself* and stamped out of the apartment. Alaine thought she might never see Tom again, and worried her old friend might even go to the police.

But after a couple more weeks passed, Tom contacted her. Despite the hour, Alaine drove straight to Milwaukee, straight to Tom's apartment, where he laid out his only stipulation. They would hold off deciding what to do with the felons they'd recruit until after the bank robbery had occurred. Alaine immediately nodded her approval. And with that in mind, the two shook hands; they even shared an awkward hug. By the time the sun came up, Tom had agreed to be what Alaine's former employer had called the *general contractor*.

And Alaine agreed to have some skin in the game. There'd be no need for more than three recruits as she'd drive the getaway car – at least until the crew exited the bank and Tom jumped behind the wheel.

Surprisingly, Alaine noted the most curious of relations vis-à-vis the back and forth between Tom and herself, as their discussions progressed throughout the month of April – she spotted the old sparkle in Tom's eye, the sense of humor she'd long thought dead had returned as they went over every aspect of their plan, again and again, from start to finish, even to the point of laughing uncontrollably at some of the crazier aspects they discarded as they plotted the smartest course to take.

Yes – old Tom was still lurking around somewhere inside the husk of a man who had returned home from Kuwait.

It only took a bank robbery to draw him out.

Alaine's former employer set down her sparkling water, cleared her throat, and said, 'You know, Alaine, in a matter such as this, emotions are bound to be heightened – passions intensified – your old friend could very well change his mind.' Her old employer added, 'Love could become . . . *requited*.'

Alaine nodded slowly.

The thought had crossed her mind.

FORTY-THREE

Aw hell, turned out it was true – the blood test came back from toxicology.

I'd been roofied.

Crystal and I stood in the backyard. I'd skipped morning class and she'd gotten home in time for the two of us to break bread – scrambled eggs and toast. I was again exhausting Alice and Rex with Frisbee fetch as I didn't have it in me to take them for a walk today. Truth be told, I hadn't felt like doing much of anything since I'd returned home from the hospital. I didn't want to see anyone; I didn't want to talk to anyone. And I half-listened as my sister told me what she'd learned this morning.

'The security camera off Putnam's front entry catches the street,' Crystal told me as I flipped a high one off for Alice to chase down.

The Putnam family lived three doors down and across the street from us. Although they'd been in the neighborhood for most of my life, I didn't know them very well on account of Mrs Putnam once screaming at me at the top of her lungs when I was a kid and Rocko – our old Australian shepherd – lifted a leg to their mailbox. You'd have thought it was the end of the world.

Armageddon.

Since then I've kept the pups on our side of the street. For all I know, I'm the guy that caused them to get a security camera.

Quite frankly, I'm still afraid of her.

My sister rarely comes home for lunch. I suspected she wanted to keep tabs on me as I continued feeling dazed and a bit hungover. I heard her call down when she headed out for work this morning but refused to haul myself upstairs to exchange pleasantries. I tried sleeping in, which didn't occur, and I spent an hour memorizing ceiling tiles before tossing in the towel. I assumed Crystal had driven in to her precinct, but now realized she'd been canvassing the neighborhood – our neighborhood. Turns out my charming personality hadn't brought her home to eat as she'd never made it more than a block away to begin with.

Crystal continued, 'The angle of their camera couldn't capture plate numbers, but it was mostly cars I recognized, you know, neighbors coming and going to work or stores.'

'Did she yell at you?'

'Who?'

'Mrs Putnam?'

Crystal looked confused. 'No, she was more than happy to help,' she said. 'Why?'

'No reason.'

Crystal grinned. 'What'd you do to her?'

'Nothing.'

'Anyway, the mail guy came the same time he does every day,' Crystal said. 'And there were quite a few Amazon Prime deliveries.'

I glanced at my sister as Alice hustled back with the Frisbee. 'Don't those Amazon drivers wear uniforms?'

'Some do.' She saw where I was headed and began working her iPhone. I flipped the disc for Rex this time, another high one toward the corner fence, as Crystal walked over and shared her screen with me. 'Check out the jackets and shirts they wear,' she said. 'Does any of this look familiar?'

I took a long look at the apparel and shrugged. Unfortunately, not much had returned since I woke up in the hospital and thought I had a brain tumor or leukemia. 'I don't know, Crys. It was all so dream-like. I'm lying on the floor and someone in some kind of get-up is sort of helping me out, and I just assumed it was an EMT.'

'I'll follow up and see if Amazon had deliveries on our street that day.'

I served the Frisbee a couple more times, one for each of the beasts to fetch, before asking, 'What's the latest on Big Albert?'

'Dave Albertson is in a lot of trouble,' Crystal said and held up a forefinger. 'His Ford Explorer was spotted near Catherine Dando's house on the night of her murder.' She held up a second finger. 'What appears to be "Al" is scribbled on the Crown National strap of cash found hidden in Dando's air vent.' A third finger went up. 'And Tom Dando's yearbooks are found at Albertson's house.' The fingers went down, and Crystal continued, 'Horton's charged him with murder in the first in Catherine's death, but we're digging for more in order to nail him for Crown National and the other deaths.'

'Albertson's in jail?'

'No, bail was set at one point five million and he made bond yesterday,' Crystal replied. 'But they've got him rigged up with an electronic monitoring system – GPS, an ankle bracelet – as the prosecutor considers him a flight risk. If he had one, they'd have taken his passport. Albertson will await trial at home. And he'll have to manage his landscaping business from there as well.'

'Weren't you unsure about him?'

Crystal shrugged. 'Dando's yearbooks hidden at his house are pretty damning. Albertson had a man crush on the guy and he wrote a slobbering piece in Dando's senior yearbook. He signed it *Your Forever Friend, Dave "Big Albert" Albertson*. It's not looking good for him . . . and this is just the beginning.'

Frisbee was finito. Alice and Rex had gotten bored, and it served more to exhaust me than them. I knelt down in the grass and scratched behind ears, under muzzles, and at the nape of their necks. Then I asked my sister what I'd been pondering for most of the morning. 'OK, Crys – who'd you piss off?'

Crystal shook her head. 'I've been racking my brain and can't think of any arrests I've made where the person would go to this extreme to get me off the case.'

'A street gang or a drug cartel?'

She shook her head again. 'They'd just shoot us both and be done with it.'

'No Hannibal Lecter hiding in the weeds?' I asked. 'Or a Professor Moriarty?'

'Here's a spoiler alert, Cor – most criminals are as dumb as a box of rocks. Rarely, if ever, do we trip over an evil mastermind, which is good for business since it makes the job a lot easier.'

'What about the mob or the Outfit or whatever the hell they're called here?'

Crystal slipped her cell phone back into her hip pocket. 'Viviana Walsh came to us. She wants us to find out who killed her son, so why would she sic her nephew on me? That makes zero sense. How would killing you to take me out of the picture profit her? I'm not even the lead detective,' she said. 'That's Horton.'

We shuffled toward the sliding glass door. I'm not much of a day drinker, but it had been a trying couple of days. I hadn't read my horoscope, yet I knew there would be alcohol in my immediate future. My only junket for the day had been to the local liquor store where I picked up a twelve-pack of Rolling Rock – a twelve-pack of Rolling Rock *cans*.

And I planned on inspecting each and every can before I opened them.

Crystal's phone buzzed and I ushered Alice and Rex inside while she took the call. The three of us worked our way up the stairs. I passed out doggie snacks and refreshed their water bowls when my sister stepped into the kitchen, a look of perplexity pasted across her face.

'What's up?' I asked.

'You know how Dave Albertson was supposed to stay at home and wear an ankle bracelet?'

'Yes.'

'He bolted,' she said. 'The ankle bracelet is there, but Albertson's gone.'

FORTY-FOUR

'He didn't do it, Matty,' Viviana leaned over and whispered in her nephew's ear. 'He didn't do it.'

'I suspect you're right,' Mattia Lanaro replied. Not only had he suspected his aunt was right, but he'd known it five minutes into the interrogation.

'I can't watch anymore.'

Lanaro noticed his aunt's face was moist. She'd been quietly crying. He nodded and waved one of his men over. 'Please take my aunt to the car.' Then he turned his attention back to Viviana. 'I'm sorry you had to witness this, Aunt Viv,' he said. 'I will be out momentarily.'

Viviana patted her nephew's shoulder as she stood, turned around, and headed across the acre or so of concrete with her escort.

They were inside an abandoned and dilapidated warehouse on the outer edge of the Fulton River District. Lanaro knew they would not be bothered here as he personally knew the owner. In fact, Lanaro *was* the owner – had gotten the place for a steal – and, in less than two years, a high-rise condominium would be sitting on this very lot.

Lanaro himself would have a penthouse suite.

Mattia Lanaro's *hunter* – a man who'd once upon a time been a high-ranking police detective himself – had notified him when Dave Albertson made bond, and that, until his trial, Albertson would be confined to his residence in Bucktown. Lanaro's team, disguised as police officers, had shown up at Albertson's house before first light this morning, under the pretext of bringing him in for additional questioning. Instead, they hustled Albertson to Lanaro's Fulton River District facility while ignoring his demands that he be allowed to contact his attorney.

One of Lanaro's men had removed Albertson's ankle monitor and appropriated his smartphone, and, while two of the faux officers frogmarched Albertson out to the waiting sedan, he'd let both items slip to the floor of Albertson's entrance hall as he made his way out.

Lanaro sat in a folding chair – close, but far enough away to avoid any splatter – and stared at Dave 'Big Albert' Albertson. Albertson sat on a green tarp atop a block of rubble, his torso swaying in slow, asymmetrical circles. His feet were bound, his wrists zip-tied behind his back. One of Lanaro's men stood at Albertson's rear, essentially to keep the man from collapsing, while another of Lanaro's men, sporting weighted-knuckle gloves – sap gloves – stood over the beaten lump of flesh, awaiting instructions on whether he should continue or call it a wrap.

Albertson's face looked like it had gone twelve rounds with a meat tenderizer. Both of his eyes were swollen shut, his cheekbones fractured, his nose broken and bloodied, and a sizable gash along his hairline refused to stop bleeding. Several of Albertson's ribs were also broken. The man had difficulty breathing; it sounded as though he was sucking air through a Pixy Stix. Worse yet, Lanaro suspected some of the man's internal organs were in the process of shutting down.

One thing Lanaro's man with the sap gloves had not done was break Albertson's jaw as they needed Albertson to talk.

And talk Albertson had . . .

First, there'd been the mass confusion as to what Albertson was even doing there, and why they kept asking him questions about some guy named Connor Walsh, whose body, along with that of Albertson's old chum Thomas Dando, had been found under several feet of dirt at Kankakee River State Park.

It took five blows to Albertson's face to convince Lanaro the man was authentically confused, that he was telling the truth. It took another three blows to Albertson's ribcage to convince Lanaro that of all the players involved at Kankakee State Park, Albertson only knew Dando from having grown up with him – from junior and senior high – from playing together on the football team.

A handful of blows later and Lanaro knew Dave Albertson had absolutely nothing to do with the robbery at Crown National and even less to do with his cousin's death.

Lanaro waved away his man with the sap gloves and inched

his folding chair closer to Albertson, until their knees were almost touching.

'Mr Albertson,' he said, 'can you hear me?'

Albertson emitted a soft and lengthy moan that Lanaro took as an affirmation.

'I am ashamed of what has occurred here today, Mr Albertson. This is not how I conduct business, and I will regret this morning's actions for years to come.' Lanaro stressed, 'I am deeply sorry, Mr Albertson . . . and I say this with utmost sincerity and contrition.'

Albertson emitted another moan as he continued swaying in uneven circles.

'You have been framed, Mr Albertson. You must know that. I bet it's eaten away at you since your arrest, and I'm sure you've discussed it with your attorney.' Lanaro leaned forward. 'People that have been framed tend to *know* who it was that framed them, wouldn't you agree?' he asked rhetorically. 'For example, I would *know* with *utmost certainty* the party responsible if someone attempted this with me.' Lanaro took a second to settle back in his chair and then said, 'Who framed you, Mr Albertson?'

Albertson exhaled slowly, an inner tube bleeding air. Finally, he mumbled, 'Sued . . . business . . . being sued.'

Lanaro sought clarification. 'Your landscaping company is being sued?'

Another lengthy moan that Lanaro took as confirmation.

'Oh, my friend,' Lanaro said and couldn't help but chuckle. 'I understand that is the world you live in, but your current predicament goes many exits beyond a crumbling retaining wall or having removed the wrong tree.'

The two men conversed another five minutes. Lanaro asked short questions, and amongst groans and frequent bouts of wheeziness, Albertson provided shorter answers. There was no more violence or threats of violence. The time for that had ended. Now it was just two middle-aged men working out a shared conundrum.

Albertson had no clue as to whom the 'Al' on the Crown National bank strap referred to. He spoke of a star running back named Alan, who had been a senior back when he and Dando were in tenth grade, and whom Dando got to know pretty well as he made varsity that same year. He spoke of another Alan that Dando had starred in a school play with, and of a girl named

Alaine whose friends sometimes called her Al. And he informed Lanaro there were several other Alans at Joseph W. Fifer High School during his attendance there.

Albertson told Lanaro he had no idea why any of his old classmates would frame him. Lanaro knew the answer, of course, but he kept it to himself. There was no reason to pile on or add to Albertson's grief. And the answer was quite simple, really. Whoever framed Albertson didn't do so out of hatred or spite, or merely for the hell of it – they did so because they knew it would work, they knew they could get away with it.

And by framing Dave Albertson, they'd sealed the poor man's fate.

Finally, Albertson informed Lanaro he'd only seen Dando a time or two after he had left the Marines and returned home, and that he had no clue who his old pal was chumming around with during the summer of 1994.

Lanaro glanced down at his watch. There wasn't any more he could get from the landscaper. Lanaro's only takeaway was to have his accountants – after all, they were the best money could buy – perform some kind of forensic accounting or financial analysis on these other *Als* that Albertson had rattled off. Find out if any of them somehow came into money in the mid-nineties.

It was a long shot, but at least it was something he could share with his aunt so the day wouldn't appear as the complete debacle it truly was.

Lanaro stood. 'You have been very helpful, Mr Albertson,' he said. 'I appreciate your honesty and, again, my sincerest apology,' he took in Albertson's face, 'for what has occurred here today.'

Albertson moaned, followed by a string of words Lanaro didn't quite catch.

'What did you say?'

'Let me . . . go home.'

Lanaro stared down at his feet. 'I wish I could, my friend. You have been honest with me, and out of respect, I will be honest with you,' he said. 'It will be quick.'

However, Lanaro hadn't been completely honest with Albertson. It would not be quick; it would not be like ripping off the proverbial Band-Aid. A firearm would not be utilized, too much clean-up involved. The same held true with a blade. There could be no DNA left at the scene in the off chance that someone, anyone, came looking.

Lanaro's man behind Albertson had already removed a strip of rope and was wrapping the ends around both of his hands.

Albertson exhaled slowly, then said, 'I'll say . . . car . . . accident.'

Lanaro patted Albertson on his shoulder, gently. 'I'm afraid they wouldn't believe you, my friend.'

Lanaro shook his head. Today had been a monumental fuckup. Albertson's disappearance would lead the police to believe he'd run for the hills, that they'd been right in arresting him, that Albertson was guilty as sin of the Crown National bank robbery, the death of Catherine Dando, as well as the deaths of those discovered at Kankakee State Park, including Lanaro's cousin Connor Walsh.

Albertson's trail would go cold, and the man's face would sit on the FBI's list of most wanted fugitives for decades to come.

Lanaro sighed. Albertson's disappearance would also signal Connor's true killer – the man responsible for framing Dave Albertson – that they were coming for him.

Any element of surprise would be gone.

Lanaro nodded at the man standing behind Albertson – it was time – and then he turned and exited the warehouse.

FORTY-FIVE

July 28, 1994
10:50 P.M.

'I don't have time for this,' Alaine snapped as soon as her former employer opened the door. 'You know where I've been all day . . . and you know what's coming tomorrow.' She repeated, more briskly, 'I don't have time for this.'

Her former employer stood in the entryway, a forefinger to

her lips. 'The kids are asleep.' Alaine had never seen the woman without her makeup before; she must have taken it off for the evening. Makeup or not, her ex-employer's face was haggard and pale, as though she were on the cusp of a cold. And her eyes were wide in what Alaine took as fear. Her ex-employer then added, 'Let's talk in the garage.'

Alaine was equal parts steamed and frightened. She returned home after a long day at Kankakee State Park, digging a grave with Tom, only to find a sequence of messages – eight cryptic messages in all – left on her home answering machine. Each message more frantic than the one before, all of them instructing Alaine to come over as soon as she listened to these messages, that her former employer dare not say anything over the telephone, and that Alaine must come over no matter the hour.

Alaine was ushered from the entryway, down the hallway, through the kitchen, and out the adjacent door and into the townhome's two-car garage. Her former employer shut the door behind them and turned to face Alaine. 'Connor Walsh is not who you think he is!'

Alaine peered back at her in bewilderment. 'What are you talking about?'

'Connor is not who he says he is.'

Alaine shrugged, still confused. 'Yes, he is – he's a college student at Marquette. I've talked to him about the classes he's been taking. He showed me one of his books on design.'

'I'm not saying it right.' Her former employer sighed and continued, 'Connor Walsh is Connor Walsh, but his uncle – his mother's brother – is Gabriele Lanaro of the Lanaro family.'

It had been a lengthy day, after a series of lengthy days, with minimal sleep to boot. Alaine had been walking a tightrope since the robbery – since that psychotic asshole Lamprecht shot and killed the security guard. She felt as though at any moment there'd be flashing lights and sirens and a dozen police officers with guns drawn that would arrest her for murder. And she seriously did not have time for whatever this was. She tossed her palms in the air. 'So the fuck what?'

'Gabriele Lanaro is the head of organized crime in Chicago,' her former employer replied. 'He is the head of the Chicago mob.'

Alaine shook her head. 'Connor's dad is an architect. Connor's studying to be an architect; he plans to work at his father's firm,' she said. 'I don't know anything about this other shit.'

'Well – you should know *about this other shit* because it's going to get us all killed.'

'Yeah, right.'

'Don't discount me, Alaine,' her former employer's voice turned cold. 'I'm not a flake and I am not an idiot.'

'I know you're not, but how do you know about Connor's uncle?'

'Easy. I did some research – a background check – like we did with the felon list,' she said. 'Connor Walsh was the only one of the three recruits I'd not looked into. I expected he'd be exactly who you said he was . . . but then I found the poison pill.'

Alaine leaned against the front panel of her ex-employer's Town & Country minivan. Although she'd taken most of the credit for compiling the felon list when discussing it with Tom – the list from which they'd recruited Lamprecht – truth be told, her former employer had done the lion's share of the research. The woman was a wizard at digging up information.

And what she'd just discovered about Connor Walsh would no doubt be true.

'If we split the money and walk away,' Alaine said, 'why would Connor's uncle come after us?'

Her former employer sighed again. 'Do you think the head of the Chicago mob is going to let us live knowing full well we could put his nephew behind bars for the rest of his life?' she answered Alaine's query with a question of her own. 'Think about it. We'd be loose ends as far as Walsh's uncle is concerned – loose ends that would have to be dealt with for his nephew's sake.'

'Why would Connor even go to his uncle with any of this?'

Alaine's former employer shook her head and began pacing the length of the Chrysler. 'I'm sure there's a certain amount of allure involved – you know, bragging rights. It's probably why Connor agreed to be involved in the first place.' She did an about-face and stepped toward the front of the minivan. 'Or he goes to his uncle for help in laundering the money because – well

– I imagine that's one of Gabriele Lanaro's areas of expertise. And then Lanaro views us as a threat to his nephew.'

'OK – so we tell Connor not to go to his uncle.'

'That might last for the short term, before he feels enough time has passed, and then goes to his uncle with his share of the money,' she replied, now heading toward the rear of the vehicle. 'More realistically, Connor moves the cash around on his own and red flags go up – maybe the IRS or the police think he's a drug dealer. If he gets arrested, his uncle finds out what *really happened*, and we're seen as a threat to his nephew.' She paused a moment as she passed Alaine. 'Or he spreads the cash around and gets picked up for the bank job, and his uncle finds out . . . and then we die.'

Silence filled the garage as Alaine's former employer continued pacing along the side of the Chrysler.

Finally, Alaine broke the stillness, 'But you're safe. I've respected your wishes to remain anonymous. Tom and the others – they don't know your name; they don't know anything about you.'

The pacing came to an abrupt halt. Her old boss looked her in the eye. 'I love you, Alaine. I truly do, but when they bring out the tin snips and tell me to either talk or they'll start with my nipples, I hate to admit this, but I'll tell them everything there is to know about you: your name, date of birth, address, whether you dye your hair, your menstrual cycle. Whatever they want to know. These are not people you cross.' She added, 'You are much braver than I am. And I'm sure you'll do your damnedest to keep my name from them when the tin snips come out, but—'

'No more,' Alaine interrupted, her voice trembling. 'We'll leave town. We'll all leave town.'

'They'd track us down, find us through our credit cards or family members or a dozen other ways I can't even imagine,' she said. 'It would only delay the inevitable.'

Alaine blinked back tears. 'So what do we do?'

'You need to tell Tom,' her former employer replied. 'You need to tell him tonight.'

'But Tom's at a motel with Connor. We each have different jobs to do in the morning.'

'Then you need to get Tom aside before it happens and let him know.'

'Even if I spring this on him,' Alaine said and shook her head, 'Tom's not going to do anything.'

'Then you'll have to find a way to convince him. Tell him the truth, exactly as I've laid it out for you. The two of you are old friends. He trusts you,' she said. 'It's a terrible, horrible, fucking awful thing . . . but this needs to end at the park.'

Alaine's shoulders began to shake, her legs felt like Jell-O; she gasped as though struck in the stomach, and sank slowly to the floor of the garage, her back against the minivan's front tire. She shuddered again and felt her eyes blur as tears warmed her face.

Alaine wanted to lie down and die.

She placed her face in her hands and began to weep.

Her former employer knelt down on the cement and took her into her arms as though she were her own daughter. 'I know, honey,' she said. 'I know.'

PART FOUR

The Scorned

Cry 'Havoc!' and let slip the dogs of war.
– William Shakespeare, *Julius Caesar*

FORTY-SIX

'Criminals are world-class bullshitters, Crystal; it goes with the territory,' Chuck Sims spoke to us over my sister's speakerphone. 'Take it from me – I spent my career listening to off-the-cuff BS that would get any actor nominated for an Academy Award. I could have retired earlier, but stuck it out a few more years because, quite frankly, when their self-preservation instinct kicked in, it brought me no end of joy to hear what these fuckers came up with.'

'I get that,' Crystal replied, 'but Dave Albertson's shock and denial at what they charged him with keeps coming back to me. The guy seemed authentic.'

'Where are Detective Horton and the others at?'

'They're pursuing Albertson, which they'd be crazy not to.'

'Yet you have reservations?'

My sister had called Sims to both pick his brain and use him as a sounding board. I sat at the kitchen table, munched on kettle chips, and pretended to be working my way through a course book on linear and non-linear data structures.

Crystal collected her thoughts. 'When it comes to lying, you remember the legal principle *false in one thing, false in everything*?'

'Of course,' Sims said, 'from Latin – falsus in uno, falsus in omnibus.'

My head perked up as I crunched on a chip. I jotted the phrase down, hoping I spelled it correctly, figuring I'd start incorporating it in daily conversations to impress friends and classmates and random store clerks.

Sims then asked, 'What of it?'

'I've called several classmates that ran in Dando's circle in high school,' Crystal said, 'and chatted with them about Dando and Albertson and some of their other friends in the in-crowd. I brought up Alaine Quinn, nonchalantly – nothing that'll raise any flags – and a couple of them remember calling her "Al" back when they were growing up.'

'*Al* – like what might have been scribbled on the Crown National bill strap?'

'Yeah, but Quinn told me she went by "Ally" in high school, like the actress Ally Sheedy who was in a bunch of movies back then.'

'You know how nicknames get bandied about, though,' Sims said. 'They called me *Upchuck* in high school. I couldn't punch out enough guys to make that fucker go away.' He added, 'I bet Quinn went by both nicknames.'

'But she made a big production out of being called *Ally* growing up – by her old friends, like Tom Dando – versus being called *Al* in college.'

'So . . . *the lady doth protest too much*?'

'Not so much that as she got overly detailed in her explanation, you know – down into the weeds.'

'She might not have appreciated Al while growing up because it's a guy's name, like Sam for Samantha,' I volunteered. 'But when she got older, she might have grooved on it because it was unique.'

There was an awkward silence, so I returned to my chips and data structures.

'I get it,' Crystal finally said. 'I'm spinning my wheels over a couple of nicknames from decades ago.' She shrugged. 'It's just the weird timing. What happened to Cory and the arrest of Albertson happened so soon after we met Alaine Quinn at Catherine's funeral, after I quizzed her on her nickname.'

'The robbers in the bank were all male, but no one got a look at the driver,' Sims said. 'Did you run a background check on her?'

'Just enough to know she never worked a day in a bank in her life,' Crystal said. 'She got her degree in business administration, and then managed a couple of businesses in the nineties – did well enough when everyone else was doing pretty well – and then married into a ton of money a dozen years ago. Living the American Dream.'

'You know, Crystal, Detective Horton is not wrong to go after the guy who took off his ankle bracelet and fled the scene.'

'But what if Albertson didn't *flee the scene*?'

'So that would mean the Lanaros, right? That's what you're thinking?'

Crystal nodded, realized Sims couldn't see her over the cell phone, and said, 'Yes – that's exactly what I'm thinking.'

'If the Lanaros were involved, that's damned fast work – snatching Albertson so soon after the guy makes bond.'

'I imagine they have ears everywhere.' Crystal sat down at the table, rotated the bag of kettle chips her way but didn't take any. 'They would have known exactly when Albertson got released.'

'OK,' Sims said. 'There were a lot of rumors and gossip and talk about Gabriele Lanaro back in my day. And the rumors and gossip and talk basically regarded how Gabriele did not take any shit from anyone. It didn't matter if you were a gang member, the mayor of the city, or the head of the local PTA. Gabriele Lanaro did not take shit. If that trait rubbed off on his son, and his son grabbed Albertson – whether Albertson's guilty or innocent, no one is ever going to see the guy again.' Sims then asked, 'Did you bring this up with Horton?'

'I expressed my concerns about Mattia Lanaro and what that might entail. Horton said that would give Albertson all the more reason to head out on the highway,' Crystal said. 'But when it comes to Albertson's disappearance, I see three scenarios. First, he is guilty as charged and he's making a run for Mexico right now as we speak. Second, he is guilty as charged, but he's been taken by Mattia Lanaro as payback for the death of his cousin, Connor Walsh. Or third,' Crystal spun the bag of chips back my way and continued, 'he has been framed, he's innocent, the guy had nothing to do with Kankakee State Park or Crown National Bank or Connor Walsh, but Mattia Lanaro wouldn't know that part and had him taken as payback for the death of his cousin.'

'And if it is scenario number three,' Sims said, 'you're thinking Alaine Quinn may be involved, that Alaine might be *Al* from the bill strap?'

'I am thinking that.'

We listened as Sims took a deep breath over the smartphone, and then he said, 'You know the background stuff you ran on Quinn?'

'Yes.'

'Send it to me.'

FORTY-SEVEN

The fixer stood in front of the entrance to Osteria Langhe on West Armitage Avenue. He heard it was a five-star Italian bistro but had never eaten there. Unfortunately, he wasn't here to savor gourmet food. Anything but. He wished to God he'd not made the phone call, but he had . . . and now he had to deal with the repercussions lest he had Mattia Lanaro on his ass.

'How did you get this number?' the voice that answered Lanaro's phone asked in a straightforward monotone.

'I have my resources,' the fixer replied and dove headfirst into the reason he'd placed the call.

'Excuse me,' monotone cut him off after thirty seconds. 'We do not know who you are, and we do not speak of such matters over the telephone.' The fixer was about to end the call when the voice added, 'Wait one moment, please.'

The fixer glanced down at his watch, considered hanging up, but he was using a burner phone, and this was Mattia Lanaro's private number. Something about being in for a penny passed through his mind. It took considerably longer than *one moment*, but the voice eventually returned.

'Do you know the restaurant Osteria Langhe?'

'I've heard of it,' the fixer said.

'Be at its entryway in one hour.'

The fixer sighed. 'What if I say no?'

'Do you really want to say "no" now that we are aware of your existence?' monotone replied and hung up.

The fixer cursed silently.

He'd seen the writing on the wall. Knocking Crystal Pratt out of play by faking her brother's suicide had been an abject failure. If anything, it would spur the detective onward. And though he'd succeeded in framing Dave Albertson, he'd been taken aback at Albertson's near-immediate disappearance. The fixer knew that all roads regarding his disappearance led to Mattia Lanaro. He assumed Lanaro would deal with Albertson once the man was in jail or serving time in prison. But his disappearance meant Lanaro now knew Albertson had been framed . . . which meant Lanaro would continue searching for his cousin's true killer.

And speaking of Connor Walsh's true killer, Alaine Quinn was not to be trusted. She was exceptionally rich, held deep, dark secrets, had killed before . . . and she had everything to lose. When the walls closed in, much like a cornered rat, Quinn was liable to lash out at anyone within arm's reach.

At this juncture, the fixer's services were null and void. He was a loose end that could sink the woman.

She would have realized that by now.

Worse yet, if Mattia Lanaro got to Alaine Quinn first – as he had gotten to Albertson – she'd tell the man everything in the final seconds of her life. And if Lanaro desired multiple layers of retribution for what had occurred to his cousin all those decades ago, the fixer would not be left with any profound sense of tranquility on account of having to peek over his shoulder for the rest of what could be a short and truncated life.

As soon as the fixer realized Quinn had him doing her dirty work on a diet of half-truths and omissions, he did a deep dive into all the players dug up at Kankakee State Park. And once the fixer became aware of Connor Walsh's relationship with the Lanaro family, he knew he had Alaine Quinn by the Achilles heel . . . and it was past time to shatter her Achilles heel into a million different pieces.

The fixer cursed again, dropped the burner phone into a trashcan, and hustled off to his car in order to make it to West Armitage in time.

Even though it was now ten minutes beyond his one-hour deadline, the fixer continued loitering outside Osteria Langhe. He scanned every face as they approached, but so far – it was still lunch hour, after all – most patrons appeared more interested in fine cuisine than in him. He even opened the door now and again and nodded at words of gratitude.

'Sorry to keep you waiting,' a voice said from behind after he'd opened the door for a group of women.

The fixer turned, spotted a fifty-something man a yard away. Though the man had just spoken to him, he noted no hand was outstretched in greeting. His initial instinct screamed *cop*. A younger man – a guerilla in a black suit – slipped out of the restaurant and stood behind him. The fixer realized he was sandwiched between the two men, and knew they were good at their jobs.

'Are you armed?' fifty-something asked.

'Yes,' the fixer replied. 'Concealed carry.'

'OK, we'll have to do something about that before you meet with him,' the man said. 'You and I and my friend are going to take a short detour into the restroom.' Fifty-something must have read something in the fixer's eyes because he followed up with, 'I could make a living as one of those age guessers you see at carnivals, and I'm guessing you were in your mid-teens when Crown National was robbed.'

The fixer nodded. 'I was fourteen.'

'Then you should have nothing to worry about.'

In the men's room, fifty-something collected his Micro 9 pistol, his cell phone, and wallet, while guerilla suit ran a wand over his body in search of any transmitter or microphone.

'You'll get these back when you leave,' fifty-something said as the two of them led him to a secluded end of the bistro's bar, to a place where there was no foot traffic, and on to a corner booth where he recognized Mattia Lanaro – expensive suit, short black hair, bifocals – who sat motionless with what appeared to be a glass of scotch in front of him.

'Please take a seat,' Lanaro said without looking up.

The fixer settled in across from Lanaro but was then forced to shuffle over as guerilla suit squeezed in next to him. Fifty-something stood in front of the booth as though he were a headwaiter, staring down at the fixer as though it were his turn to order.

'We will be here five minutes, much less if I'm not pleased,' Lanaro said. 'Now it's been brought to my attention that you have something you want to share with me.'

And share the fixer did.

From Alaine Quinn seeking his services, from her keeping him in the dark until it became exceedingly clear that she was the architect of the Crown National bank heist, that she had brought in Thomas Dando to lead the crew, that she was ultimately behind his cousin's death . . . and that Alaine Quinn was the only one to walk out of Kankakee River State Park that summer day three decades ago.

When he was finished, Lanaro took a long sip from his scotch before saying, 'And now you're selling her out.'

The fixer stared at the table in front of him. 'In a chess match, you acknowledge defeat by expressing your wish to resign, often by offering your hand to your opponent,' he said. 'Otherwise, you waste everyone's time by having the victor chase you around the board.'

Lanaro sipped slowly at his scotch.

Fifty-something broke the silence. 'Did you kill Catherine Dando?'

The question caught the fixer off-guard. 'Of course not,' he said, a bit too quickly. 'Quinn went to visit her and then panicked when she found out Catherine could place her with her son that entire summer.' The fixer knew to keep his lie as close to the truth as possible. 'That's when Quinn first contacted me – to help clean up her mess.'

Lanaro set down his whiskey tumbler. 'But you did set up Dave Albertson?'

The fixer nearly sighed with relief when he realized the head of the Chicago mob – unlike Mr Fifty-something – didn't give two shits about Catherine Dando. To Lanaro, she was just the mother of one of the pricks that was involved in his cousin's death. He glanced from the guerilla suit blocking his exit from the booth to fifty-something, still standing in front of the table, still staring his way, reading his face as though it were the morning paper, and then back to Mattia Lanaro.

'I did,' he confessed.

'That was *regrettable*,' Lanaro said. 'It triggered a most *unpleasant encounter*.'

The fixer nodded slowly but said nothing. Any kind of apology would ring hollow. He put his odds of surviving this meeting at fifty-fifty. In the abstract, he wondered how they planned on getting his body out of the eatery.

The fixer imagined they had ways.

'As a result of that unpleasant encounter, you will pick up Alaine Quinn for us – you will be our ticket in.' Mattia Lanaro finished his scotch and slid out from the booth. The meeting had lasted longer than five minutes, but less than ten. Lanaro then added, 'That will be your penance for Albertson.'

The fixer nodded again. Clearly, there was no other response.

Lanaro held his eye a long second and said, 'What do you think happened in the park that day?'

The fixer shrugged. 'As far as I can tell Quinn and Dando took out their own crew – including, unfortunately, your cousin – so nothing about the robbery or the murder of the bank guard could come back to bite them in the ass,' he said. 'And then, when it comes to that second grave, Alaine Quinn took out Dando in order to close the circle.'

FORTY-EIGHT

July 29, 1994
11:14 A.M.

'Why'd she . . . shoot me?' Connor struggled with his words.

''Cause she's a greedy fucking pig.'

'You don't even know who he is, Tom.' Alaine was surprised she could still speak. She'd never been in this much pain. Her face felt as though it were on fire. She used an elbow as a crutch to prop herself up in the dirt, her other hand clamped tight against the side of her head, the spot where Tom had smashed her with the Beretta M9.

Dando ignored her, focusing his efforts into working on Connor's wound.

'Tell him who your uncle is,' Alaine shouted at Walsh, making her head pound, a hammer on anvil. She waited on a reply that never came, and then continued in a softer voice, 'His uncle is the head of the Chicago mob.'

'I don't care if his uncle's the King of Siam,' Dando said, not even bothering to look in her direction.

'Tom,' Alaine persisted, blood dripping down her cheek. 'His uncle will have us killed.'

'No,' Connor finally spoke. He looked up at Dando, his eyes glazed over, his face a washcloth of perspiration. 'Uh-uh.'

Alaine slowly shook her head. 'If he shows his uncle a million dollars, we'll be dead in a day.'

'No,' Connor said again. He held Dando's eye. 'This was never about . . . my uncle, Tom.'

'He's suddenly a millionaire, but they'd never piece together Crown National and the dead guard?' she said. 'Tom – we'd be killed in a day.'

Connor gripped Dando's hand. 'No – I'd never give . . . names.'

Dando squeezed back at Connor's hand. 'Don't worry about it, kid,' he said. 'I know you wouldn't.'

'Jesus Christ, Tom – you've always been the practical one.' Alaine pointed a blood-smeared finger at Connor. 'His uncle would have our names out of him in twenty seconds flat.'

Dando continued to ignore her. Alaine stretched across the dirt and picked up Tharp's firearm. She watched as Connor was lifted into a sitting position. 'If Connor leaves here, Tom,' she said, taking a deep breath and lifting the handgun, 'we're dead.'

Dando glanced back her way, his eyes widening at what she held in her hand.

'You fucking—'

Alaine pulled the trigger. The bullet burst a hole through Connor Walsh's left eye.

Dando was on her in an instant, swatting aside Alaine's pistol, his fingers wrapping around her throat, squeezing, tighter and tighter still. Tom's eyes were ablaze with hate and fury as Alaine lay on the forest floor, staring up at her old friend, eyes bulging, and her hands on the dirt as she offered no resistance.

This is how it ends flashed through her mind when suddenly Tom rolled off her and sat upright.

An eternity passed as Alaine gulped for air, as she massaged her neck, as tears washed silently down her cheeks. 'What happens now?' she said finally, her voice a gravel truck.

Dando stood, emptied a backpack of phone books and used it to collect the handguns strewn about the forest floor. 'What happens now is you're going to drag Tharp and Lamprecht to the grave we dug for them.'

'What about—' Alaine didn't finish her query as Dando read her mind.

'Connor won't be sharing a hole with those two scumbags.'

'We're going to dig another one?'

Dando shook his head. 'I will be digging another one, not you,' he said. 'Make sure you empty all their pockets,' he pointed toward the dead felons, 'before you roll them in. Then wipe the blood off the side of your face,' he said and added, 'because you've now got three bikes to ditch.'

'Look, Tom,' Alaine said a minute later, as she dragged Tharp past him, but Dando kept moving. He was back to ignoring her as he began digging a grave for the friend that she had shot.

Alaine returned to her tasks and grunted as she lugged Lamprecht's dead weight over dirt and undergrowth to the grave they'd spent yesterday digging. Getting rid of three mountain bikes was a drawn-out pain in the ass; however, it kept her busy – it kept her moving – and it kept her from thinking her thoughts.

Alaine rode with one hand on the left side of her handlebars while her other hand cupped the middle of the handlebars on a second bike. She rode that way until she worked her way down to the river. Once there, she tossed the bike in, as far as she could.

She followed this procedure three times.

Perhaps the bikes would be found; perhaps they wouldn't.

It didn't matter.

When Alaine returned from dumping the third bike, she was surprised at the progress Tom had made. Connor's grave was already the correct length and width. Tom dripped with sweat as he now worked on deepening the cavity. He knew she was there, but he didn't acknowledge her presence, glance her way, or request help.

Alaine found she couldn't look toward Connor's remains. She understood – at least in the abstract – that it was either him or them. Her former employer had made it exceedingly clear last night, had walked her through every possible scenario.

Nevertheless, Alaine felt shame and guilt . . . and horror and nausea.

Alaine felt evil.

She felt Tom should not have paused in strangling her, that

what she'd done to Connor merited death . . . that you had to pay for blood with blood.

And she knew for shit sure, deep down in her heart, Tom was going to kill her.

Alaine knew after they'd completed all of the bullshit tidying up out here in the middle of nowhere, she'd be asphyxiated or shot or stabbed or maybe even beaten to death, and then haphazardly tossed in a hole for an eternity spent with Tharp and Lamprecht.

Alaine got off her bike and sat cross-legged on the ground next to the deepening grave. She racked her brain, but there was nothing she could say in order to defend her actions, in order to convince Tom that for them to survive . . . Connor had to die.

He wouldn't listen, anyway. He'd made that abundantly clear.

Dando finally glanced her way. 'Did anybody see you?'

'A couple of hikers,' she replied, 'but I just smiled and flew past.'

'No one saw you chuck the bikes in the river?'

'No. I was able to shove them a good ten feet in, all submerged.'

Dando nodded.

'What now, Tom?' she said, a student asking a teacher about the day's assignment.

He glanced around. 'Get that backpack,' he pointed at the bloated one that'd been left untouched, 'and all the phone books and the other shit back to your car,' he said. 'When we leave, I don't want so much as a toothpick left behind.'

Dando went back to shoveling as Alaine set the backpack and phone books and other odds and ends inside a heavy-duty construction bag. She'd toss it in her trunk when she got back to the parking lot. If anyone spotted her doing that, they would assume it was trash from a campfire.

Alaine set a bottle of water next to Dando's pile of dirt before, once again, riding off toward the trail.

After putting the construction bag into her trunk, she walked her bike to a rack that sat at the entrance to the park trails. She didn't bother locking it as she'd not need it again. She returned to the car, sat in the driver's seat, and shut the door. She'd come up with a plan on the ride back to the parking lot. The plan was simplicity personified – she would get behind the wheel of the car and drive, and keep on driving, and maybe see what the East Coast had to offer this time of year.

She had enough bank straps of cash on hand to take care of herself well into the foreseeable future.

Alaine turned the key and started the car when the tsunami hit. At first the sobbing was almost soundless, her shoulders shuddering, tears spilling down her face. But then it got louder, and louder still, as she wept and cried out. The windows were shut and there was no one nearby or within earshot to either witness or hear her meltdown, but she wouldn't have cared one whit if there was.

Her brain was a kaleidoscope of pain and horror and loss.

Everything. Was. Lost.

She felt it in her soul.

Everything.

And she couldn't run away.

What was the old saying?

She'd be living on borrowed time.

Because her dear old friend from way, way back would come looking for her.

Or – perhaps even worse – Tom might say *fuck it all* and turn himself in to the police . . . and tell them everything.

Five minutes later Alaine turned off the car's engine.

And sat still.

She could not remember a time when she hadn't been in love with Tom. She'd tossed herself at him on more than one occasion. And even though it crushed her to see him with one girl after another in school, she hung out on the periphery as some kind of dopey, platonic friend when she wanted to be anything but.

And she'd been heartbroken at the shell of a man that returned home after his time in the Marine Corps, after his stint in the Gulf War. She'd tried everything she could to pull him out of his stupor, but nothing worked. And then from out of nowhere came this totally mad scheme – insane from the get-go – to rob the Crown National Bank in downtown Chicago. She'd only approached him, partly to be with him, but mostly as some kind of shock treatment to yank Tom out of the empty husk he'd become.

It was either a lark he'd instantly dismiss and they'd chuckle about later . . . or a tie that would bind them together . . . forever.

And, as crazy at it seemed, she'd never seen him be *back-to-normal Tom* more so than in these past several months. Damned if it somehow hadn't worked, committing a major felony as a form of psychotherapy.

What would Freud and Jung have to say?

Sure, there'd been bumps along the road. Her former employer had initially broached the idea of eliminating the felons recruited for the robbery as a way to protect themselves from physical harm or potential blackmail or prison time once the bank heist was complete. Alaine hinted at the notion with Tom during the planning stage. In response, he'd gone ballistic and stormed out. When they'd reconnected, the two decided to table the idea, most likely forever.

But then that fucking Lamprecht ruined everything by killing a bank guard for no reason whatsoever, forcing them to deal with that situation. And deal with it they had. Tom was not only now on board with it, but he'd become the active driver. Then, at the eleventh hour – and out of the clear blue sky – another threat reared its ugly face. An existential threat concerning Tom's new friend Connor Walsh . . . and Tom made it exceedingly clear whose side he was on . . . and it sure as hell was not Alaine's.

If only she'd had a week to make him understand what they were up against with Connor's family. If only she'd had a day to make him understand, instead of three minutes, instead of being forced into taking care of the threat in real time. She'd done all of this to save their lives, and in response, he'd smashed her across the face with a pistol and damn near choked her to death.

Alaine ran the back of her forearm across wet eyes.

Why did she have to die or go to prison for keeping them safe and sound, for doing what had to be done? Why did she have to run and hide from a man she'd loved since they were children . . . run and hide from this man who now wanted her dead?

She'd hoped Tom would come to his senses and understand she had no choice in the matter. Instead, he beat and strangled her.

Worse than any of that . . . Tom had broken her heart.

Repeatedly.

She'd never have him now. They would never be together.

Never in a million years.

He didn't love her.

And the truth of the matter was he never had.

She'd given everything for the man she loved . . . everything . . . and it all came crashing down around her ears.

Alaine reached for the glove compartment.

When she returned to the gravesite, she stepped off the mountain bike and used the kickstand so it would stay up. She handed Tom another bottle of water. Digging a hole for Connor all by himself – he had to be thirsty.

Tom twisted the cap and pounded the water as Alaine slipped around to the rear of the grave. Tom leaned his head back, splashed the rest of the water over his face, and shook his head. Then he stood motionless a long second before saying, 'Fuck.'

Even though Alaine knew it was because she'd moved behind him, she said, 'What?'

Tom leaned forward against the shovel. 'You had another gun in the car?'

'Yes,' Alaine said. 'You made sure we were well armed, Tom. Driving those packets of cash around, I stuck the extra SIG Sauer in my glove compartment just to be safe.'

Tom nodded slowly. 'Smart move.'

Alaine said nothing.

Dando tossed the empty water bottle near the other one. 'Can I ask you something, Al?'

'You can ask me anything, Tom.'

'Was there ever a scenario where I'd be leaving here today?'

Alaine said nothing.

Tears streamed down her face as Tom pivoted with the shovel . . . and as she pulled the trigger.

FORTY-NINE

Alaine held the diamond – the round brilliant, the gold standard – in the palm of her hand. Her thoughts centered on a summer day three decades back, and to a dark place she could never find a way to shake no matter how many years had passed. And to its aftermath, which lingered in the here and now because, quite frankly, her life had been *a living hell* since the bodies had been discovered – rather, had been unearthed – at Kankakee River State Park.

A . . . living . . . hell.

Alaine had been a machine – detached, moving forward, getting it done – that afternoon in late July of 1994. She'd driven her car to Bourbonnais, the city nearest the state park, and called her former employer from a payphone outside a gas station. The two then worked in tandem to get the Ford F-150 from the parking lot at Kankakee to the concealment inside her former employer's garage at her executive townhouse in Hinsdale. Then the two drove back to Bourbonnais in silence – not a word was spoken – to retrieve Alaine's car, return again to the townhome, and put a horrendous day to rest.

That was when Alaine broke.

That was when Alaine marched into the townhome's guest room, shut the door behind her . . . and didn't come out for a month.

Alaine lay in bed. Sometimes she ate a little of the soup or the oatmeal or wheat toast or fruit her former employer brought in several times a day. Sometimes she drank the herbal tea or freshly squeezed orange juice or glass of wine left on the tray that had been set up next to the guest room bed.

Sometimes she ate . . . but more often she did not.

And sometimes Alaine sat in the bath her former employer drew for her until the water turned cold.

But more often than not Alaine never left the bed.

The first few nights her former employer lay beside her on the queen size, making sure Alaine didn't do anything rash. She wrapped her arms around her and whispered words of support and encouragement, comfort and affection that she appeared too catatonic to comprehend or respond to.

As far as Alaine was concerned, she would lay in the guest room bed until the earth broke off from its orbit and spiraled into the sun.

At the end of the month, her former employer strode into the room, a five-star general ready to address the troops, and flung open the curtains, showering the room with natural light. She stood at the foot of the guest bed, stared down at Alaine's prone figure, and said, 'This cannot go on. You need to get dressed, Alaine. Right now. We need to get you out of this . . . *this mausoleum*.'

It took another half-hour of prodding and needling, a stern voice, and an active hand in getting Alaine into a clean pair of jeans and a white blouse and tennis shoes, but an hour later found the two wandering the jewelry stores and gem shops along Wabash Avenue, between East Washington and East Monroe streets, in Chicago's diamond district known as Jewelers Row. It was the fifth store they'd drifted into where they found the round brilliant. A minute later Alaine's former employer paid cash on the barrel for the perfectly cut stone – the first item in which the spoils from the Crown National bank job had been employed.

Alaine had said all of four words during the shopping trip; most responses came with a quick nod or shake of her head. Back home, back in the guest room, back under the covers, Alaine had her head on the pillow and eyes shut when her old employer marched again into the room, sat down, shimmied next to her on the bed, opened Alaine's right hand, and pressed the newly purchased diamond into the center of her palm.

'Every morning I come in here half-expecting to find you with your wrists slit open or on the bathroom floor after having guzzled a bottle of drain cleaner,' she said. 'I know you hurt, Alaine. I get that. And I know of the crushing sense of guilt and shame and grief and self-hatred that's eating you alive, that's drowning you, but, honey – it has to stop. You're shedding weight. The kids are terrified. *I'm* terrified.' She wrapped Alaine's fingers around the jewel. 'Tom was a diamond in the rough. You told me that on more than one occasion, so I need you – I require this of you – to transfer all of your heartache and guilt and pain into this gemstone. Keep it with you at all times; talk to the fucking thing if you have to.' She stressed, 'I need you to compartmentalize the horror and the hopelessness and keep those feelings stuck inside this talisman or amulet or whatever the hell you want to call it.' She wrapped both of her hands around Alaine's closed fist. 'If you hadn't done what you did, we would all be dead by now. We would not have survived the Lanaros; Tom *would not* have survived the Lanaros. You know that.' Alaine's former employer slowly stood up from the bed. 'You're going to live here, Alaine, for as long as it takes to get your head together. I will not allow you to be a basket case. You are not a body in a morgue drawer, and you can't go on living as though you were, so I need you to put all of this torment and angst into that stone,' she took a heavy breath and continued, 'or else we both drive to the police station first thing tomorrow morning and turn ourselves in.'

Alaine shut her eyes; her fist remained wrapped around the diamond.

Her former employer hovered above her another minute, sighed, and shut the door behind her as she exited the bedroom.

The next day, when her former employer woke, put on her robe, and shuffled out to the kitchen, there sat Alaine, alone at the island. She was fully dressed, her hair brushed, her makeup on. And a full pot of coffee had been brewed.

'Where's the F-150?' Alaine asked as if an entire month had not passed by, having noticed the pickup truck Tom had gotten for Kankakee was no longer hidden in the garage.

Her former employer poured herself a cup of coffee and added cream. 'That's long gone. I drove it to a parking lot in Milwaukee, left the windows open with the keys on the front seat, and took a bus home,' she said. 'It was not a pleasant afternoon.'

Alaine sipped at her coffee and set it down on the island. 'You told me at the start of *all of this* that you got your Bachelor's in accounting – it was where you met your husband – and that you had ideas about what to do with the cash, how we can make it clean,' Alaine said. 'How we can make it ours.'

Her former employer nodded. 'Let's go into my office.'

It took several years and a series of cash-intensive business ventures to launder the four million dollars. By that point the two of them were living comfortably. Her former employer's husband had, in fact, not made bank president. He resigned from Crown National within six months of the robbery. Within two months of that he found employment at an investment management firm, making more money than he had as a regional bank manager – the old boys' network in all its glory.

On the night her former employer heard the news, she and Alaine split a bottle of Cabernet Sauvignon and toasted to Pyrrhic victories.

The years passed. Eventually, Alaine met Paul Quinn at a charity event for the American Heart Association. He asked her out that first night.

Six months later they were married.

Did she love Paul Quinn? Did she have the ability to love? Good questions.

Paul had a brilliant mind; he was witty, creative, and unconventional. He had been the polar opposite of Alaine. He'd also been attractive, photogenic, and wealthy. And good Lord – now and again the man could make Alaine laugh out loud . . . and take her away from the world.

Perhaps that was love.

Perhaps.

Alaine continued staring at the perfectly cut diamond in the palm of her hand. Her thoughts then turned to Tom's mother.

Having Catherine killed should have sent her back to bed for another month . . . but it hadn't. Alaine was not that girl anymore, which, to be honest, she found more terrifying than comforting. Alaine cursed the day the bodies had resurfaced, cursed what it forced her to do. Though getting up in years, Tom's mother was as sharp as she'd ever been, and she would have remembered Alaine and Tom hanging out together throughout both the spring and summer of 1994 – the two of them spending a great deal of time together, practically inseparable, right on up until Tom's disappearance, right up until Tom had truly disappeared, that is. Catherine would have ruined everything. She would also have let the authorities know how she continued receiving phone messages from Tom on her home answering machine all the way through Thanksgiving of 1994, several months after Alaine had informed Catherine she couldn't be friends with her son anymore as Tom didn't have the same feelings for her as she held for him, that Tom had made that point abundantly clear . . . that her feelings were unrequited . . . that it crushed Alaine, and for her own emotional well-being, she couldn't see him anymore, not even as a friend.

Catherine had understood because . . . well, because it was the truth, and Catherine knew her boy.

But also because the script for the *challenging* phone call had been penned by Alaine's former employer, and though Alaine imbibed in a couple of stiff drinks before she'd made the call to Catherine, it had gone perfectly. Later still, in the first week of October of 1994, she'd called Catherine again to let her know she'd met someone new, someone she felt special about.

Alaine even got Catherine's blessings. Catherine wished her well. She told Alaine to follow her heart.

Her former employer thought of everything; she even came up with the idea of editing Tom's voice off Alaine's old answering machine in order to leave snippets of messages on Catherine's home answering machine when the two knew Catherine was away at work or church. *This is Tom, I'll call you back* and *we need to grab a bite soon* and *phone tag, you're it* had been left on Catherine's machine in her son's voice, but, by this time, Tom had long since left his job and apartment in Milwaukee and poor Catherine had no number in which to return her son's phone calls.

Alaine had fought this ruse at first, but her former employer thought it best that she remove herself from Tom's life several months before Catherine got around to reporting him as missing. It would also serve to keep police detectives or the FBI from connecting Tom's disappearance with the disappearances of Tharp and Lamprecht and Connor Walsh.

And it had worked so flawlessly that Catherine had not even contacted Alaine before she reported Tom as missing.

Time had, in fact, moved on . . . and Alaine was out of the picture.

But if Catherine were questioned by CPD detectives about the phone messages and how they could possibly have been left after Connor Walsh and the others involved in the bank robbery were noted as missing, Alaine would have topped the list of those who could have pulled it off.

Yes, Tom's mother would have ruined everything.

It broke Alaine's heart – another unspeakable act to compartmentalize inside the round brilliant – but Catherine's *unfortunate* death had saved the poor woman from ever finding out what had really become of her only child.

The ring chime brought Alaine back into the present moment. She placed the diamond back into her pocket for safekeeping and checked the doorbell app on her smartphone.

Alaine cursed silently.

He had a lot of nerve showing up unexpectedly.

FIFTY

I studied the man's profile as he slowly drove past Crystal's car.

There was something familiar about him. I figured he worked at Quinn Chevrolet – upper echelon, a general manager or head accountant – and had fun moonlighting as an extra in a few of the dealership's TV commercials. He was probably one of the guys in the background shaking his head and looking exasperated at Paul Quinn's antics.

I set my smartphone back down on the unopened UNIX textbook that sat on my lap and glanced around to make sure the pups still hovered about nearby. McCullough Park required dogs be kept on leashes, but no one had yet to stop by and enforce said edict. Alice and Rex roamed free, behaving themselves, of course, and staying within twenty-five yards of the park bench on which I'd nested for what had already seemed the better part of my lifespan.

It was only fitting that Alaine Quinn lived in Burr Ridge, one of Chicago's wealthiest neighborhoods, a suburb which had even gone so far as to knight itself a village. Living in Burr Ridge allowed Quinn easy access to the Loop as well as the local airport, expensive establishments in which to dine, and all the upscale shopping the owner of the Quinn Chevrolet dealership could shake a stick at. Burr Ridge was located in both Cook and DuPage counties; McCullough Park lay in DuPage. McCullough purports to cover nine acres, including a good-sized pond and a pedestrian pathway. I sat on a bench along the pathway, shrouded by a patch of bur oak trees, and within a hundred yards of the spot on Kenmare Drive where Crystal had parked her Honda HR-V. I sat sidesaddle on the edge of the bench in order to keep an eye on the road leading into Kenmare Drive as Kenmare contained a driveway that circled another hundred yards – I'd brought Street

View up in Google Earth – before dead-ending on a four-acre lot and the Queen Anne in which Alaine Quinn lived.

OK, so why in the hell am I sitting on this uncomfortable bench for hours at a stretch?

Crystal may have gone a bit Ahab and the whale over Alaine Quinn. She spent one evening out here in McCullough Park by herself, five hours, before enticing me with Taco Bell to perch outside and monitor any cars that turned up Quinn's driveway and/or let her know if I saw anything shady or suspect.

Turns out my dogs are not the only ones driven by food.

At least Crystal didn't have me going through the woman's trash bins. Not yet, anyway, but I'd probably do that as well if my sister promised to spring for dessert.

I wore a Cubs baseball cap and sunglasses as I'd met Alaine Quinn at Catherine Dando's funeral. She might get tipped off if she cruised by in her car or went for an evening stroll around the pedestrian path, only to spot me camped out on a nearby park bench. In this get-up, any passersby would only see me as a nose and a chin.

Crystal's rigged a high-def video recorder the size of your forefinger on the far corner of her passenger-side headrest. It's aimed in the direction where Kenmare Drive meets Quinn's driveway, but the camera also provided a reasonably clear shot of a vehicle's driver as well as the vehicle's plate number as they drove past Crystal's HR-V. My job was to monitor incoming traffic and then check the recorder app on my iPhone to note if any of the vehicles curved into Quinn's driveway.

I didn't disagree with my sister's suspicion regarding Alaine Quinn's involvement in recent events, and I was excited to take part in a stakeout when Crystal first broached the topic yesterday morning – what red-blooded American male wouldn't be? – but now that I was hours into my second afternoon-to-evening shift . . . well, grass grew quicker.

Crystal runs the license plates to find out who's been visiting Quinn. In this third day of spy games, we've only noted a singular visit from her gardener, a gentleman in a different truck that turned out to be from her pool service, as well as a lengthy visit from Quinn's personal secretary, or perhaps administrative assistant is the more politically correct job title.

In other words, the stakeout had been a complete bust and my Taco Bell dinner could not get here fast enough.

Crystal has the passenger window of her Honda down a third of the way for added clarity – no recording through glass – so my secondary job was to make sure no one dicked with her car. No such luck. There'd been no break in the mind-numbing boredom demanding the beasts and I hustle over to her parked car and chase away any neighborhood brats hoping to find money or knickknacks inside the HR-V's glove compartment.

Alice and Rex provided great cover for me to loiter endlessly in the park, but if any cops were summoned after complaints about the debonair young gentleman sitting forever on a McCullough Park bench, I'd have them phone my detective sister. Crystal also made dang sure her Honda wouldn't get towed or ticketed by having a CPD tag lying atop her dashboard.

My sister thinks of everything.

Hopefully she'll remember to bring extra packets of hot sauce.

Crystal has my truck. She took it back to the station to complete some paperwork and catch up on other tasks. She said it'd take too much time re-rigging the video camera on the Silverado. That makes total sense, but there was another factor at play. Dad's ancient Chevy pickup didn't exactly fit in with the Burr Ridge demographics. I should have felt insulted, but it was fine by me. Feel free to borrow my truck whenever you want, just come back with a ton of hot sauce.

I glanced over at the pups. Unlike yours truly, Alice and Rex were in hog heaven, having a complete blast at the McCullough Park stakeout. And why wouldn't they? The pair got to act as park bouncers for any wayward squirrels or rabbits that wandered into their vicinity; they got to sniff and pee on an entirely new universe of objects; and the twosome ate it up whenever some kid came by and asked permission to pet them. Currently, Alice and Rex were taking an involved interest in something near a trash bin. I raised my head to verify it wasn't dropped food or a squirrel they'd managed to catch and were in the process of dissecting.

It wasn't, and I turned my head back in time to catch a black sedan with a police officer behind the wheel cruise along the frontage road. I grabbed my iPhone, tapped quickly enough to catch the vehicle as it passed Crystal's Honda. Sure enough, there was a cop at the helm. I also caught a glimpse of the man in the passenger seat – an older gentleman, suit jacket not uniform. I watched as the vehicle slowed, signaled . . . and swung into Alaine Quinn's driveway.

'I don't know, Crys. I think the older guy was plainclothes.'

'It wasn't Horton, was it?'

'No, but if other cops were heading to Quinn's address, you'd know, right?' I asked. I thought it smart to contact my sister and tell her what I'd just seen. 'You'd know if anything was up?'

'Not necessarily,' she replied over speakerphone. 'I spoke to Horton a couple hours ago and he's still searching for Albertson. Quinn's not on his radar.'

'OK – so maybe Quinn called the police for some reason?'

'No lights or sirens, which means it's not an emergency.' I listened as my sister thought out loud. 'A cop chauffeuring a detective in an unmarked car?' she said. 'But we don't get chauffeured. Only bigshots do.'

'He was in the front seat with the driver, though. Wouldn't a bigshot be in the back?'

'You said another guy drove up ten minutes ago?'

'Yeah. He wasn't a cop, but he did look familiar. I think he works for Quinn at the dealership,' I said. 'I can work the app and try to get plate numbers if you'd like.'

'Don't bother. I'll be there in five.'

'You got the tacos, right?' I said, but she'd already hung up.

FIFTY-ONE

Alaine blocked the doorway, not a pleasant look on her face. 'What are you doing here?'

'Mind if I come in?' the fixer said. He had to handle this delicately. Knocking Crystal Pratt out of play by faking her brother's suicide had been a complete fiasco. And though he'd succeeded in framing Dave Albertson – Alaine, knowing of Albertson's innocence, had to be highly suspicious of the man's disappearance. He then said, 'I wouldn't have stopped by if it wasn't important.'

Alaine sighed and stepped aside to let him in. Without another word being spoken, she led him down the hallway and into her office, where she slid behind the cherry wood desk, took a seat, and motioned at the guest chair for him to sit. 'What fresh hell now?'

The fixer cleared his throat as he sat down. 'The police will be pulling into your driveway any minute now,' he said. 'And they will be arresting you for the murder of Catherine Dando.'

Alaine sat upright. 'Uh-uh – there's no way.'

'I've got a man in CPD who let me know.' The fixer put a leg over a knee. 'I drove straight over.'

'What happened?' she snapped. 'What did you screw up now?'

The fixer stared back at Alaine Quinn. Any reservations he had about what he was doing – about setting her up for Mattia Lanaro – melted away in a flash. He finally said, 'My guy doesn't know any specifics beyond they will soon be here to cuff you and bring you in for questioning.' The fixer scratched at a cheek. 'I've got an attorney – a defense attorney – who'll meet us at the station. He's the best there is—'

'I don't need your guy,' Alaine interrupted. 'I've already got a lawyer. More importantly, I've got an alibi. I worked late at the dealership that day, well into the evening, and then went to a friend's house for dinner, drank too much wine, and I stayed overnight.' She added, 'I've got witnesses at both places.'

'Then you go with the police, you don't say one word, and you have your attorney walk them through all that.' He held up a forefinger. 'You'll be out in an hour.'

Alaine leaned back in her leather office chair and studied him as though she would an equation that didn't add up. 'Why are you really here?'

'To give you a heads-up,' he said, returning her gaze. 'I didn't have to come.'

She glanced at his upper body. 'Are you wearing a wire?'

'No,' the fixer said and damned near laughed. 'I doubt a wire could save me from you at this point.'

'You need to be saved from me?'

The fixer shook his head and silently cursed himself. He'd

shared too much with the viper seated across the cherry wood. But it didn't matter; it was too late . . . for her, anyway.

A ring chime saved him from having to respond further as Alaine switched her attention to her smartphone. She then stood and began walking back toward the entryway, speaking to herself as the fixer fell into step behind her. 'It's not Detective Pratt,' she said, staring into her iPhone. 'Or Detective Horton – and he heads up the investigation.'

The fixer had to hand it to Alaine. She certainly knew who she was up against.

'It doesn't make any sense,' she said, coming to a stop in front of the double entry doors. 'Pratt and Horton would be here in person if they were arresting me for Catherine Dando.' Her attention turned back to the fixer, and he was able to spot what she'd been viewing on her iPhone security app. A large policeman in a CPD uniform stood next to a fifty-something gentleman in a dark suit jacket and gray fedora – the men from the Italian restaurant – on the porch outside. Both looked serious, gravely serious. Alaine tilted her head in thought. 'Unless these men aren't the police.'

The two of them locked eyes for the briefest of seconds.

Then Alaine spun around to flee to the interior of the house, but the fixer was on her in an instant; he had her elbow locked behind her back.

It felt good, real good . . . he owned the conniving bitch.

'Femme fatales gotta femme fatale,' he whispered into her ear, 'but there's no fucking way I'm going down with you.' The fixer pressed Alaine against one of the entry doors so he could twist open the other one with his free hand and let the two men inside. 'Welcome to the day the piper gets paid, Alaine.'

FIFTY-TWO

Crystal inched the Silverado up to the drive-thru menu board, her mind occupied as to why there'd be a police presence at Alaine Quinn's residence. She would have been clued-in, and actively participating, if it had anything to do with the bodies at Kankakee State Park, Catherine Dando's murder, or the Crown National bank robbery. Could there be a local Burr Ridge issue at play – nearby break-ins, vandalism, homeless squatters in the park? Or, if Cory was right that the man who'd arrived earlier worked for Quinn, had something occurred at the car dealership – stolen or damaged vehicles?

Crystal ordered a high-enough quantity of tacos to keep her brother satisfied, a couple of soft drinks, requested enough sauce packets to sink a battleship, and crept the pickup forward. It was still suppertime and the line of cars wormed along at a snail's pace.

Crystal's smartphone buzzed. She peeked down to where it lay on the passenger seat, saw the caller ID indicated Chuck Sims, and tapped both answer and speakerphone.

'I've got the link,' the retired parole officer said, skipping any salutation. 'Turns out the inside man was a woman.'

'What are you saying?'

'That background shit you sent me on Alaine Quinn. What you sent was sparse; there wasn't much to it. At first I didn't notice a damned thing; there were no thunderbolts,' he said. 'But being the meticulous son of a bitch I am, I went back and reread all of my files on Crown National. I combed through everything, Crystal, every goddamned word.'

'And?'

'Get this – the Crown National regional bank manager at the time of the robbery was a man by the name of James Schorr.'

Crystal's blood froze. 'Oh my God.'

'Fuckin' A right,' Sims said. 'Your file lists Alaine Quinn's executive admin at the Chevrolet dealership as Teresa Schorr. And guess what? James and Teresa Schorr got divorced the year before the bank robbery – in October of 1993 to be exact.'

'Oh my God,' Crystal said again.

'I'm thinking the divorce may not have been Teresa's idea,' Sims said. 'What's that old adage? *Hell hath no fury like a woman scorned.*'

'Jesus, Chuck, we got her,' Crystal said. 'We got both of them.'

'If it's not connected, it's one hell of a coincidence.'

'It's no coincidence. And I bet they've been joined at the hip all these years.' Crystal no longer had time for dinner. 'You're a genius by the way,' she told the retired parole officer. 'I've got to call Horton.'

Crystal was boxed in by cars in front and behind her, but she was also in a pickup truck. She drove over the curb to escape the fast-food drive-thru and headed to McCullough Park to pick up Cory and the dogs.

FIFTY-THREE

Immediately, Lanaro's hunter knew the fixer had messed up.

As soon as the front door opened, Alaine Quinn screamed and twisted and scrambled to break free of her captor until the slab of muscle stuffed inside a policeman's uniform slapped her hard across the face. Hard enough to take the fight out of her, giving them time to cuff Quinn's hands behind her back, frogmarch her out to the rear of the sedan, and get her buckled into the backseat.

Lanaro's hunter glared at the fixer, who, in response, tossed his palms in the air and shrugged as though it were just another day at the office.

Lanaro's hunter despised him, he despised being in the man's proximity, despised what the man did for a living, despised what the man stood for – which was for nothing at all . . . well, nothing except for himself. Though the man's betrayal had worked in their favor, he despised how easily he turned on a dime and fed his client to Mattia Lanaro in order to save his own sorry bacon.

Most of all, Lanaro's hunter hated being part of this asinine charade, but Mattia Lanaro had looked him in the eye and requested he personally go along with the fake officer – the mountain range of biceps, triceps, deltoids, and pectorals – in order to add gravitas to Alaine Quinn's arrest, but it was all for naught as the fixer had bungled his role from the get-go.

The man had one job to do, he had one job, and . . . well, now they'd have to listen to Quinn whimper and whine all the way to Lanaro's Fulton River District warehouse. And even though Alaine Quinn had enough blood on her hands to paint the broad side of a good-sized barn, Lanaro's hunter didn't like violence, especially against women. It was all he could do to keep his hands at his sides when the beef slab finished buckling Quinn into the backseat and then smacked her across the face a second time for good measure, or whatever, and said, 'You better shut the fuck up or I'll be riding in back with you.'

Turned out the trip to Fulton River might not be so shrill, after all.

Christ wept.

Lanaro's hunter sighed and closed his eyes. He thought of sunsets and exotic beaches, how the fish in Hawaii looked as though they'd been painted by Dr Seuss, how much he enjoyed keeping box score at baseball games, and how much he loved sipping bourbon out of a Glencairn glass, but no amount of positive thinking tricks was going to make him feel better about today's task. The hunter would prefer not to venture within ten miles of the Fulton River District warehouse as he knew what happened there, but when Mattia Lanaro asks for your help . . . well, there is really only one right answer.

And Mattia Lanaro had not been pleased with Dave Albertson's fate, how that had gone south . . . how they'd been tricked by Alaine Quinn and this fixer son of a bitch into killing an *innocent* man.

The hunter could not blame Lanaro. Dave Albertson's death rubbed him wrong as well.

In fact, the only way Lanaro's hunter could stomach working for the head of Chicago's mob was because he got paid, and paid generously, to find men whose absence from planet earth would prove a net benefit. In a manner, he was doing the world a favor . . . at least that's what he kept telling himself.

He caught the sound of an engine – great, what now? – and glanced across the driveway.

An aging pickup truck came to a stop and parked on the far side of the asphalt, blocking in the fixer's vehicle. He recognized the person behind the wheel – Detective Crystal Pratt. And riding shotgun was her dog handler of a kid brother.

He blinked his eyes. There weren't enough memories of Maui and baseball and bourbon to contest the way this evening was turning out.

Lanaro's hunter tilted his head toward the slab of fake cop and the fixer, and said in a no-nonsense whisper, 'Follow my lead.'

Detective Crystal Pratt stepped out from the pickup . . . and the three men walked over to meet her.

FIFTY-FOUR

'They got her in the car,' I said as Crystal parked the pickup on the far side of Alaine Quinn's four-car driveway. The uniformed policeman shut the sedan's back door and glanced our way, as did the older man I took to be a plainclothes detective, as did the middle-aged man who appeared oddly familiar, whom I took as some upper management guru in the Quinn Chevrolet universe.

'Yeah, but what the hell for?' She added, 'Stay put, Cor.'

Crystal stepped down from the Silverado, held up her badge as though a priest holding a cross, and introduced herself as a CPD detective as the trio slinked around the unmarked police car and headed to greet her.

I didn't get why my sister couldn't have waited in line another minute to grab the chow. The cops were already here, picking Quinn up for something or other, and Detectives Horton and Andreen and Crystal could sort all that crap out later in the evening. Per Crystal's rushed call with the lead detective, Horton and Andreen were breaking the sound barrier in order to get to Alaine Quinn's Burr Ridge residence. Once here, the detectives will burn up another hour as the right hand ferrets out what the hell the left hand's been up to.

Meanwhile, I'll be stuck in the pickup, sitting on my ass and twiddling my thumbs. That's fine and dandy, I guess, but it'd be a hell of a lot finer and dandier being stuck in the pickup with a bag of tacos. Plus, once we do get to leave, we won't be able to return to that nearby Taco Bell as they'll remember my Silverado as the one that jumped the curb and tore up their strip of grass.

Way to go, Crys.

Even though I was starving, I had to admit that Chuck Sims's revelation was a solid kick in the backside, that the genius behind the Crown National bank robbery – the inside man – was actually a woman. That it was Alaine Quinn's right-hand, her executive assistant, and that this Teresa Schorr lady had been married to some bigwig at Crown National and gotten divorced a short time before the bank heist.

I glanced across the driveway at Alaine Quinn as she sat in the backseat of the unmarked sedan, her hands cuffed behind her back. Quinn looked scared as she watched the police officers powwow in the middle of her driveway. And she had good reason to be frightened; she'd been caught, after all. She must have sensed my gaze as she slowly turned her head and peered in my direction. Alaine Quinn not only looked scared . . . the woman looked absolutely terrified.

Quinn caught my eye and shook her head. She mouthed something my way, but I was unable to read her lips.

And that's when Alice began to growl.

The pups had been slacking about in the backseat, probably also wondering when they were going to get fed, but my bloodhound's paws were now draped over the seatback as she stared through the windshield at the conversing officers. Alice's attention was focused on one of the figures in particular – the gentleman that looked vaguely familiar. Rex leaned against the other seatback and began to growl as well, joining Alice – offering his two cents on what was going down in the driveway.

Why would my pups alert to Mr Familiar?

What were they telling me?

And why did I feel as though I should recognize the man?

With those queries came an answer . . . an answer that couldn't have struck harder had it been a bolt of lightning.

Someone had knelt over me as I lay on the floor between the kitchen and the living room. Someone had carried me out to the garage. And that someone had done their damnedest to end my life and make it appear as though I'd committed suicide, but that someone hadn't bargained on my execution being interrupted by a MENSA-level bloodhound and a happy galoot of a springer spaniel.

My dogs damn sure knew who Mr Familiar was . . . and now I did as well.

All thoughts of hunger and tacos and driving over curbs vanished in a flash as I watched the situation unfold in front of me. I noticed Crystal had put her badge away, her stance had changed, her right hand hung near her holster as though she were an old-time gunslinger. And I got the feeling if I were standing behind her, I'd spot the hair on the back of her neck begin to rise.

Oh shit!

I stepped down from the Silverado and held open the door as Alice and Rex leapt on to the blacktop with me. The dynamic changed as all eyes switched my way. Mr Familiar's jaw dropped at the sight of the two dogs; it was as though he'd seen a ghost.

Could he be more obvious?

'Settle down,' I said. Alice, still snarling, was on my left, closing in on my sister's position, while Rex stayed on my right. 'What's going on, Crys?'

'I was telling these gentlemen why we were here, and this *detective*,' she nodded toward the oldest of the three, 'was telling me they're with the Burr Ridge Police Department, and that Mrs Quinn was involved in a car accident earlier today.'

The trio stood in a row, facing us. On the left was the man in the CPD uniform who may or may not be a police officer. The man was about my height but had biceps the size of propane tanks – gym muscles, I figured. He had a head of short black hair and stared my way with great disdain. I think he was the one that tripped my sister's trigger; that made her edgy.

'Is that so,' I said, my gaze settling on Mr Familiar, who stood in the middle. 'My dogs seem to know you from somewhere,' I added, wanting Crystal to know exactly what we were up against, though I suspected she already did.

'I bet they smell my cat on me,' Mr Familiar said in a dry voice, understated, rebounding from his initial look of alarm.

The older guy on the right turned my way. 'Shouldn't those dogs be on leashes?'

'They're just fine.' Actually, Alice and Rex tracked Mr Familiar's every move. I wouldn't be able to break their focus if I used a crowbar. The pups remembered Mr Familiar, all right, and appeared as though they'd like nothing more than to chew his face off.

'They're not going to attack, are they?'

'Not as long as everyone remains calm and collected,' I said, 'if you know what I mean.' My pups weren't pit bulls or German shepherds or Dobermans, but they were putting on a damned good show. At least Mr Familiar knew what they were capable of.

The older man nodded slowly, turned his attention back to Crystal, and continued, 'As I was saying, Alaine Quinn was involved in a hit-and-run. Several witnesses reported her plate number.'

Crystal said, 'But you never answered my question. Why would they send an unmarked and a detective instead of a squad car to pick her up?'

'Alaine Quinn is a pillar of the Burr Ridge community.' The older man shrugged. 'I know it sounds terribly elitist, but her standing comes with certain advantages.'

'Does being a pillar of the community mean there's no tow truck?'

'What?'

'If you're picking Quinn up on a hit-and-run, you'll need a tow truck to take custody of the vehicle involved in the incident.'

He nodded again. 'The truck is on its way.' The older man appeared to be in charge. He did all of the talking, anyway.

I was confused. If these were the men that had *disappeared* Dave Albertson, that meant they were Chicago mob – that they worked for Mattia Lanaro. And if Mr Familiar worked for the Chicago mob . . . then Lanaro wanted me dead.

What the hell could I have possibly done to piss off Mattia Lanaro?

I train dogs and attend computer school for Christ's sake.

'Is the damaged car in the garage?' Crystal glanced around the driveway, empty except for my pickup, the car parked in front of it, and their unmarked sedan with Alaine Quinn in the back. My sister was stalling, playing for time. She had to know if they left with Quinn, then Alaine Quinn would never be seen or heard from again. Crystal then said, 'If Quinn's got it parked in her garage, you'll need a search warrant.'

The uniformed cop glared at Crystal in open hostility. Mr Familiar shuffled from one foot to the other, his eyes locked on Alice and Rex. The older man, however, remained motionless, staring back at Crystal, all pretenses now gone.

'So,' my sister continued, 'have you got a warrant?'

The five of us stood in complete silence. Tension hung in the air like humidity before a storm. Where in the holy hell were Horton and Andreen? We needed them here to put an end to this Mexican standoff. These *police officers* Crystal thought we could use as backup for picking up Alaine Quinn had turned out to be anything but. And the dog bluff could only carry us so far with this live wire of a phony cop.

An ungodly shriek from the back of the unmarked broke the stillness.

All eyes turned in that direction.

Alaine Quinn screamed a second time. 'They're not real cops!'

And the man in the uniform went for his firearm.

FIFTY-FIVE

'Sic!' I screamed at the top of my lungs. Alice and Rex weren't police dogs, but the two were mainstays of my training sessions, show dogs to usher the class along.

And the two of them knew each and every command by heart.

Alice blasted off like a roller coaster, spurred by the motion of the fake cop reaching for his sidearm. Her teeth latched on to his wrist and pressed down like pliers. A shot went wild, the bullet spit into the driveway where Alice had been an instant before. My bloodhound hung to the man's arm, a canine appendage, as Crystal launched herself into the fray.

Rex's focus never left Mr Familiar. He went for him, diving in and out, shadowboxing, snarling and snapping. If her pack was threatened, Alice turned carnivore. Rex was more vegan. He'd clamp on to a pant leg with the best of them – but my springer spaniel's bark was far worse than his bite and I threw myself into Mr Familiar as though he were a tackling dummy.

The two of us tumbled and fell, bowling pins to the asphalt. Rex was on him a second later, had the bastard by his jacket sleeve, but Mr Familiar's other hand was jerking a handgun out of his pocket.

There was no way I'd get to the bastard in time as his hand cleared leather. The weapon swerved my way.

'Kill!' I screamed.

Mr Familiar's eyes widened in horror. He tore his trapped sleeve from Rex's jaw, covered his throat with that arm, and scuttled backward, his gun swaying toward Rex's head. But I was on him, pinning the gun barrel to the ground, and bashing the side of his face with a right hook.

My bluff paid off. I have no 'kill' command.

I hit him again, and then again.

I caught bits and pieces of Crystal and the fake cop in my periphery; they were up-close and heated – headbutts, twists and gouges, elbows and incisors. Alice spun about, sinking her teeth into the man's kneecap, deep. The fake cop screeched in pain, dropped his pistol – it scattered across the blacktop. My sister rode the bastard to the ground, smashing her Glock against his face, splitting lips, breaking teeth.

Thank God – Crystal had all but won the scuffle.

Then I was in a world of hurt, the air knocked from my body. Mr Familiar had sacrificed his face to pummel me in the kidneys. My mouth lurched open, a silent oval, like in an Edvard Munch painting. He knew how to hit and kept after my abdomen. I rolled off him, losing my grip on the gun barrel. Mr Familiar swung his weapon toward me again, a smirk on his face, with Rex a fading tempest between us.

I prayed for air. It wouldn't matter for much longer. Mr Familiar's pistol was inching toward my forehead.

I'd let my sister down.

After me, he'd shoot her, and then maybe my dogs.

There was a flash of movement, another shape beside me – the older man.

He stuck his pistol against Mr Familiar's temple . . . and pulled the trigger.

FIFTY-SIX

'Ahhh!' I screamed and jolted backward, my hands in front of my face.

My ears rang from the gunfire. Crystal raised her weapon in alarm. Rex fled as though shot from a cannon, darting about the side of Quinn's house in search of sanctuary, but Alice stayed put. She faced down the older man, snarling, baring her teeth, ready to attack. Mr Familiar lay face down on the driveway, motionless – a light switched off – dark blood and other matter pooling about the blacktop.

The older man's pistol now pointed upward, toward the sky, the palm of his other hand held up in a calming gesture. 'I am not a threat,' he spoke directly to Crystal. 'I just saved your brother's life.' He added, 'And yours.'

'Then place your gun on the ground,' Crystal said. Her Glock 22 aimed at the man's torso, center mass. 'Right now.'

He nodded once and obeyed.

As Crystal flipped the fake cop, groaning and bleeding, on to his back, her eyes never left the older man. I lifted a hand to settle Alice, who let her snarl fade to a low growl. She wasn't ready to forgive or forget, not yet. Rex peered around the corner of Quinn's house, saw the commotion – the fireworks – had subsided, and trotted back my way. I imagined the poor kid's ears were ringing, worse than mine as he'd been closer to the gunfire.

Crystal said, 'You with Lanaro?'

'No,' the older man replied. 'Occasionally our paths have crossed, but I am most definitely not with Lanaro.'

'What about these two?'

'You're not going to get one word out of him,' he aimed a forefinger at the fake policeman, 'and, until a couple days ago,' he glanced at the dead man on the driveway, 'this gentleman worked for Alaine Quinn.'

Crystal squinted in disbelief. 'What?'

'He is what's known as a professional fixer – he makes problems go away for money, a hefty amount of money. Which means he works for rich people.' The older man looked toward the sedan where Alaine Quinn still sat, her eyes wide open, gazing back our way. 'He framed Dave Albertson for her,' he said. 'And if I were a betting man, I'd say he killed Catherine Dando for Quinn as well. I'd put the probability of that at about ninety-nine percent.'

Crystal cuffed the fake officer's wrists behind his back. There was no fight left in the man; he was going nowhere. He lay there in pain and crimson, likely praying an ambulance would be in his immediate future.

I took the moment to crab walk backwards from the body, the lifeless remains of the *fixer guy* who had now attempted to end my life on two occasions.

The older man continued, 'If you drill into his cell phone, dollars to donuts you'll find a link to Quinn. And if you turn over whatever rock this scumbag crawled out from under, you may find other links to her as well, maybe on a laptop or something.' He paused in thought and then added, 'I'd look at his bank records. Maybe you could make something out of the deposits made.'

Crystal voiced what I'd been thinking. 'Why are you helping us?'

'Because I don't do police,' he said. 'And I don't do civilians.'

Crystal stared at the man a long second. 'You were a cop once.'

He shrugged off the suggestion. 'I hope saving your lives has bought me a bit of goodwill as I'm about to pick up my gun by the barrel and place it in my pocket.'

'No, you're not,' Crystal replied, her voice steel, her Glock pointing his way.

'Then you're going to have to shoot me.' The older man reached beyond his firearm, retrieved the ejected shell casing from his nine-millimeter, and placed it into the inside breast pocket of his suit jacket. Then he held Crystal's eye as he gently picked up his pistol by the gun barrel and eased it into the same pocket as the shell casing.

Crystal sighed . . . and holstered her handgun.

Sirens sliced through the night air, getting closer. Whether it was Detectives Horton and Andreen finally making an appearance or a squad car responding to the sound of shots fired . . . well, we'd soon find out.

The older man rose to his feet. 'I'm going to cut across Quinn's yard now. Into the clump of trees,' he said, turned, and stepped on to the front lawn, '. . . into the ether.'

My sister called after him, 'You know I'll be looking for you.'

'I would expect no less,' the older man called back as he disappeared from view.

A minute later both detectives and two squad cars arrived at Alaine Quinn's.

FIFTY-SEVEN

Mattia Lanaro sat again on a folding chair inside the deserted Fulton River District warehouse. He glanced down at his watch; Aunt Viv would be arriving shortly. Lanaro knew, after today, he'd not be back here again until the grand opening of the high-rise condominium he was having built on this site, some two-plus years in the future. In fact, this decaying facility would be under the wrecking ball by this time next week . . . leaving all of its secrets entombed in a mound of rubble and brick.

As they should be.

Across from the head of the Chicago crime syndicate sat a singular figure, a female this time – Alaine Quinn's executive admin, Teresa Schorr. Although that job title was somewhat misleading. Schorr had been anything but Alaine Quinn's personal assistant. Lanaro had his sharpest pair of accountants dig in on Alaine Quinn – perform a forensic audit – after the tipoff from Quinn's own man at Osteria Langhe. And what they discovered tied Quinn's early fortune to Teresa Schorr. The two were more or less equals, like birds of a feather – scheming hand in hand – over these past several decades. Quite frankly, Lanaro wouldn't be able to say where Schorr began and Quinn ended . . . or vice versa.

Nor would he care to waste another second of his life trying to sort it out.

This extended nightmare had begun with a robbery gone bad, all roads led back to Crown National . . . and Teresa Schorr had been the inside man – she'd been the silent partner all these many years.

Teresa Schorr had gotten the ball rolling that led to his cousin's death.

Schorr sat on a green tarp atop the same block of debris Dave Albertson had once perched upon, but she wasn't as bound up as he had been. Only Schorr's hands, petite as they were, were trussed, and loosely at that. One of Lanaro's men stood behind her. Not so much in the off chance Schorr attempted to make a break for it – she wouldn't – rather, he was there to keep her honest during today's *get-together*.

Perhaps *reckoning* was a better word – as today's reckoning was all about honesty.

Schorr had been sitting there, silently weeping, since Lanaro's arrival. She knew her road had come to an end. She spotted Lanaro gazing her way and opened her mouth to speak, but Mattia shook his head and pressed a forefinger against his lips. The man behind Schorr placed a hand on her shoulder, firmly, so she'd get the point.

Mattia Lanaro would give Teresa Schorr a chance to make her case after his aunt arrived, but, quite frankly, he didn't have the stomach to listen to her denials, her blame-shifting, her begging and beseeching . . . and her eventual pleas for mercy more than once.

The news about the massive fuckup at Alaine Quinn's residence had irked him, at first, but the man he employed as his *hunter* explained that Quinn was being arrested for the Crown National bank job as well as all subsequent crimes and, though it would eat up more than a year, the woman would no doubt wind up in prison, where Mattia, if he so chose, could have another bite at the apple. The Lanaro family had lengthy tentacles, even so far as into a women's penitentiary. Personally, Mattia felt life in prison was a fate far worse than death, at least it would be for him, anyway . . . but he would let Aunt Viv be the final arbiter.

Lanaro's foot soldier in the CPD uniform wouldn't utter a

word, of that Mattia was certain. And as for the man Lanaro used for hunting, well, he would be on a beach a thousand miles away, under a different name, by this time tomorrow.

The *incident* at Alaine Quinn's would have no long-term fallout.

Needless to say, picking up Teresa Schorr from her home in Hinsdale had gone far smoother.

At least they'd gotten to her first.

Lanaro heard footsteps and turned in his chair. There came his aunt, dressed in black, as was her habit, and striding across the acre of concrete on her journey to the day's reckoning, her escort trailing in her wake. Then it dawned on Mattia – his aunt had been dressed in black for as far back as he could remember. He figured her somber attire had come into being about the same time her son went missing.

The poor woman; she'd been grieving for over thirty years.

'Aunt Viv,' he said, and rose to meet her.

'Matty,' she replied softly, and cupped a hand against his cheek.

He saw that she'd been crying, but he also noted steel in her eyes. He waited until she took her seat on the second folding chair before he spoke. 'There is no *inaccuracy* today, Aunt Viv,' he said. 'This is Teresa Schorr, and Teresa Schorr is the person – the brains, the mastermind – behind the Crown National bank robbery.' He then stressed, 'Teresa Schorr is the person behind Connor's death.'

Viviana Walsh's eyes were dark – they were unblinking – and they focused like a laser on the woman seated atop the green tarp.

'So nice to finally meet you,' she said softly.

FIFTY-EIGHT

One Week Later

'The fixer's name was Warren Brings,' Crystal said. 'And Brings had both his real phone and a burner on his body as well as his authentic ID.'

'Not too bright of him.'

'I doubt Brings woke up that morning and made arrangements for dying on Alaine Quinn's driveway.'

I nodded; I couldn't fault Crystal's logic.

My sister continued, 'Quinn called Brings's cell phone the day the bodies found at Kankakee made the headlines. That conversation lasted four minutes, so it wasn't a wrong number. But Quinn, through her attorney, states she was returning a call from a gentleman interested in a Chevy Blazer – as if Quinn worked on the sales floor of her own car dealership.'

'But a jury could buy it,' I said.

Crystal shrugged. 'It's total bullshit. I figure the two of them switched to clean phones as soon as Brings came on board.'

We were taking the pups for an evening stroll about the neighborhood as Crystal had just gotten home after another twelve-hour shift. Alice and Rex weren't complaining about the additional workout and, after wolfing down an entire sausage-pepperoni by myself – I hid the pizza carton in the outside bin a half-hour before Crys got home – neither was I.

I should probably circle the block all night to work off those calories.

Crystal pointed to where Rex had taken care of his personal business on the sod next to a fire hydrant, as though I were going to blow it off, and I reached inside my pocket for a waste bag. 'But here's the thing, Cor,' my sister continued, 'Quinn had a burner phone in a desk drawer, and we've got two calls linked from her burner to the burner in Brings's pocket.'

'She should have crushed it with her heel and tossed it in a storm drain, you know, like they do in the movies.'

'Well, I also doubt Alaine woke up that morning and anticipated Brings dying in her driveway,' Crystal replied. 'Quinn's got her lawyer maintaining you and I broke up a kidnapping in progress – that *three strangers* showed up at her house unexpectedly, pretended to be police officers, placed her in handcuffs, and shoved her into the back of their car.' Crystal shook her head when I tried handing off the bag of Rex's waste and said, 'She's going down. Brings had a condo in the city and we got into his laptop. His history has a Google Earth search on Catherine Dando's house as well as searches on Dave Albertson and his landscaping business.'

'What an incredible coincidence.'

'Yeah, what are the odds?' Crystal said. 'But Quinn's in even deeper shit because our forensic auditors are tearing into Brings's bank accounts – the man had several – and there was a large amount deposited from a numbered account on the day Kankakee hit the news.'

'A down payment?'

Crystal nodded and said, 'Alaine Quinn has no cards left to play.'

'What do you mean?' I asked, U-turning the four of us around in order to begin our trek back home.

'She got out at the arraignment, but so did Dave Albertson, and since Quinn set Albertson up, she knows exactly what happened to him . . . Lanaro happened to him. And she knows her partner in crime, Teresa Schorr, suffered a similar fate. So even with whatever security or bodyguards Quinn hires, she'll always be watching her back.'

Teresa Schorr vanished without a trace the same day my sister and I broke up Alaine Quinn's kidnapping. Crystal mentioned Schorr's car remained parked inside her garage; her bank accounts and IRAs and money markets have gone untouched; and Schorr's son and daughter have not seen hide nor hair of their mother in over a week.

Alaine Quinn knows Lanaro got to both Albertson and Schorr . . . and she knows just how close he came to getting her.

We took a few more steps before Crystal said, 'If Quinn gets convicted, she goes to prison, and it might be easier for Lanaro to get at her in there. She's in a Catch-22 situation – damned if she goes to prison, damned if she doesn't.'

'Can't she spill her guts for protective custody?'

Crystal shrugged again. 'I'm sure Quinn would like some kind of guaranteed safety in return for a guilty plea, but with nine dead, including a bank guard and an elderly woman, I doubt the prosecutor will be in the mood for any kind of special deal.'

'So where does it go from here?'

'Well, Quinn's been letting her attorney do all the talking until we informed her of Teresa Schorr's disappearance. She turned white, ghost white, Cor – no kidding. I thought we were going to have to call a medic, but once her color returned it's been a long stroll down memory lane. Nothing incriminating. Her lawyer sits next to her, sipping Diet Pepsi and counting billable hours as Alaine blathers on about Tom Dando this and Tom Dando that. Clearly, she loved the guy,' Crystal said. 'Still does.'

'Loved him?' I replied. 'She killed him.'

'I get the feeling she wants to tell us why.' Crystal snatched the leashes from my hands, leaving me alone with the bag of Rex's waste as we rambled homeward. 'Protective custody or not, I think it's just a matter of time. I give her a week before she comes clean.' Then Crystal said, 'You want to know something else?'

'What?'

'Quinn's step-kids can't hide their delight in her arrest.'

I raised my eyebrows. 'They don't like her?'

'I don't think there's an ounce of love lost between Alaine and Paul's kids. After their father died, things didn't turn out as well financially as they'd anticipated.' My sister then explained, 'If Quinn gets convicted, the car dealership reverts to them.'

'Interesting – maybe they'll start in with the zany ads again.'

As we approached the house, Crystal said, 'I talked to Chuck Sims.'

'How's Chuck doing?'

'To be honest, he sounded disappointed it was all over,' she replied. 'He said he'd wished he could have been there with us at the end.'

'Retirement may not be all it's cracked up to be.'

'On the other hand,' Crystal said, 'Todd Surratt called to pass on his congratulations. In fact, he wanted me to tell you something.'

The hair on the back of my neck stood as Crystal mentioned the special agent in charge of the Chicago Field Office. 'Out with it.'

'He said he'll see ya next time.'

'Great,' I replied. 'I can't wait.'

We trailed Alice and Rex as they cut across our yard, heading for the front door. I split off, heading toward the side of the house, to the outside bins to dispose of Rex's bag, when Crystal said, 'One last thing, Cory. When we brought Quinn in, she had a diamond – no ring, no jewelry or anything – just a single diamond sitting in her front pocket. From the looks of it, it had to be expensive. And by expensive I mean *real expensive*. I asked her what that was all about, but she didn't respond.'

I paused in my tracks. 'Why would she lug a diamond around?'

My sister shook her head. 'I guess we'll never know.'

Ten minutes later and the pups were loafing about in the living room while Crystal was in the kitchen, boiling pasta and heating sauce for spaghetti. 'Do you want a plate?' she asked.

'No,' I said, 'I'm good.'

She stopped and stared my way. 'You're turning down food?'

'I'm good,' I said again.

Crystal returned to her cooking but continued speaking. 'You've been through a hell of a lot, Cory – what happened in the garage, what happened in Quinn's driveway. And I've been meaning to ask how you've been doing . . . how you're processing all of it?'

'I'm fine, Crys,' I replied. 'Really, I am.'

'But you've been acting all antsy and weirder than normal, and now you're turning down food,' she commented. 'Not to mention you cut our walk in half.'

Actually, I tend to eat when I'm nervous, hence the sausage and pepperoni pizza, and I cut our walk in half due to something entirely different than what had occurred in our garage or in Alaine Quinn's driveway. 'I cut the walk short,' I said, 'because I've got a study partner coming over any minute now.'

'A study partner?' Crystal again looked my way. 'That girl you were telling me about, the one from class?'

I nodded right as the doorbell rang. I turned toward the entryway to hide the look of abject terror in my eyes.

'A study partner,' my sister repeated. 'Is that what you young folks call it these days?'

'Don't embarrass me, Crystal,' I said as I headed for the front door, Alice and Rex trailing in my wake. 'Do not embarrass me.'